Red My Lips

Stained Heart Series: Book One

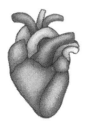

LILA HERRON

Red My Lips

Stained Heart Series: Book One

ASIN B0D6N7DV7N

ISBN 9798332173462

Edited by Cassidy Hudspeth and Hannah Landoe

Cover design by Disturbed Valkyrie Designs

Interior formatting for print by Hannah Landoe

To all the girls who's had life bite them in the ass;
it's time to bite back.
You think the men get to have all the fun? I think not.

CONTENTS

CONTENT WARNINGS

- Stalking
- Use of guns and gun violence
- Knife violence
- Explicit physical violence including blood and murder
- Mention of drugs and drug use
- Fatphobia
- Mental health topics such as past trauma
- Mention of addiction and alcoholism
- Torture
- Graphic sex scenes
- Explicit language
- Mention of child abuse and neglect
- Excessive alcohol consumption
- Mention of intended rape
- Knife and blood play
- Mention of physical abuse
- Gambling
- Organized crime

PROLOGUE
GAGE

The clink of the poker chips landing on the growing pile punctuates the silence of the room. All eyes are zeroed in on the man sitting opposite me while they await his next move.

Will he call? It'd be an interesting move, considering he's out of chips. But if he folds, he'll be lying down to let me win. And he can't do that after the trash he's been talking all week leading up to this game. No, Jonas has dug himself into a very deep hole.

And I'm about to bury him in it, alive and screaming.

The blonde curls hanging over his forehead don't hide the sheen of sweat on his brow that belies his calm expression. He's trying to play it cool, but I can read him like a book, and I know exactly how this next scene plays out because I'm the one writing it.

"Go ahead, Jonas," I say as I casually lean back in my chair. "There's no shame in folding. Forty million dollars is a lot of money to lose, no need to add your dignity." The condescension in my voice lets him know what I really think of him. His lips press into a firm line as he looks between me, the pot, and what he's sure is a winning hand.

He's fucking wrong.

"Nice try, Lawless." His attempt at returning banter falls flat under the pressure of the situation. "You might have more chips, but you can't beat my hand."

"Then it's a pity you have nothing to bargain with. Cards mean nothing if you can't pay to play." I can see when my words spark the idea. He's a puppet in my hands.

"I have something to play, and it's worth plenty," he counters.

"Oh, really? Is it as worthless as your nonexistent chip pile?" I ask and the other players chuckle around the table.

"It's not fucking worthless," Jonas spits through clenched teeth. "It's the hottest nightclub in Chicago. I'm putting up Inferno."

I tilt my head in consideration. Unlike him, my poker face is unreadable, masking the exhilaration coursing through me. That saying about horses must be bullshit, because I just led this ass to water *and* made him drink. Now, the real fun begins.

"You think one club covers everything?" I scoff, looking around the room like I don't believe it.

"It's worth plenty."

I remain skeptical, playing it up just to piss him off a little more before I sigh goodnaturedly.

"Alright, you can put up your little club. But not just the building—the employees, the vendors, the backroom deals. Everything." I know how Jonas does business, and I don't want any surprises. He doesn't get to leave the building and take all the furniture with him when he moves out.

There's hardly a beat of pause as he considers the offer.

"Deal."

"Put it in writing."

Jonas is offered a napkin, which he uses to write out the terms of the deal in full. At the bottom, he signs his name with the date. Then he tosses the napkin, worth millions, onto the pile of chips in the center of the table.

"Alright Jonas, time to show your hand." When he lays his cards down, adrenaline runs through me—dark, twisted, and thrilling.

He has a full house, which would usually be a good hand—a winning hand even. If I didn't have a straight flush. The color drains from his face as I show what I've been holding. A satisfied grin slowly spreads across my face as I stand to lean over and collect my winnings. Jonas' hand shoots out to snatch up the napkin before I can. I stare into his eyes, watching the five stages of grief warring in them.

"Are we going to have a problem?" I ask, a sharp edge to my voice. Playing with such high stakes leads to severe consequences, and you always pay up. There is no other option. He can grieve all he wants as long as the stage he lands on tonight is acceptance.

Jonas stares at me for a moment, his mind reeling, before he finally pulls his hand back. Picking up the napkin, it carries a weight far heavier than a scrap of paper. I have so much planned for this contract and everything it represents.

This is the beginning of everything.

CHAPTER ONE

JILL

The next man to ask me what I'm doing after work is getting stabbed.

Violently and repeatedly.

You'd think they'd learn, because I'm definitely not the first female bartender at the club they've asked to do a shot with them. But they never do. I'm not here to party or dance. I'm fucking working. And if they refuse to learn, I'm happy to be their final lesson.

"Three shots of Patron, and pour one for yourself, sexy."

I suck in a calming breath before looking up at the man leaning over the bar, tapping his credit card against the counter. He's as generic looking as they come—the leering eyes that stare none too subtly at my big tits, the cocky smile meant to be charming, and the plastic credit card he's trying to stretch past its default limit.

"No can do, handsome. I'm on the clock." The practiced line flows from my mouth with ease. I've worked here at Inferno—Chicago's most popular and expensive nightclub —long enough to know not to bite the hand that feeds me. Telling off every man who makes me want to grab a sharp

object and start slashing—however tempting it might be—
would severely affect my tips. And I need to make as much
money as I can right now.

Working at this nightclub isn't my idea of a good time.
It's not my idea at all. I miss bartending at the luxury hotel
bar I worked at up until a few months ago—before everything happened. But I'm here to work off my brother
Tommy's debt to the owner of the club. The loan sharks
didn't exactly give me a choice in the matter. The money
isn't coming from Tommy, so it was either pay up or suffer
the consequences. So now I belong to Inferno, and whatever money I earn goes towards the debt.

Walking into Inferno feels like stepping through the
gates of Hell—if Hell was full of people fueled by booze and
had seven-star service. The entire building is shrouded in
red lights, dancing off the matte black walls like flames that
engulf the space with hedonism. Fog machines in the
rafters above the dancefloor meet red lasers that cast a red
haze over the dancers. The music is alway blasting, and
energy is always high.

Inferno is never lacking in work or tips. The sheer
number and caliber of clientele that walk through the doors
every night keeps the drinks flowing and the minimums
high. You have to pay to play here, something even basic
frat boys are learning the hard way with every swipe of
their credit cards.

Filling orders left and right—a muddled cocktail here, a
round of shots there—I keep an eye out for any familiar
faces in the crowd. Having worked in the service industry
for a while now, I know that regulars mean better tips. They
might be annoying, but you know what they say about
making deals with the devil you know.

My eyes lock on the blond man moving through the

crowds past the bar, greeting partiers like a king greets his subjects—his self-importance is astounding. Jonas Firth is the previous owner of Inferno, up until about two weeks ago. Rumor has it he lost ownership over a high-stakes poker game. I don't doubt it for a second. The bastard thinks he's invincible, and I know how much he loves a poker game. Even after losing the best nightclub in the city, he's strutting around like he's untouchable.

Fucker.

The image of my brother's ransacked apartment, covered in blood and damage that the police called 'evidence of foul play' in Tommy's disappearance, has hatred bubbling through me like acid. He's the reason my brother is missing and assumed dead. Up until recently, Jonas had been my living nightmare.

When my brother got in too deep with his gambling debts, it was Jonas and this club that he lost to. My brother dug himself into a three hundred and twenty-five thousand dollar hole he couldn't climb out of. And when he couldn't come up with the money, they took his life instead.

The authorities think there's a possibility Tommy is still alive, and they promise they're looking into it. But a gambling addict with a history of skipping out on his debts isn't exactly a top priority on their list of missing persons.

I believe Tommy's dead. I know my brother better than anyone—the good and all the bad—and he wouldn't have gone this long without trying to contact me if he were able. He's gone, and I know who's responsible.

My eyes track him as he makes his way past the dance floor. Jonas Firth is the farthest thing from invincible. He doesn't know it yet, but he will. I'm going to show him just how easy it is to make him bleed. My heart rate spikes with excitement, adrenaline rushing through my veins until I'm lightheaded. It's been a long time coming. I've bided my time, and tonight is it.

Tonight, Jonas Firth dies.

I'm going to enjoy this.

"Jill, go change." My manager's voice pulls me back into the moment. "The new boss wants you on service." I open my mouth to agree as a habit before realization sets in.

I've done bottle service before, and there's a reason I like to stay behind the bar. I have no qualms about doing what needs to be done to earn the good money. A desperate woman can't be picky. But if I'm going to be forced to work in Hell's Inferno, I would prefer a good three feet of counter space between me and the customers. I thought Jonas being gone meant I was safe from pimping myself out.

"I'm a bartender, Miranda. Jonas is gone. I don't do bottle service anymore."

"You do tonight," she states. Noticing my glare as I place my hands on my hips, she sighs. "Please, Jill. This isn't my decision. They asked for you specifically, and new ownership means a whole new set of rules."

"Fine," I concede.

"Thanks, doll. I don't want either of us getting fired tonight. I can't handle this place without you."

Not that I would get fired. Or even *could* get fired from this place. I'm already working here against my will.

"Which table?" I pull my apron from around my waist and toss it below the counter.

"VIP."

"Gold?"

"Executive lounge." High rollers. "You have fifteen minutes. Go get changed. Trinity will meet you in the stairwell with the bottles."

I huff out a sigh, making sure to get dramatically louder

as I pass her on my way out from behind the bar, laughing as she swats me with her towel. "Tits up."

"Ass out," I call over my shoulder, finishing the mantra of the Inferno bottle girls. Pushing through the door marked *Employees Only,* I make my way to the bottle girls' dressing room. Pulling a change of outfit from my locker, I strip out of the black bodysuit and black jeans I wore for my bartending shift.

Luckily, I don't have to wear one of the usual bottle girl outfits of a black sequin bikini top, high-waisted thong bottoms, and fishnets with thigh-high boots. Those outfits don't come in a size with double digits, and I have more body than most people know what to do with. The closest I get to wearing a size two is if you add another two in front of it. Hot as I am, I'm a big girl, so I bring my own attire when I'm forced to be a bottle girl.

My black two-piece set consists of a long-sleeved crop top that sits off my shoulders and ties at my breasts, and a little black mini skirt. I have absolutely no issues showing skin, I have a lot to show. But I choose who gets to see my assets and when. I slip on some sexy strappy black heels with red bottoms before walking over to my vanity.

Rifling through my makeup bag, I pull out my lipliner and lipstick combo, both in the Inferno signature blood red. Red lips are part of the bottle girl uniform, along with a headband adorned with glittery red devil horns.

Pulling my dark hair out of the high ponytail, I shake out my waves. Getting this long, 70s-inspired shag haircut was the best decision I've made in a long time. I finger brush through my full bangs, fixing how they sit on my forehead and accentuate my eyes. A few spritzes of perfume has me smelling delicious.

Stepping back, I twist to check myself out in the mirror from every angle.

Fuck, I'm sexy.

Time to go drain a couple of men's bank accounts until it's raining down on me. The more money I make, the sooner I'm free of this place.

Trinity's waiting for me at the bottom of the private stairs. She turns to flash me a smile, and it's genuine— which isn't something I can say for all of the girls working here.

"Could you possibly be any more beautiful?" I ask.

"You're a total bombshell," she says, making me smile. I almost wish I could hate Trinity, with her silky blonde hair, legs that go on for miles, and the type of body lingerie is designed for. But she's honestly one of the most genuine girls I've met in this city, and her beauty matches her brains. She's gorgeous inside and out. If I have to do bottle service, Trinity's the one I want to partner with. She loves her job and knows how to have a good time. Not to mention, she rakes in the tips.

"I know," I say, giving a little shimmy that sends my tits swaying and earning a laugh. "We're a couple of show-stoppers."

"What did they order?" I ask, looking at the bottles she's holding. Inferno has a fifteen thousand dollar bottle minimum just to sit in the executive lounge for the night, so I'm not surprised to see over twenty grand worth of champagne and cognac in her arms.

"Two Louis Roederer Cristal and Remy Martin Louis XIII," she responds, handing off one of the champagne bottles to me. As one of the regular girls, she'll be taking lead on this group.

"Damn, mo-*ney*," I comment.

"Tell me about it," she laughs.

The sound of our heels clicking echoes through the stairwell under the pulsing music playing from the DJ booth. The stairwell leading up to the Executive lounge is one of my favorites. Arches made of black lights lead up the stairs every four steps, with flickering red lights that climb the matte black walls like red flames on both sides of each stair. It feels like you're in a tunnel that leads straight to hell, and I like it.

We pause on the landing at the top of the stairs to prepare the sparklers on the champagne. Taking a deep breath, I look at Trinity. "You ready?"

"Let's get these tips." Her straight white teeth glow under the black lights as she grins. "Tits up."

"Ass out," I reply, pasting on my own smile—it's the one designed for male customers, specifically the ones with real money. I press the lighter to the sparklers, setting them ablaze as the sparks fly dramatically.

Pressing the button near the door, music pumps through the lounge with a heady beat that sets our pace as we strut into the lounge with the bottles raised over our heads. Pumping our arms to the rhythm, sparks flying, we make our entrance. All eyes are on us.

The Executive lounge is a glass box that overlooks the club above the dance floor, the privacy glass allowing the VIP guests to see out without being on display themselves. Soundproofing gives the option to sync the speakers up to the house music or select something different. A large, tufted blood-red sofa curves around a circular table that faces the club below, the rest of the space decorated in decadent matte black. A small bar sits in the corner closest to the door, with a fully loaded bar cart situated near the guests.

Five men sit scattered around the sofa. Jonas Firth smirks at me from the end closest to me. Just the sight of his blond curls makes my blood boil. He doesn't know what's coming for him, but for now I need to do my job. At least while there are witnesses.

The four other men I haven't seen before. Sitting next to Jonas is a man with the term 'hipster' written all over him —dyed black hair peeking out from under an olive green fisherman beanie, mismatched ginger mustache, and brightly colored new-school tattoos placed like patches on the visible skin of his lanky limbs.

Another man sits in the center of the couch, his black hair cut close to his scalp with expertly trimmed facial hair. Tattoos climb up his bulky biceps like snakes on his rich, dark brown skin. He flashes a smile of dazzling teeth when he spots me and Trinity, his eyes bouncing between us.

The man next to him has a grizzly, overgrown appearance—wavy brown hair curling over his collar, and facial hair that looks several days overdue for a trim. His black button-up shirt gapes open to show symmetrical black patchwork tattoos scattered across his hair-littered chest.

At the end of the sofa, next to the grizzly, is a man who sucks up all the energy around him like a black hole. I've felt his eyes on me like a spotlight since I stepped foot into this room. Reclining on the couch, long jean-clad legs outstretched, arms spread across the back of the couch on either side of him, he tracks me with half-lidded eyes that pierce my very soul. He watches like the Grim Reaper, waiting for people to throw their souls at his feet, and I'm sure they do.

Tattoos cover every inch of visible skin, climbing up his neck to his jawline and down the backs of his hands. I have no doubt that the ink continues to cover the rest of his built body beneath his black t-shirt and worn leather jacket. Several silver necklaces hang from his neck, a heavy silver cross catching the flashing club lights. His dark brown hair is buzzed short to his head, a clean stubble covering his strong, angular jaw.

Ripping my eyes away from the man stealing the air from the room, I focus on finishing out the song, the heavy bottles above my head giving my arms a workout. Taking the lead, Trinity steps forward to greet the men.

"Hello, gentlemen. My name's Trinity, and this is my friend, Jill." I give them a sultry wink. "You ordered some bottles and a good time, and we're here to deliver. Let's get these drinks flowing." She sets out to open the bottles and starts pouring drinks while I focus on the mixed drinks at the bar.

Making my way through the men on the couch, I take drink orders. When I hand Jonas a rum and coke, my smile is genuine as I picture what I have planned for him. The patchwork man next to him—who introduces himself as Dane while he feels me up with his eyes—orders a whiskey sour. The gorgeous black man, Anders, and the grizzly man, Messer, each order a vodka on the rocks, along with premium champagne. Trinity makes a show of pouring the bubbly for each of the men. Then she gets to *him*.

He doesn't introduce himself, he simply reclines on the couch like he owns the room. There's an air of arrogance about him, a slight smirk on his unbelievably gorgeous face. Placing a glass of champagne on the table in front of him with a dazzling smile, Trinity addresses him in her best money-making voice.

"What else can I get for you?" she asks.

"Cognac straight," he replies simply before his gaze moves back to me. Opening the Remy Martin, I pour him a glass. His eyes don't move from me once. Not when I hand him the drink, not when I move away when Anders calls for some of the cognac. Not when Messer leans over to say something to him, making him smile in a way that sparks between my legs. I can feel his eyes on me, heady and unrelenting, for most of the night.

Most clubs have strict rules about touching the bottle girls, or at least they claim to. And most tables on the floor are monitored by security, so the girls have an easier time with the men who get too handsy. But Inferno is more 'hands-on,' especially for the VIP tables. Touching is allowed, and bottle girls do what they have to in order to get the men to empty their wallets and max out their Amex cards. Short of having sex on the sofa or standing on the table and stripping, everything goes.

When Dane wants me to dance with him, I do. I let loose and move my body with his to the thrumming music. He presses close behind me, his arms wrapping around my waist as he grinds against my ass. I'm good at shaking my ass, and there's a lot of ass for me to shake. It's definitely one of my best assets.

Trinity and I dance, mingle, and keep the drinks flowing. With every movement, every laugh, every appeasing smile, I can feel *his* eyes on me. His gaze follows me like a shadow–dark and knowing.

"Do you need anything? More cognac?" Trinity asks him. He looks up at her in consideration for a moment before responding.

"I want a venom shot." His dark gaze moves from Trinity to lock on me. "From her." Trinity backs off as I grab the bottle of tequila from the bar cart, along with the salt and lime wedge. His eyes skate over my skin, making my nerves go haywire. My heart rate jumps, and my core clenches with desire. He's as hot as he makes me feel.

Strutting over to him, I swing one leg over his lap to straddle him. If he minds my full weight in his lap, he doesn't show it. This is what he asked for, and his hardening cock against my thigh tells me exactly how he feels about it.

Sticking two of my fingers into my mouth, I suck on them before dragging them back out slowly to draw an x over my heart in my saliva. His hooded eyes track my movements carefully. Taking the salt, I pour some onto the dampness on my left breast.

Tossing my hair, I make a show of arching my chest towards him in offering as I lift the tequila to my mouth. He doesn't hesitate to lean down and run the flat of his tongue across my salted skin. The heat of his mouth makes my breath hitch before I take a big swig.

Pushing him back against the couch and leaning over him, my hand circles his throat under his jaw and tilts his head back. I lean in as he parts his lips for me to spit the shot of tequila into his mouth. His groan is lost in the music, but I feel it vibrating in his chest. Reaching for the lime wedge, I place it between my teeth. When I lean in to let him take the fruit with his own mouth, he lets it drop between us as his lips claim mine.

Goddamn.

The way his mouth moves against mine feels like he's waited a million lifetimes to kiss me. Taking in long pulls, deep and hungry—he devours me until I can feel it all the way down to my toes. He draws me closer until I'm sinking into him as I let him take my mouth with unrelenting passion. Our breath mingles, passing oxygen back and forth until I'm lightheaded. His hands—big, strong, tattooed hands—grab handfuls of my thighs and ass, greedy to own and explore.

Demanding entry, his tongue plunges into my mouth, pulling a soft moan from me. Potent chemistry sparks between us until we're engulfed in white-hot flames. I rock against him, my pussy wet and needy for the massive erection I can feel growing beneath me. My hands run down his chest to fist the lapels of his leather jacket, pulling him impossibly close.

I need more.

I've never been so overtaken by a man before, never been drowned in so much lust that I'm left gasping for air. A growl vibrates through his chest when my teeth catch his bottom lip, giving it a sharp tug before licking the pain away. When my teeth graze his tongue, it's like I've unleashed something inside him. His hips grind up against me, his rock-hard cock rubbing me right where I need it, earning a soft gasp.

Sure fingers are slipping under the hem of my dress on a mission when a percussive sound rips us back into our surroundings.

Bang!

Breaking away from each other abruptly, I'm suddenly being hugged to a strong, solid chest.

The pop of a champagne bottle is followed closely by a bang of the cork hitting the ceiling and a chorus of excited shouts. Everyone else has migrated to the other end of the sofa, where Trinity is opening the second bottle of champagne. As realization sets in, I can feel his body relax against me, his arms loosening their protective hold.

Pulling out of his grasp, I slide off his lap onto the sofa

next to him. Forcing a deep breath, I look up at the ceiling as I regain my composure—or at least the appearance of it. Glancing over at the man I almost fucked right here in front of a bunch of people, I can see he's doing the same thing. Resting against the back of the sofa, he tilts his head to look over at me, his chest rising and falling with heavy breaths. Smiling, his tongue runs along the bottom of his top teeth in a way that's both self-satisfied and begging for more. My red lipstick has transferred onto his lips, making them look even more tempting. I bite my bottom lip to stop myself from leaning back in for round two.

Without a word, I stand from the couch. Ignoring the intense gaze I can feel touching every inch of my body behind me, I readjust my skirt and run my fingers through my hair.

I make eye contact with Trinity across the room. She looks pointedly at the mirror behind the bar, and I know I need to clean up my lipstick. That's the only thing her eyes tell me before she turns back to the guests—no judgment or disapproval. That's why I love her.

Stepping behind the bar, I take a moment to fix my lipstick where it's smeared. Luckily, this lip combo is fairly makeout-proof and cleans up with a few swipes of my finger. I take this time to fluff my hair and straighten my bangs as well. Lust still thrums inside me, making me wish I could turn around and have the sinful man finish what he started.

I don't feel a single ounce of regret. There's nothing for me to feel bad about. If I were a real employee, I might have something to worry about—there are certain lines bottle girls and guests aren't supposed to cross. But I don't give a single shit about this job. In fact, I'd love to be fired.

So if the mysterious new owner has a problem with me fraternizing with their hot-as-fuck guests, that's their problem.

They can kiss my fat ass.

I release a cleansing breath and force myself to refocus. As much as I need to be railed into oblivion, my energy needs to be directed at another goal tonight. Jonas can have a great time drinking at the club tonight, but it'll be his last. He's going to feel every bit of pain he's inflicted on others, and I'm going to enjoy every second of it.

Gazing at my sexy reflection in the mirror, the pulsing club music dances through me. I can see the tattooed god checking out my ass in my peripheral vision. I suck in a deep breath, soaking in the attention and the energy around me. Turning around, I swipe a bottle of vodka off the bar along with a couple of shot glasses. I'm ready to take on the rest of the night.

Bring it on.

I exhale a sigh as I sit in the chair in front of my vanity. It's been a long night—lucrative, but long. My feet are killing me, my bra straps are digging into my shoulders, and this horned headband is giving me a headache. I'm exhausted and *so* ready to get out of here. Anticipation runs through me at the thought of my plans for the rest of the night.

Pulling out my money bag, I toss the crumpled pile of cash onto the vanity. Most of my tips from tonight were on cards. I wrote down the exact amount of my card tips, not that I'll ever see that money. It's already gone, just like this cash is about to be. But if I'm going to be forced to work off my brother's debt, I want to know exactly how much this place is getting from me. I'm not giving a single cent more than I have to.

Since I need money to live, the club pays me a small salary that goes straight toward my expenses. It was a fight with Jonas to have any type of pay at all, even the small amount I'm getting. The amount of money I'm taking home right now is abysmal—I can barely cover my bills. I've been living mostly off savings and credit cards. And I'll admit I use the attention I get from men for the luxuries they offer me that I can't afford for myself right now.

What can I say? If a man is going to be a douchebag, he might as well do it while I'm eating a three hundred dollar steak.

Letting out an exasperated breath, I refocus on the task in front of me. I count out each stack of money, flattening and organizing as I go. Being a bartender, I rarely see bills larger than a twenty. Turns out bottle service brings in the fifties and hundreds because these stacks are larger than I expected.

I sit back in my chair and breathe out a laugh. This is *a lot* of money. More money than I've ever made in a single night. More money than I've ever heard any of the other bartenders and servers making.

More money than they would ever expect me to make.

Even a fraction could really help me right now. I never agreed to how much would be taken from me, and I fucking earned this money. Every cent of it.

I count the money again, pulling a few bills from each pile to set aside. Folding the smaller stack of contraband bills, I tuck it into my bra cup until it's no longer visible.

"Those horns suit you perfectly." The deep voice from behind me vibrates over my skin. Movement catches my eyes in the mirror as a large figure emerges from the shadows. The blood freezes in my body, every one of my muscles tense, as a man steps forward from where he stood against the lockers and into the glow of the vanity lights.

Every inch of visible skin up to his chin is inked with tattoos, his deep brown eyes catching mine in the reflection without letting go.

The tattoo god from the VIP lounge.

"You can't be in here." My voice sounds as tense and surprised as I feel.

He stalks closer, his approach slow like a predator toying with its prey. I sit frozen, tracking him with my eyes in the mirror.

He chuckles—deep, rich, and dark. It's both arousing and alarming.

"I wouldn't bet on that." His choice of words picks at me and my situation, making my shoulders straighten in defiance.

"Do you always go to clubs and lurk in the women's dressing rooms?" I challenge, my voice cold. One of my hands slips into the shelf beneath the vanity, past my makeup bag, and grips the handle of the four-inch switch-blade I keep hidden. The cool metal in my hand is calming, reassuring.

"Only the ones that I own," he responds easily.

Realization runs through me like a chill. He's the new owner. *The new owner of Inferno just had his tongue down my throat and his hands on my ass.* I'm still wet from that kiss, and my pussy pulses at the thought of it.

He stops behind my chair, holding my eyes in the mirror. Leaning forward, he plants his hands on top of the vanity on either side of me, his arms caging me in. I press my thighs together as the scent of leather hits me.

His hands are large and strong, the ink covering everything all the way to his fingernails. Several silver rings adorning his fingers glint in the light. I can feel his necklaces falling against my hair, the weight of his heavy silver cross pressing against the nape of my neck. He's completely engulfed me.

My eyes hold his in the mirror, equally thrilled and terrified.

"Looks like you had a good night." He nods down to the cash, innuendo heavy in his voice.

"It could've been better," I respond simply. I don't know where this is going, so I'm not giving anything more than I get.

"Count it for me." There's a demanding edge hidden in his calm tone. I reach for my pile of tips before his next words stop me. "All of it."

I freeze.

He knows.

Of course he fucking knows. He saw me take the money and hide it.

"If you don't give me the rest of the money, I'll enjoy taking it from you, little devil." His hands stay firmly planted, but I feel as if he reached into my top and fondled me.

Heat spreads through me—whether from fear or arousal, I'm not sure. After a second of hesitation, I reach into my top and pull out the hidden cash. His eyes break from mine to follow the movement of my hands as they reach beneath the mesh and lace to produce the evidence of my crime. Caught red-handed.

Damn.

"Well, would you look at that?" His face lowers, his mouth close to my ear. "Some of my money made it into your bra. I guess that means you need to start over."

"You're really just going to loom there in my personal space?" I shoot back, staring him down and quirking my brows. He grins, and I swear my panties dissolve.

"Seems like I've gotta keep a very close eye on my money around you. Besides, I *really* like being in your personal space." His eyes move back to my hands. "Go ahead."

I count out each stack of bills carefully, then count again to be sure. Once I'm satisfied, I move to the receipt with my tips from credit cards. The total comes out to just over two thousand dollars.

"Not bad, only three hundred and twelve thousand dollars to go." His smirk doesn't falter when my glare snaps to the mirror to meet his gaze. "We're going to have a lot of fun together, little devil."

"Don't count on it," I snap. "And my name is Jill."

"I know exactly who you are."

A thrill runs through me, my body telling me to run. But I'm not going anywhere. I simply narrow my eyes at him, unamused.

"I'm Gage Lawless. It's not a name you'll ever forget." He leans in so close his nose brushes against my hair, sending goosebumps over my skin. "I own you now, Jillian Hart."

CHAPTER TWO

JILL

I didn't expect to enjoy taking a life the first time I did it. Killing my abusive shithead of an ex-boyfriend, Carter, wasn't supposed to spark this urge inside me. It was meant to be a one-time thing—and he had it coming.

I'd been with Carter Long for a little over six months the first time he hit me. He claimed it wouldn't happen again, he promised me, begged me. Then he did it again. We'd fight a lot, and I'll admit I'm a fairly volatile person, so I excused his violence as emotional outbursts during a heated moment. But that excuse didn't last long when he started hurting me just for the hell of it.

One day, about eight months ago, after he tried to strangle me for disagreeing with him about what movie to watch, I snapped. He'd put his hands on me for the last time, so I threatened to end his life if he ever touched me or any other woman ever again. Then I left him.

Carter was an arrogant prick who thought rules didn't apply to him—something I should've seen as the raging red flag it is. When I saw him out with his new girlfriend four months ago, I knew he hadn't taken my threat seriously.

He should have.

When his young, admittedly gorgeous, new girlfriend raised her arms over her head, and I saw the bruises, I knew. The rage inside me burned white hot that night. The next night, I found him at the dock where he liked to smoke, all alone.

Plunging the knife into him wasn't the best part, and neither was knowing my face would be the last thing he'd ever see. It was watching the arrogance fade from his face as the life drained from his eyes. It was the sight of his blood, so beautiful and perfectly red, against my skin as he paid for his sins.

The police had chalked it up to a random mugging gone wrong, and none of the suspicion ever landed on me. Carter's wealthy parents—who turned a blind eye to their piece-of-shit son's abusive tendencies and excused his behavior away—offered a ridiculously big reward for information about his death. No one ever came forward.

Pity.

His then-girlfriend is currently thriving. I follow her on social media to keep an eye on her.

But Carter, as it turns out, isn't the only person I want to kill. Not even close. And now I know how good it feels—stealing one life to take back my own. Call it what you want: acts of revenge, sickness, the pure darkness of evil. Maybe all of the above. But that doesn't change the reality.

I *really* like killing. And I have plans for who's next.

The sound of footsteps catches my attention. And there he is, my next target.

Jonas strolls towards me like there's no stopping him from getting what he wants. He'd murmured as much to me at the party earlier, saying, "I spent too long without sampling the goods. It's about time I get some of this sweet ass of yours."

I let him think that's why we're here. Being the man he is, so used to getting his way, he didn't even question why I would tell him to meet me at the old loading dock behind an abandoned warehouse at three in the morning. All he heard was *sex*.

That's his problem, not mine.

"Are you ready to get messy?" His eyes run over me. "I'm finally going to use that big mouth of yours for the only thing it's good for."

I've changed out of my bottle service set back into my all-black bartending outfit. Black is good at keeping secrets. Things are about to get real messy, but not for the reason he thinks.

"You have no idea how much I've wanted to do this." I've never spoken truer words. Excitement courses through me, all of my senses heightening.

"I always knew you were an eager little slut, throwing that ass at anyone with a dick," he says, adjusting himself in his pants. "Now come here."

"What if I told you to wait?" I give him my best bedroom eyes, watching as he licks his lips.

"I'm done waiting."

Jonas stalks closer, aggressively invading my space. I recognize the look in his eyes, the intent to take me whether I want it or not. He's so close I can smell the cognac on his breath and the smoke that clings to his clothes. He grabs one of my hands and places it on his crotch, his dick hardening beneath the material of his pants. Yanking me against him, my left hand is pinned between us as his arms wrap around me to grab my ass.

"You never take no for an answer, do you?"

He lets out a grunt as he grinds against me, the sound drowning out the chink of my switchblade springing open in the hand down at my side.

"You like forcing people to do what you want. You get off on it."

"Stop fucking talking and take your pants off. This doesn't have to be unpleasant for you. If you're good, I might even let you get off too." His hands grow rough on me, moving to pull on the waistband of my black jeans.

When he pushes me back against a wooden pallet to yank my top up, I use the space created between us to position my knife. With a step forward and a strong thrust, my knife sinks into his abdomen. My four-inch blade is met with resistance, but with an extra shove, I break through his muscular wall without too much trouble.

"Oh, I'm definitely getting off tonight," I murmur, reveling in the warmth of the blood coating my hand. Jonas stands still as a statue, his body locked in shock. His eyes go wide, looking down to where I've stabbed him. Taking advantage of his stillness, I pull the knife out and ram it back in—this time angling it upwards to pierce his liver. I know I've hit the right place when another rush of blood starts pouring out of him.

"What the fuck—" Jonas stammers, a range of emotions flashing across his expression. "You fat fucking bitch." The color is already starting to drain from his face. But I'm not done yet.

"What's the matter? You don't want me anymore? You can't seem to get it up." My free hand palms his semi-hard dick through his pants, giving it a punishing squeeze. "Not that it would make a difference. You're way too small to make it past my ass."

Pulling the knife from his torso, his shaky hands grab at the wound as if his fingers can stop the bleeding and undo the internal damage. I take the opportunity to slash his thigh, severing the femoral artery. With a shout of agony, he claws at his leg before falling to his knees. A string of curses spew from his mouth, mixed with slurs and insults. His angry words fall on deaf ears.

"You look good on your knees, Jonas. This is where you've belonged all along." He's bleeding out fast, right before my very eyes—but it's still not enough. The adrenaline that spikes through me is intoxicating, and I'm riding the high until I'm drunk on it.

His stammering and sputtering are silenced with a gargle when my blade slices across his throat, cutting both his windpipe and jugular vein. Taking a step forward, I press the ball of my foot to his shoulder and give it a shove that sends him falling backward onto the ground. His eyes widen up at me, gulping for air to no avail. Moving closer, I tilt my head and look down at him.

The dying part takes longer than I originally thought. I remember it took a good forty-five minutes for Carter to bleed to death. This time, I've made a few adjustments to my technique by improving my aim and knowing where to cut. I still have a lot to learn, but a girl's gotta work with what she's got.

Losing his strength, Jonas' arms fall to his sides. I'm not an expert yet, but with how much he's bleeding, I'm guessing he only has a few more minutes left.

I better make them count.

Stepping over his neck, I stand over him before lowering my full weight to be sitting on his chest. His eyes no longer follow me, instead gazing distantly at the ceiling. His chest struggles beneath me for what little air he can get.

Taking my knife, I lightly trace the lines of his face with the blade to toy with him. His eyes find me again when I start to speak.

"I like you so much better this way," I state. "Silent and hurting." He wheezes as his struggling breaths become short and erratic. I can quite literally feel the life draining out of him. And it feels fucking amazing.

"Oh, don't give me that face, just be grateful I'm so generous," I patronize, weaponizing words he's said to me on more than one occasion—usually while forcing me to service his heinous clients. "You should smile more, put that pretty face to good use." His attempt at glaring at me is pathetic, but I applaud the effort. I huff out a dramatic sigh and shake my head at him. "Here, let me help you."

Dragging the tip of the knife, I watch his skin split under the blade. Jonas' eyes bulge, his face twitching against my artistry—but I don't stop until I've carved a bloody smile onto his face. "There we go. Now, is that so bad?"

Seeing he's about to draw his last stunted breath, I lean in closer and lower my voice until it's barely above a whisper. "I know you're lying here wondering why this is happening to you, and I don't want there to be any confusion. This is for what you did to my brother, Tommy—taking his life before stealing mine. You better hope whatever pit of hell you end up rotting in is so deep that I can't reach you when I get there."

With one last shudder, Jonas stills. His eyes stare through me, now lifeless and unseeing. The silence is beautiful, and I soak it in. I feel so powerful, absolutely unstoppable. My right hand is coated in sticky blood, and it's a lovely shade of red. I'm going to enjoy wearing it to work tomorrow.

Reaching my clean hand into my bra, I pull out a mini vial. Unscrewing the top, I drag the rim up Jonas' neck to collect several drops of blood. Replacing the lid, I hold the vial up to the light of the nearby lampost to get a better look. Satisfaction settles inside me, filling me until there's no room for regret or remorse.

I'm not sorry, and I'm only getting started.

CHAPTER THREE

JILL

"**W**hat about this one?" Lana asks, holding up a tube of red lipstick. I gaze at the color for a moment in consideration before shaking my head.

"Close, but no. It's a little more maroon than that, more vampy," I say as she puts the lipstick back where she found it on the makeup display. Strolling down the aisle, my eyes scan each lip product that I pass in search of the perfect shade.

"Don't you already have, like, five red lipsticks?" Lana asks from the next aisle over.

"Yeah, so? I have to wear them to work a lot, and I get bored." My eyes catch on the last color in the display next to me. "This one, this is the color I'm looking for."

"Damn. Okay, now I totally see the vision. You need that," Lana says from behind me, peering over my shoulder as I swatch the dark red lipstick on the back of my hand. The formula is creamy, and I'll definitely need the matching lip liner to keep it in place. But the color is perfect.

Finding lipsticks the exact shade of the blood I've shed

is addicting. The thrill when I find what I'm looking for—when the shade matches exactly what the tiny vial looked like when I collected my victim's blood—is intoxicating. The first swipe of the bright red lipstick that matched Carter's blood had felt like a hit of the best drug on the market—the high only second to the actual kill. Now I'm determined to grow my collection. With each new man I make bleed, a new lip combo will make its way into my makeup bag.

And now I've found Jonas.

Lana doesn't know what this lipstick represents. I haven't told her about my newest violent obsession—I haven't told anyone. Lana would never turn on me, as my true ride or die, I know she'd be first in line to help me bury the bodies.

Literally. There's no question of loyalty.

I trust Lana with my life—and my kills—but the only way to ensure something stays a secret is not to tell a single soul about it. Plus, it gives her plausible deniability and all that shit.

Since the day I met Lana Love five years ago, we've been inseparable. We grew close insanely quickly and never looked back—she's my other half. Not to mention, she's absolutely gorgeous with platinum blonde hair cut bluntly just above her shoulder, charming dimples that decorate her megawatt smile, and lots of body to work with.

We're the same in that aspect, wearing the same size clothing with almost the exact same measurements. The only difference is where I have a little extra ass, she has more tits. Nothing beats having a best friend you can share clothes with, especially another plus-size baddie with great style.

"Red is definitely your color," Lana states, and I agree.

"It's a good thing, too. Red seems to have taken over my life lately." It's the truth. Between the red lipstick, the interior of Inferno, and the blood I crave to shed—there's no escaping it. So I embrace it instead, and it does look damn good on me.

"Now help me find a lipstick for my date with Christos tonight," she announces, picking up a plumping peach lipgloss to get a better look.

"You're seeing Christos again? This is your third date with the guy in a week." I give her a sly look over my shoulder, but she just rolls her eyes and shrugs.

"So? It's not like it's serious between us. He's only in town a few more days, and he gives good dick. Why not get it while I can?"

"Okay..." My voice trails off, not the least bit convinced.

"Besides, he's an arms dealer. You know I don't do relationships with men who deal with guns—not after Nico. Never again." The smile tilting her lips tells me I can't believe a word she says. She's drawn to dangerous men. Men who can't file an honest tax return and are often on some sort of federal watch list. It's one of the many things we have in common—we like to flirt with darkness.

"You can't even say that with a straight face," I point out. She flashes me a big, dazzling smile.

"I'm thinking tonight I wanna do a pink and pouty look." She purses her full lips into an exaggerated pout, widening her big hazel eyes. "A look that says *I deserve another Chanel*."

I tilt my head back and laugh. Lana does well for herself, we both do—or at least I did. Now that my paychecks are being taken for my brother's debt, I'm left clutching at the lifestyle I've grown to love.

Lana knows my predicament, and she's very generous.

But I can't let her act as my sugar mama, I can't enjoy things knowing they're draining her bank account. So if men want to buy us pretty things or pay for expensive trips, we let them.

"I'm sure we can find something that'll do the trick," I assure her. Lana doesn't have any trouble getting what she wants and looks stunning in everything. Her sense of style ranges between glam streetwear, clubbing Barbie, and early 2000s with an urban twist. She reminds me of a Bratz doll if it were a fat babe with expensive taste.

I turn to show her a gorgeous pink lipstick when my eyes catch on a figure standing in the parking lot. A man is casually leaning against my car, tattooed arms crossed over his chest with silver rings glinting in the summer sun, looking into the store through the front window.

Looking at *me*.

Gage Lawless' dark eyes follow my every move as I put the lipstick back on the shelf. When our eyes meet, he smirks and looks me over from head to toe. He's completely relaxed, his presence like a dark cloud on a sunny day.

He looks out of place in this shopping center—it's obvious he's not here to buy cosmetics, get his hair done at the salon next door, or get a facial at the med spa.

He's here for me.

And with how he's standing out in the open so brazenly, it's obvious that he wants me to see him. The sight of him picks at me, making annoyance itch under my skin. It feels like he's trying to get a rise out of me, but I'm not going to give him the satisfaction. He doesn't get to ruin my day.

The best way to deal with someone demanding attention, someone who's trying to force your hand, is to ignore them.

Pulling my eyes away, I continue my shopping like I never saw him. Lana and I browse while she tells me about the restaurant her date's taking her to tonight—sampling products and tossing things into our baskets—until we've both racked up quite the beauty haul. Stress claws at me with every swipe of my credit card, and I have to force myself not to cringe against the numbers being added to the balance.

Today was a shopping day, and this is our last stop after clothing and accessories. When we're finally done shopping, we check out.

Walking out the door, I can see when Lana registers our shadow. "There's a man on your car," she murmurs, leaning in. "Is he yours?"

"Yeah, just ignore him," I say, staring straight ahead. Stowing our shopping bags in the trunk, Lana climbs into the passenger seat without a word. When I approach the driver's side, there he is.

His massive frame leans against my vehicle, taking up space and drawing me in like gravity. The closer I get to him, the more my body responds.

I want him to wreck me.

I don't spare the man a glance when I reach for the handle. He doesn't budge an inch, simply standing with his hands tucked under his crossed arms to display the rich ink covering his beautiful, bulging biceps. After a moment of trying—and failing—to get my door open, I finally give him a taste of what he wants.

"Gage."

"Jill."

"You're in my way," I say, keeping my tone and expression neutral. He doesn't like being ignored, and despite his calm demeanor, I can feel the tension radiating off his body.

Instead of backing away, he leans in, speaking intimately into my ear.

"I want to be in more than just your way, little devil." He gives me a cocky grin when he finally steps back with a dark promise. "I'll see you around."

I open my car door as soon as there's enough room, not bothering to make sure it doesn't hit him on my way in. Unfortunately, he's faster than me and dodges it effortlessly. I climb behind the wheel, shutting the door soundly behind me.

"Is that Gage Lawless?" Lana asks, pushing her vintage Prada sunglasses down her nose to look at him over the frames.

"That's him," I confirm, starting the car. I told her all about last night, all the way up until the part where I met up with Jonas and killed him. I spared no details about what happened between me and the new owner of Inferno. There are no secrets between me and my best friend—aside from the ones too dark to see the light of day.

Gage tucks his hands into the front pockets of his jeans as he walks backward towards a motorcycle, only taking his eyes off me to tilt his head and grin at Lana before his gaze locks back on me.

"Goddamn," Lana murmurs, echoing my thoughts the first time I saw Gage. "That man wants you so bad. Are you gonna fuck him?"

"Probably," I say, putting the car into gear. I rev the engine and peel out of the parking spot, but not before flipping him the bird. "If he's any good, I might even let *him* fuck *me*."

The question isn't if I'm going to fuck Gage. It's whether or not I'm going to kill him.

"Here you go," I shout over the club music. "Four Hellfire shots." Placing the tray on the counter in front of the group of girls, I grin as their eyes widen. The red shots look so pretty, with flames dancing on the tops of each glass. They exchange glances before grabbing a shot each to clink in cheers and down in one gulp.

They each cope with the effects differently—one shouting with a whoop, one screwing her eyes shut tight and clenching her fist in front of her, one hopping around in a little dance, and one taking it with a straight face like she'd just taken a sip of water.

"Another round?" I ask, but they shake their heads.

"No, I wanna go dance," the hoppy girl says, tugging two of her friends' arms. "But we'll definitely be back. That shit is good."

"Thanks, girl," the straight-faced girl says, laying down some bills. They paid when they ordered the shots, so this is for me. I accept it with a smile.

"My pleasure, ladies. Enjoy yourselves." I'm off in ten minutes, so I won't be here when they come back. But Billy will take good care of them when he takes over behind the bar.

As soon as they walk away and disappear into the crowds on the dancefloor, I let out a deep breath. My eyes lift to scan over the crowd, half expecting to find a dark figure standing amongst the partiers—watching me.

Gage has appeared several times since my shopping spree earlier today, always watching me like it's his favorite thing to do. Every time, he makes himself known— standing out so there's no confusion about what he's doing.

I don't try to avoid his attention. In fact, I meet it head on. I never shy away from meeting his gaze, but I won't let it affect how I live my life. He can watch me, try to get inside my head and toy with me. But I'll decide when it's really time to play.

Seeing nothing in my perusal of the dancers, I focus on collecting my receipts and cash tips. Tonight has been hectic, to say the least, and I'm glad I'm not closing. There have been some big and rowdy groups here tonight.

I'm not working at the main bar, which is a blessing and a curse. Tonight, I'm at the smaller second bar Inferno has off the dancefloor. We only serve shots over here, so the work is faster and much simpler. But the chaos is so close to the DJ booth, with sweaty throngs of dancing partiers, that it can be overwhelming, and the tips are a lot smaller.

Either way, I'm almost done for the night. After I finish here and I'm off the clock, I'm getting out of this outfit and letting loose.

My phone vibrates in my pocket, alerting me to a notification. Pulling it out of the back pocket of my jeans, I see it's a text from Lana.

> We're here. Christos got us the Sinner's Suite. Now get your big beautiful ass out here so the party can start!

I can't help but laugh. I wasn't planning on staying out tonight after my shift, but Lana insisted. She demanded I meet up with her and Christos after their dinner so her boy toy could buy us bottles and treat us to the VIP experience. It's not nearly the first time one of our dates has taken us out to 'treat' us—it's usually a requirement for Lana to even consider letting them take her out in the first place—but I'm never one to say no to a good time on someone else's dime. Especially if Lana's going to be there.

I send her a quick text to give me twenty minutes to clock out and change, and I'll meet her at the table. Clocking out on the computer and saying goodbye to the other bartender, Jordan, I weave my way through the club toward the dressing room.

Stripping out of my work clothes, I wish I could take a shower to wash my work off before I play. But that's not an option, so I pull out the packet of baby wipes I keep in my locker to scrub myself down before I get dressed.

Gotta stay fresh.

The dress I brought to change into is a slinky gunmetal gray number with thick spaghetti straps, a square neckline that cuts low across my breasts, and a tie that sinches in my cleavage. The corset bodice accentuates the curve of my waist, the short skirt flairs around my full hips and flutters to just below my round ass. The heels I picked for tonight are chunky black knee-high platform boots with a five-inch heel.

I love these boots; they're fun, sexy as hell, and remind me of the shoes my Bratz dolls had when I was growing up. They also bring me from my five-foot-seven-inch height to a full six feet tall—and I like being tall. I'm a statement that can't be ignored.

I lean over the vanity and reapply my lipstick in the mirror. The deep maroon color is rich and vampy, drawing the attention my full lips deserve. Swiping the color on my skin fills me with the same power I felt last night, and the exhilaration makes me smile.

Red my lips, Jonas. And rot in hell.

Popping the cap back on with a click, I unzip my makeup bag to toss the tube back in. It clinks against the other tube inside, one that's a true vibrant red—Carter. They can get cozy in there together. More will be joining them soon enough.

A few swipes of anti-chafe stick to the insides of my thighs, and a spritz of my favorite sultry perfume are the finishing touches before I'm off to meet my best friend.

The Sinner's Suite is a private table on an elevated platform above the dance floor with the other VIP Gold tables. My best friend is sitting with a fit man dressed to the nines. Lana stands from the curved red velvet sofa to meet me at the bottom of the stairs.

"There you are! I was about to come find you, you look gorgeous," she gushes, grabbing my hand and pulling me towards the table. "Come get some champagne. We got the good stuff. And you *have* to meet Christos. He's dying to meet you."

"He's dying to meet me?" I repeat with some added skepticism. From the way Lana has talked about him, the only two things the man is obsessed with are her and himself.

"Duh! I never shut up about you, so it's only fair that he gets to meet the real love of my life." Lana looks over her shoulder to flash me a wink and blow me a kiss, making me laugh.

"Alright then," I say, flipping my hair over my shoulder. "Let's go meet my competition."

It's Lana's turn to laugh as we approach the table. She leans in closer, lowering her voice as much as she can with the music.

"Trust me, babe, there's no competition." Her smile turns dreamy. "Although, he does call me his 'star'. *Astéri.*" With that, she turns on her megawatt smile and addresses the man of the hour—greeting him like they've been apart for weeks instead of minutes. "Christos! Hi, baby."

Christos pulls Lana in for a kiss, his arm circling her waist to rest on her round hip. When he pulls back, he turns to focus on me. His thick black hair is styled back from his chiseled face, perfectly suited for his bronze complexion and mediterranean features. He's tall, meeting my eyeline in my heels, and I can tell that he's well-built—and from what Lana's told me, well endowed. There aren't any labels on his clothes, but there's no question that they're designer —he has real money, it's not just for show.

"This is my other half, Jill," Lana says brightly.

"Hi," I say with a smile.

"Jill, it's nice to finally meet you." Christos' whiskey-brown eyes sweep over me from head to toe, and he gives a little nod of appreciation.

He's obviously obsessed with Lana's plus-size body, so I'm not too surprised that he finds me attractive in some way too. I have no problem being appreciated by a man, especially as handsome and rich as Christos is.

But if he's looking for a threesome, that's not going to happen. I don't fuck with my best friend—I value our friendship too much to jeopardize it for a messy *ménage à trois*. Christos is Lana's boy toy, so letting him buy me a night of drinks and dancing is as far as I'll ever go.

"Let's get you some champagne," Christos announces, gesturing over a bottle girl named Remi to fill a glass for me. As I accept the glass and take a generous sip, Christos continues. "Lana said you just got off work, and I figured you might be hungry, so I had some sushi delivered."

Some is not the word to describe the amount of sushi arranged on the table in front of me. Between the assort-ment of sushi rolls, sashimi, nigiri, and temaki, he clearly ordered one of everything on the menu. I lift my eyes from the table to meet Lana's, and she nods—a delighted sparkle in her pretty hazel eyes.

"I don't like very many people, Christos. But you're off to a good start." I reach for a piece of an unagi roll and eat it in one bite. A proud grin lights up Christos' face when my eyes roll back in exaggerated appreciation at the flavor.

That is damn good.

"Excellent," he says, turning to Lana as the song changes to something with a heady beat. "Dance with me, *astéri*."

Lana joins Christos, plastering her body against his as she moves with the music. I toss back the rest of my champagne and pop another piece of sushi into my mouth before I stand up to join them. The beat pulsates through the air, vibrating through the floor until it resonates in my chest.

Accepting another glass of bubbly when it's offered to me, I don't stop moving. Lifting the glass to my lips, my gaze collides with a dark pair of eyes and I falter. Awareness prickles over me at the sight of the man watching me so intently that I can feel his eyes on my skin.

Gage sits reclined on the sofa at the VIP table a few yards away, sharp eyes following my every movement as if I'm the only other person in the world. Even when his friend—Anders, from the VIP lounge the other night—walks up to join him at the table and greets him, Gage's eyes never stray from me.

He's watching me again.

Again? No, *still*.

The unadulterated attention settles through me until every nerve is standing on end. It's both intoxicating and irritating. When he cocks his head to the side and smirks at me, annoyance sparks into anger as liquid desire pools between my legs.

Fuck him.

Fuck me.

A fiery cocktail of lust and indignation pour through me, making me both horny and spiteful. Ripping my eyes away, I turn back to my friend and her date. By the time I see the bottom of my second glass of champagne, some of the tension has eased from my body.

After the third glass, I don't care so much that he's watching as I dance and laugh. And the first round of shots leaves just me, my friends, and the music.

Gage can lurk and watch me all he wants, I don't mind. I'd watch me too. Every time my eyes meet his, the desire to fuck him grows stronger. Just like the urge to end him.

CHAPTER FOUR

GAGE

F*uck, she's perfect.*
Carefree, living life on her whims and letting nothing stand in her way. Jillian Hart couldn't be more perfect if I designed her myself. The fire blazing inside her threatens to scorch everything in her path, and I plan on burning like the damned.

She moves with the music, dancing and laughing with the group she's with. She doesn't shy away from being the center of attention, not once. She embraces it, feeds on it. My eyes touch every part of her beautiful body, admiring the art of her. When our eyes meet, dark satisfaction brews deep inside me.

Absolute perfection.

Finally being touched by the weight of her stare, feeling the focus of her attention after all this time, was worth the wait. After five long months, she sees me—because I let her.

Jillian Hart has been mine a lot longer than the debt she owes me, whether she knows it or not. But she'll learn. She'll see that there's no escaping me, no amount of money

that can sever our connection. There is no other option—
I'm an omen of the inevitable.

Jill will love me, crave me, *breathe* me. She'll feel me
rooted so deeply inside her she won't know where her soul
ends and mine begins. She'll *be* for me.

Just like I am for her.

Until then, I'll watch her and enjoy the way her bombshell body moves with the music. I'll take pleasure in
knowing she sees me.

"She sees you watching her," Anders comments, though
his eyes have barely strayed from Jill's blonde friend all
night. I've had my eyes on her for months, always just
staying out of sight. But not anymore—it's time I make my
plans a reality.

"I know." I lean back against the sofa, ignoring the
flashing red lights and the thrumming bass of the music.
Tilting my head, I let my beer dangle between my legs as I
watch her.

She arches her back and shakes her juicy ass to the beat
next to her best friend, Lana. Lana's interesting enough—
it's not painful to watch her with my Jill—especially with
the company she keeps. The man dancing up against Lana's
back with his hands on her waist, Christos Alexandris, is a
war criminal and arms dealer with connections to the mob
both here in Chicago and in New York. I don't give a single
fuck if Lana's dating him seriously or not, as long as he—
and his mess—doesn't touch Jill.

"You're staring again," Anders says. I never stopped. He
knows that. I could sit here for the rest of the night without
moving an inch, just watching her breathe, and not regret a
single second.

"So are you," I point out. He can't seem to tear his dark
eyes away from the blonde.

"They're both fucking hot." He takes a swig of his beer, rolling his bulky shoulders and settling back on the couch to get comfortable. He's attracted to Jill, but I don't give a shit about that. I don't fault him for recognizing how stunning she is, and I don't mind other men looking. I want them to look—to admire, and desire—to witness how brightly she burns. But they won't touch.

I don't share.

Anders knows exactly who Jill is to me—he's known all along. He knows what kind of a man I am.

He was with me the first night I saw her. She'd been on a night out at another club, Helix, with Lana and her brother Tommy. Anders and my other best friend, Messer, had dragged me out for my birthday that night to celebrate my 30th. That's when I saw her.

One of the bookies her idiot brother owed money to had tried to hassle him on the dance floor, but there she was, coming to her brother's rescue. She'd verbally cut the goon at the knees, and he'd left in a huff. I'd seen the violence in her eyes, a shadowed soul just longing to be recognized and set free. Then she'd gone right back to dancing like nothing had ever happened. That was all I needed to see.

Happy birthday to me.

I took my present and never looked back. Following her home was easy. She never even glanced over her shoulder —I'll have to spank her for that later. Her apartment is on the ground floor, something that both thrilled and infuriated me—she's not safe there.

Every moment I spent watching her was infectious— thrumming through my veins until she consumed me entirely. Every detail I learned about her was a hit of a drug that became my lifeline.

Jill has her own demons, twisted and beautiful. Her

darkness calls to mine, and I like that—I'm going to use it. I'll pull all of her shadows to the surface, warping them around us until I'm the only one she sees.

"What's her name?" Anders asks, trying to act casual when I know he's not. His darkness might not be as visible as mine, but it's there. We're opposite sides of the same coin.

"That's Lana Love," I respond, glancing over at him. His jaw is set as he gazes at her, and I know he's clocked how the Greek man's hands are all over her.

My phone buzzes in my pocket, reminding me that I have other responsibilities outside of the club. It's a text from my employee Stevie.

> Are you ever planning on coming back to the shop, or can I start redecorating now? This place could use a big splash of color. I'm thinking yellow.

My thumbs fly across the screen, typing out a message before pressing send.

> I'll be in tomorrow morning. Touch a paintbrush, and you're fired.

Her response is almost immediate.

> Yeah, right. And leave this place to be run by tweedle-dee, tweedle-dumbass, and tweedle-asshat? I don't think so.

She's not wrong. Firing her would mean having to leave my tattoo business in the hands of a bunch of shitheads. And I'll be dead and buried before I let anyone taint my reputation as a tattoo artist.

I'm not just a tattoo artist, I'm an ink master. My business, *Stained Heart Tattoos*, is the best there is. Over the last twelve years, I've been perfecting my craft and building a portfolio of clientele that NDAs keep me from talking about. People from all over the world come to me for their tattoos. No one comes even close to what I can do with a tattoo gun. Half of the tattoos that cover my body were done by me, and they're damn good.

Tattooing was also my introduction into the world of high-stake poker. One of my clients invited me to a game, and that was it. I've sat along side the world's most wealthy and powerful people with a drink in one hand and the winning cards in the other. After a few years, I don't just know everyone there is to know in the gambling world—I run it. Anders and I host some of the most exclusive games in the country with pots worth millions. And that success is only growing.

My eyes lift back to find Jill. She's accepting another glass of champagne from her server. When she does a twirl, her sexy little dress flares out, and I catch a glimpse of the sweet spot where her ass cheeks meet her thick thighs. I can't wait to get my hands and mouth on her.

She's got a body a man could sink into and get lost in.

She stays out with Lana and her date until almost three in the morning—drinking, dancing, and laughing. When they decide to call it a night, Lana goes back to her criminal's hotel room and Jill orders a car for a ride home. I know she's not listening for the rumbling engine of my custom black Thunder Stroke as she walks up the steps of her apartment building.

I sit on my bike to watch and wait. After a few minutes, the light turns on in her living room. Her blinds are drawn almost all the way, but a decent gap in the curtains allows me to track her.

She dumps her phone and bag on the counter before she fumbles around in the kitchen to chug a glass of water. After she's drained the glass, she turns off the lights, and her bedroom light turns on a few seconds later. Eventually, the apartment goes dark. I wait for several minutes before I climb off my motorcycle.

The latch on the gate leading to the alley along the side of her building clicks open easily once I remove the padlock with the key on my key ring. The first time I came here, there'd been nothing to stop someone from opening the gate.

Darkness cloaks the side of the building as I walk to the set of French doors that lead into her apartment. Lifting the keyring in my hand, I slide the correct key into the lock and it clicks open without issue. It's an older building, so the door sticks when I push it open and the floorboards creak under my weight.

Quiet stillness fills the apartment. The only light is the faint glow from the streetlight filtering through the small opening in the curtains. I don't need light. I know every inch of this apartment—the small sectional sofa in the living room to my left with the black and white checkered throw blanket, the circular coffee table that always has some sort of half-finished drink perched on it. Three pairs of high heels are scattered between the living room and kitchen, and a bag of her work outfits is lying haphazardly on the floor next to the door to her bedroom.

My girl is messy. She likes her place to look, feel, and smell like her. Every once in a while, she'll get on a tear and clean the place spotless, but that usually only lasts a few hours before her sexy bras are slung over the back of the couch, and her Red Bull cans and half-drunk coffee cups are cluttering the coffee table again.

I know that the ice maker on the fridge doesn't work, the silverware drawer gets jammed if you don't use the handle properly, and the ceiling fan in the living room clicks when the blades start to collect too much dust. I know this place as if it were my own. I've spent almost as many nights here in the last five months.

The first thing I do is head to the kitchen and grab a chilled bottle of water from the fridge and a couple Ibuprofen from the cabinet above the sink. The only sound in the bedroom when I enter are the two fans Jill keeps going at all times.

I walk over to the nightstand and place the water and pills next to the lamp. Standing next to the bed, I gaze down at the woman sleeping soundly. Jill lies sprawled in the sheets wearing only an oversized band tee, laying on her stomach and hugging the pillows with one shapely leg hitched up to reveal her little black lace panties.

She's so still—she always is when she sleeps. As soon as her head hits the pillow, she's completely dead to the world. I could start singing and jumping on the bed, and her eyelids wouldn't even flutter. Sleep is the only time she's still and silent. Peaceful—like the calm before the storm.

Because with Jill, there's always a storm brewing.

Walking backward four steps, I lower onto the chair at her vanity. My eyes trace the glorious curves of her—the way her back dips, how her plump, gorgeous ass leads to round hips, thick thighs, and shapely long legs.

I have plans for that ass, those hips, and those legs. I have plans for every sinful inch of her.

She sleeps sprawled in the center of her king-sized bed until there's no room for anyone else—we'll have to fix that. Soon, I'll be in that bed with her, and she'll be the first thing I see when I open my eyes in the morning. I'll sleep feeling every beat of her heart.

I sit and watch her breathe, shift, and sigh for hours. Just like I have most nights since I first saw her. And just like all those nights, she'll sleep soundly until one of her many blaring alarms wakes her up to an empty room with no idea I was ever here.

I can picture how her hair will look when she sits up in bed, the grogginess in her voice while she mutters to herself about how she's 'never drinking again' as she searches the apartment for wherever she left her phone. But I know better.

Because I know Jill.

I know her past, I own her present, and I *am* her future.

CHAPTER FIVE

GAGE

"**O**h, so you *are* alive." The female voice carries over the buzzing of tattoo guns as I walk through the door. Fuchsia flashes out of the corner of my eye as I turn to see Stevie standing by the reception desk, her hand on her full hip.

"You've moved on to pink, huh?" I ask, taking in her bright pink hair. Stevie reaches up a tattooed arm to touch the ends of her freshly dyed shoulder-length hair.

"The white was a moment, but I was ready for a change. You know how much I love to play with color." She's wearing all black to match the uniform of my shop, but her body is covered in brightly colored tattoos. As young as she might look, Stevie is a master at saturation and color blending. That's why I hired her, and it's because of her tattoo abilities that I keep her around, despite her insistence on splashing her eccentric style in my otherwise all-black shop.

"It suits you," I comment.

"Connie's been calling," Stevie adds, making me pause. "She said to tell you *'if you don't get your ass over to the club-*

house to spend time with your family, she's gonna come bang down your front door.' I look up at the ceiling and huff out a deep breath. My mom has always had a flair for the dramatics, but it seems to be getting worse as she gets older.

"This is exactly why I didn't join the Chained Saints. If she calls again, tell her I have businesses to run. I can't be hanging around an MC clubhouse all the time," I say, walking past the front desk towards my office. My eyes catch on a pink vase full of bright yellow flowers. "And get that shit off my reception desk."

"Oh, come on, boss," she protests behind me. "They look nice."

"No yellow," I call over my shoulder before walking back through the shop towards my office.

The interior of my studio is designed to be simple and classic, with black-on-black walls, fixtures, and furniture. The only colors on the walls are featured in the framed tattoo design options and client photos. Each artist is allowed to personalize their workstation, but the theme remains throughout the space.

This building used to be a Catholic church, and I paid a pretty penny to restore the tall, arched, stained glass windows and hardwood floors that are original to the building. I'm not a religious man, but people come from all over the world to worship me as their tattoo god.

I have five tattoo artists working for me, each with their own chair in the main bullpen that we call The Chapel. Three additional chairs sit along the back wall in separate booths—The Confessionals—with heavy black curtains for clients wanting more privacy.

I pass three empty chairs—one of them being Stevie's colorful workstation. It's still pretty early, and I usually only require one tattoo artist per shift to be in the shop available for walk-ins. The rest come in to handle their appointments. Today will be fully booked.

Once in my office, a decent-sized room featuring the biggest and most ornate stained glass window in the building, I walk past my tattoo station to my desk. With a few clicks, the surveillance feed appears on my computer screen with a grid view of several cameras. Placing my palms on the desk, my eyes scan each feed until my focus lands heavily on what I'm looking for.

Her.

Just the sight of her—even black and white and pixelated—hits my bloodstream like a drug.

The door to my office swings open without warning, and two massive figures enter unannounced.

"I told you he'd be creeping on her when we got here. Pay up," Messer says. He holds his hand out to Anders, who smacks it away as he trails in behind him.

"I was the one who said that, dumbass. I'm not giving you shit." Anders turns his attention to me and pulls his shirt over his head. "Take a break from being a peeping tom to get this tattoo finished." Lowering his bulky frame onto my tattoo chair, he makes himself comfortable, looking at me expectantly. Taking one last glance at Jill on the screen, I push off the desk to walk over to my tattoo station.

Anders' deep brown skin has healed fully from our last session, and he's ready for the final ink to finish off the angel wings across his chest.

"Have you let her see you yet?" Messer asks, strolling over to my desk to look at the security feeds. He's known about Jill from the moment I laid eyes on her since he was with me that night. Unlike Anders, Messer doesn't share the same dark possessive qualities as me—at least, they don't present the same way. He might obsess over one woman, but he doesn't mind sharing her. In fact, he gets off on it.

"Yeah, I have."

"Understatement of the year," Anders laughs.

"And she likes it," I say. The memory of Jill soaking up my attention last night has me itching with need. The need to see her, feel her.

Fill her.

I force myself to focus on the task at hand while I prep my station to finish Anders' tattoo. Sitting on the stool, I roll closer and pull on my disposable gloves.

"That's unexpected," Messer says thoughtfully, gazing at the screen, probably at my Jill. "Out of all the outcomes you've been planning, that wasn't even on the list."

He's right, at least not one I said out loud. After watching Jill for so long and fantasizing about the day she'd finally see me, I'd braced myself for every possible outcome —screaming in fear, violent anger, calling the cops. I was ready for anything, I still am. Everything except arousal. Jill being turned on by my unrelenting presence proves that we're made for each other. And I intend to take full advantage.

"I didn't hate watching her either, especially with her hot blonde friend shaking her ass like that." Anders grins at the memory. "Lana Love. She was bangin'. I'd put my lovin' on Lana, believe that." Despite his easygoing tone, there's a sharpness in Anders' eyes that tells me his interest in the blonde is more than casual. I won't be surprised if I hear her name out of his mouth a lot more in the future.

"Shut up and stop fantasizing about her. I'm not touching you if you get a boner in my chair." I pull my tray over and turn on my tattoo gun. Anders shuts his mouth and lets me get to work while Messer updates me on Jill's movements.

Messer tries to get me to elaborate on Jill, but it's none of his business. They don't need to know Jill the way I do.

No one ever will.

I zone in, diving into my work as I weave artistry on my canvas. With Anders' deep skin tone, it's essential that all of my blacks are saturated and precise without being muddy. While I work, Messer tells us about the restoration project he'll be working on—an estate from the Gilded Age on the East Coast.

"How long are you gonna be gone for this one?" Anders asks. Messer is an architect and a fucking talented one at that. When I bought this building, it was just a crumbling church full of dusty pews. He transformed it into the tattoo shop I'd always pictured.

"Right now, the plan is six weeks. But knowing these types of projects, it'll probably end up being at least twelve. I leave in four days," Messer explains, leaning back in his chair. He travels a lot for his work, so spending a few months across the country doesn't faze him. I'm not stoked that he's going to be gone again, our friend group isn't the same without him. But he's pursuing his own art, and I would never fault him for that.

"We're gonna have to video chat for twelve whole weeks like a couple in a long-distance relationship? Damn," Anders jokes, even though he's half serious. The three of us are in constant contact with each other.

"You know I'll always make time for you," Messer says, blowing Anders a kiss. We might all be laughing, but we're dead serious.

We're not just friends, we're brothers. Family.

Back when we first met, I'd hated both of them. I was an

angry teenager who had been taken from my parents and forced into the foster care system. My mom and dad were in and out of prison for everything from petty crimes to grand larceny. For most of my adolescence I had no contact with my parents or my younger brother. I'm on good terms with them now, but those relationships didn't happen until a few years ago.

Back then, my lack of family ties made me volatile and reckless. The boys group home didn't know how to handle my temper, so I was thrown into the room for the more 'troubled' kids. Those troubled little assholes were Anders and Messer.

We fought at first—verbally, psychologically, and physically. Anders was always the biggest, so I knew better than to get in the way of his fists. I'd play mind games instead. Messer didn't give a shit about anything, so the only way to get to him was when things came to blows. Eventually, us versus each other shifted to us against the world. We were stuck in a shitty situation together, but we all wanted the same thing.

To be someone. To build something.

We got out together, doing whatever it took to make names for ourselves and build the lives we wanted. I was going to be an ink master, and become the best tattoo artist in the world. Anders built his elite private security company, Obsidian Security Solutions, from the ground up and became one of the best in the business. And Messer is now one of the top architects in the country, specializing in historic restoration and modernization.

Now, the three of us are unstoppable and unbreakable.

CHAPTER SIX

JILL

I'm squinting against the daylight in my room before my eyes even open. Every one of my muscles aches, either from the amount of alcohol I consumed last night or the intense amount of dancing—probably both. A low groan leaves me as I sit up slowly and prop myself up against my backboard. Inhaling a deep breath, the faint scent of leather blended with tobacco, and a warm musk fills my nose.

Gage.

I inhale again but can only pick out my amber room spray, making me question what I thought I smelled before. Am I still drunk? No, I'm too miserable.

Damn, I've completely lost it.

My head feels like a ball of lead, and fatigue pulls at my limbs until they're heavy. I huff out a breath and rake a hand through my wild hair. Last night is a blur of drinking, laughing, dancing, and more drinking. And now my body is revolting against it.

Woof.

What time is it? I'm never drinking again.

Looking over at my nightstand in search of my phone, my eyes snag on the bottle of water and pain pills waiting for me. Wow, drunk Jill has really been on top of her shit lately. It feels out of character, but I'll take it.

Reaching for the Ibuprofen, I toss the pills into my mouth before cracking open the bottle of water. Tilting my head back, I gulp the water to swallow the pills and chug the rest until the bottle is empty. The liquid feels so good going down my dry throat.

Dragging myself out of the bed, my body screams at me for partying so hard. Nausea rolls in my stomach, and I have to cover my mouth to fight the urge to gag. Shuffling towards the living room, I scowl at the bright sunlight bathing my apartment.

"I'm never drinking again," I mutter, looking around my apartment. Walking around, I lift pieces of clutter in search of my purse. Hearing the faint ding of a notification coming from the kitchen, I finally find my bag on the floor behind the kitchen island. Digging through it, I pull out my phone to find several notifications, including three texts from Lana and one from my friend, Sierra, inviting me to a pool party at her luxury apartment.

Lana's off work today, and I could use a day poolside, so I respond to my best friend's text and invite her to the party as my plus one. After hitting send, I put my phone down and brace myself on the counter against the pounding in my skull.

Spying a mini bottle of Jack Daniels out of the corner of my eye, I snag it and crack it open. A little hair of the dog will ease the pain, and what's one more drink? Bringing the bottle up towards my mouth, I halt before it touches my lips.

The image of a rancid memory has my gut churning

painfully. *My dad stumbling into the kitchen in the morning and hunching over the counter while he added three ounces of brandy to his coffee. His hands shaking and a permanent scowl on his face until he was on his second cup.*

I knew better than to try and talk to him before he'd had his first beer of the day, which was usually around ten in the morning. When I was six years old, he backhanded me for trying to get him to drink a glass of water instead— it's how I lost my first tooth. I never made that mistake again.

Disgust twists inside me as I lower my arm and walk across the kitchen to the sink. Tipping the mini bottle upside down, I watch the amber liquid disappear down the drain.

I won't be like him.

Instead, I make myself a chai latte and plop down onto the couch. It's gonna take a nice long rotting session in front of the TV before I'm able to function like a normal human being, let alone go to a party.

Strolling out into the party, arm in arm with Lana, the pool deck is buzzing with music and partiers. Spotting Sierra at the drink station, we head her way. The leggy brunette lifts her drink and does a little shimmy when she sees us coming.

"Hey," she calls, drawing the word out dramatically. Lana and I dance up to her, vibing with the music for a moment before bursting into laughter. "Glad you could come."

"Are you kidding? A party with you at this nice pool? We wouldn't miss it." Lana pushes her sunglasses down the bridge of her nose to check out a hot guy walking by. "This building is nicer than I thought. Maybe I need to move."

"You could try, but the waitlist is currently three years long, and they vet their tenants more thoroughly than the state senate," Sierra laughs. "I only got in because the owner of the building had a crush on my mom in college."

"Damn, with a wait time like that, by the time I get to the top of the list, I won't be hot anymore." Lana replaces her glasses and flips her hair. "I'll just stick to flirting with the residents."

Sierra tilts her head back and laughs. She opens her mouth to say something but gets interrupted before she gets the chance. "Sierra, Taylor is looking for you," a guy calls from across the pool.

"Coming!" she yells back, turning back to us. "You two get some drinks and have fun. I'll find you later." With that, she's walking around the pool.

Snagging some sparkling water, Lana and I find some lounge chairs in a nice sunny spot to settle on. Setting down our drinks, we pull off our coverups before laying down to soak in some rays. Pulling the crochet mini dress over my head to stand in my bikini, my eyes can't help but look over enviously at the lack of cellulite on Lana's thighs and round ass. I know that the sunlight is harsh against the dimples, creases, and stretchmarks on my skin, and the idea of putting my coverup back on crosses my mind more than once.

But seeing Lana standing so boldly, embracing her body in the pink monokini without a second thought, empowers me to toss the dress aside before lowering onto the chair. Laying in the sun, Lana and I chat a little bit while we watch the other partiers around the different parts of the deck.

Several people surround the pool, sitting on the edge, standing in the water, or messing around on floaties. Clusters of people dance and drink while others eat tacos from the food cart in the corner. Lana's head moves as she scans the crowds, her eyes catching on someone off to the side.

"You have eyes on you," Lana says, nodding to my left. "Gage really has his minions following you around?" I follow her gaze to find Anders standing on the other side of the pool. But I'm not the one his eyes are zeroed in on.

"He's not looking at me," I inform her with a knowing tone.

"He's coming over," Lana murmurs, replacing her sunglasses and situating herself on the lounge chair like she doesn't have a care in the world. A moment later, a tall figure stands at the end of our chairs. Anders stands shirtless in a pair of orange swim trunks, the sunlight glowing against his melanin-rich skin. I look up to see him smile at me before his gaze latches on the blonde next to me.

"Jill, what a pleasant surprise seeing you here." His eyes remain boldly on Lana. "How you doing?"

"Hi there." Lana's fingers flutter in a flirty wave as she slides her sunglasses to rest on the top of her head.

"Anders, this is my best friend, Lana," I introduce. "He's friends with Gage."

"Are you a psycho stalker, too?" Lana asks, looking him up and down. Her tone hasn't lost its flirty undertone, but her gaze has sharpened.

"I'm definitely considering it now that I've met you," he replies smoothly, licking his bottom lip in appreciation as he openly checks her out. "Let me get you ladies a drink."

"I'm not drinking today," I inform him. My skin is overheating, and I spot Sierra in the pool. "I'm gonna go for a dip, but you two have fun." Standing up, I make intentional eye contact with Lana before sauntering away.

Joining the others in the water, I strike up a conversation with Sierra and her girlfriend, Taylor. Splashing around in the water, we laugh and dance, and I soak up as much sun as I can before it's time to get ready for another night at work.

Nothing gets rid of the buzz from a fun day by the pool like going into work. Walking into the empty club, I let out a heavy sigh. Being called in early with the instructions to 'clean and prep the bar' adds insult to injury. Miranda didn't specify *who* wanted me here by myself before anyone else arrives, but I can guess.

"Are you going to just keep lurking in the shadows watching me?" I call over my shoulder, not bothering to look back at the man I can sense behind me as I wipe down the counter.

"You know how much I like to watch," Gage says, getting closer. "You're in quite a mood tonight."

"I don't know what you mean," I say, adding some false sweetness to my tone. "I'm a bartender. Why would I be in a mood when I get to come into work early to clean and play barback?" My movements as I clean are more aggressive than needed, but I don't give a shit.

"And you're doing such a good job." His comment is bait for my attention, but I don't bite. I ignore him instead. The irritation underlying his taunting is satisfying. "Don't be like that. I was just about to have you make me a drink."

My hands still and I suck in a deep breath as I force

myself to remain calm. Pasting on my best customer service smile, I turn to face him.

"What can I make for you, sir?" Gage stands with his arms crossed over his broad chest, eyes smoldering and head slightly tilted as he watches me.

"I'll have a Boulevardier."

His drink order is a complex mixed cocktail that calls for bourbon. Pulling the necessary bottles from the shelves, I add the ingredients in balanced measurements into an ice-filled shaker. I don't miss how Gage's eyes wander when I lift my arms to mix the cocktail in the shaker. His phone rings and he turns his back to me as he answers. I pull out a chilled glass to pour the cocktail into, adding an orange wedge as a garnish.

Placing the drink in front of him, I wait for him to hang up and turn around to grab it before reaching under the counter for my knife. He takes a leisurely drink as if he's enjoying a quiet moment with a friend. The metal handle bites into my palm as I squeeze the weapon, my hand itching to lash out and see what color Gage bleeds. A simple red seems far too commonplace for a dark entity like him. I bet the color of his blood will look great against my complexion.

"Getting rid of me won't wipe out your debt." His words have surprise trickling through me, though I don't show it. "It just means you'll answer to someone else—someone a lot less attentive to your *needs*."

What would make him say that to me?

He tilts his head back with a lazy smile, looking down at me with heated hooded eyes, making my urges swell and my pussy throb. "Plus, I'm a lot harder to kill than you think, little devil."

"I don't know," I reply easily, casually offering him a falsely innocent smile. "You took that drink awful fast."

Gage's gaze burns into mine as he presses the glass to his lips again. But not before I've seen it—the hesitation. The flicker of doubt as his mind races with the possibilities of what I might have done. What I can still do to him at any time.

As he tips his head back to swallow the last of the liquid to prove his point, I know it burns differently going down.

"Then again, men aren't usually the ones worrying about what's in their glass." I lean onto the counter, my self-satisfied smile wide as I flash him my cleavage just for the hell of it. "But maybe they should be. It really could be anything."

"You didn't put anything in my drink. That's not your style." His choice of words creep under my skin. Gage thinks he knows me after following me for a few days? He has no idea who he's dealing with.

"Maybe I did, maybe I didn't. I guess you'll just have to wait and see."

"Hey, boss, the truck is here to pick up the old ice machine." Jax appears in the doorway to the back hallway. "What do you want me to tell them?" Gage looks over at the bouncer before glancing back at me. I meet his stare head-on, raising my brows expectantly.

"Sounds like you should go," I say, adding an extra thick layer of sarcasm when I add *"boss."* Gage stands in silence for a moment, in no hurry to move from his spot, watching me. Picking up his glass off the bar, his eyes remain locked with mine as he drains it down to the very last drop.

Then the fucker licks his lips.

"See you later."

CHAPTER SEVEN

JILL

Being told to go to the owner's office at work feels a lot like being called to the principal's office, and I don't like it. When I walk into Gage's office to find him waiting for me with that fucking grin of his, I want to slap it right off him.

And rip his clothes off.

The tension in the air that settles in the room around us feels electrified, sparking my defiance. I don't know what he called me into his office for, and I don't care. Because now that I'm here, I'll be running the show.

"Why are you following me?" I demand, crossing my arms over my chest and glaring at him. A pleased smirk appears on Gage's devastating face as he leans forward in his chair and places his clasped hands on the desk in front of him. The pure self-satisfaction in his expression confirms that this is what he's wanted all along—my attention.

No, not just my attention.

Me.

"Because when I'm not with you, there's an itching in my veins that only the sight of you can fix."

I blink at him, processing his words. That wasn't the answer I was expecting, and I'm not sure how to feel about it.

"You're not just trying to get into my pants?" I ask skeptically. I'm not buying it.

"I never said that."

"You're attracted to me," I state as his hungry gaze sweeps over me.

"Like you wouldn't fucking believe," he says, standing from his chair. The sexual desire radiates off him and thickens the air around us. "If you don't have a god complex, I'll give you one."

"What do you want? What are you getting out of this?"

I don't trust a single word coming out of his mouth. If he wanted to fuck me, why hasn't he done it already? I've had plenty of men desire me before, but this feels different —amplified. It's hard to wrap my head around.

"Isn't it obvious, Jill?" He steps from behind the desk and walks over. "I want you."

"You get off on watching me, don't you?" My barb of accusation hits Gage without inflicting any damage. Instead, a wicked smile crosses his face.

"Yes," he states, stepping closer to me. "Yes, I do. Watching you was my favorite thing to do in the entire world. It was my reason for existing." His words douse my body in gasoline, his dark eyes promising to set me ablaze.

"Was?" I ask, desire itching through me until I'm overtaken.

Gage's passionate gaze on me is intoxicating, and I can't seem to get enough. There's something addictive in the way he looks at me, like I'm the only thing that keeps his heart beating—a being looking at its life source.

A man looking at his god.

I like being his deity.

"It was," he confirms, taking another step towards me. He's waiting for something—a sign? "Then I kissed you. Kissing you will be my reason for living until I fuck you."

Those words are the spark that has me going up in flames.

"Fuck me," I repeat, making his eyes flare. "You really think I'm going to let some psycho stalker fuck me?"

"I know you are." There isn't a drop of doubt in his voice. "You like that I follow you, watch you, *want* you. You feed off my attention, my need. It makes you want, makes you hot—makes you *wet*. And I'm the only one who can give you what you need. Isn't that right, little devil?"

"You think you can handle all of me? I'm a lot of woman."

"Let's get one thing clear." He inches closer to tower over me, his eye contact deeply intentional. "You're my warmup weight, Jill, so watch that pretty little mouth of yours and remember who you're talking to. We're made for each other. I'm the only man who will ever be able to handle you the way you deserve to be handled." His eyes dip lower, trailing down my body like a caress. "All of you."

My breath catches in my chest and arousal pours through me until I'm throbbing for him. Gage doesn't miss any of it.

"I bet your pussy is throbbing and needy for what only my cock can give you. You're wet for me right now, aren't you?"

"I'm soaked." The words come out breathless.

"Show me," he commands, coming closer. He's just inches from me now, his eyes latched onto me like he won't ever look away. Like he *can't.*

"Come find out for yourself."

That's it, the sign he's been waiting for. Those four words, and he's been unleashed.

In the blink of an eye, he's on me, his lips descending on mine as one of his hands slides down into my shorts. When his fingers find my pussy—drenched and without panties —an animalistic groan sounds deep in his chest. "Fuck, baby."

"I'm no one's baby." I gasp as his lips trail along my jaw, his teeth tugging and nipping against my skin. My hands grasp his broad shoulders, clinging to him as his hand toys with my pussy lips. He runs his fingers through my arousal, teasing my swollen clit until I'm squirming, begging for more.

"Is that right, Menace?" he murmurs deeply in my ear. Two of his fingers sink into me, making me arch against him.

"Mmm, much better," I sigh, falling back against his desk. Gage follows me like a magnet, his unrelenting body pressed to mine. His lips leave mine briefly as he uses the hand that's not playing my pussy like a violin to swipe everything on his desk out of the way, sending papers and books flying. His fingers withdraw from inside me to pull off my shorts until they're falling down my legs onto the floor, leaving me naked from the waist down.

"If I were a patient man, I'd feast on your pussy like it was my last meal," he growls as I pull him closer by the waistband of his jeans. "But I'm desperate to be inside you, to finally have what's mine. I want you more than I've ever wanted anything in my entire life, Jill."

"Then don't make me wait," I pant. My hands make quick work of his pants and briefs as he reaches behind his head to pull his shirt off, his muscled torso rippling beneath dark ink. Reaching for the condom he pulled out of his pocket, I take it out of his hand to rip open the package and roll it down his stiff cock. His impressive erection stands tall, already hard as steel—all for me.

"Take it off," he demands, his voice rough with barely bridled need. Tugging at my halter top, I pull it over my head. My strapless bra is last to join my clothes on the floor, allowing my heavy breasts to fall free.

"You're the most beautiful thing I've ever seen." Gage's all-consuming eyes devour me from head to toe, the muscle in his angular jaw ticking.

The admiration in his eyes as he takes in my fully naked body does nothing to detract from the dark desire swirling around him. There's a split second of hesitation, a moment of indecision—should he fall to his knees and worship me as his idol, or ruin me until I'm so stained by his touch that no man will ever stand a chance to see my full beauty again?

His hands fondle my large breasts, kneading them roughly with a groan before trailing down to caress my soft stomach, palm my thick thighs, then cup my fupa.

"Christ, you're a fucking dream. My walking wet dream." My pussy throbs with desire, already so wet and swollen, more than ready for him to fill. "Look at this pretty pussy, already crying for my cock."

"If you don't fuck me right now, I'll go find someone who will," I threaten, impatient and horny. I can't wait any longer. I need him to stop playing with his food and fucking eat it. A shadow crosses Gage's face, anger darkening his eyes. A tattooed hand circles my throat, pushing me back on the desk as the broad head of his cock presses into my pussy.

With one rough thrust, he's inside me—filling me, stretching me to capacity. I hiss out a breath at the twinge of pain that radiates through my body, not fully prepared for his girth. The discomfort mingles with an undeniable pleasure, making me moan.

Holy shit.

"Is this what you wanted, little devil?" Gage growls, pulling out almost all the way before thrusting in to the hilt, making the pain melt into pleasure.

"Yes," I moan. "More." The hand on my neck adds pressure as he pulls out and slams back in again and again. His pace is punishing, overwhelming my body until I'm delirious. His free hand palms my ass, pulling my thighs to wrap around his waist to hold me closer. He lowers his lips to my right breast, sucking my nipple into his mouth. I gasp as his tongue circles me before his teeth clamp down roughly. The bite of pain flares through me like a fuse, igniting a breath-stealing orgasm.

My back arches off the desk, my mouth parting as a helpless cry escapes me. The aching bliss that tears through my body has me gasping for air against Gage's hand. His assault on my senses is unrelenting and unrepentant as he drills my greedy pussy with his cock.

"Oh, fuck," I gasp, my thighs clamping around him. His mouth moves across my chest, sucking and biting until my skin is tender and raw beneath his lips. "Don't you dare stop."

"I'm just getting started with you, Menace." The hand necklace around my throat releases me to wrap my arms around his neck, and I'm being lifted. He carries me like I'm light and dainty, but his touch is anything but gentle. His cock pulses inside me, making me so overcome with need that it doesn't even register that he's walking us across the room until I'm being lowered onto the sofa, and Gage's body is covering mine.

I rock against him, chasing the friction that's building between us. Gage looks down at me, his eyes blazing over my skin until I'm singed. "You are so fucking gorgeous, it's unreal," he murmurs deeply. "I'm going to mark every inch of your glorious body so there won't ever be a question about who owns it."

"You talk too much." I tighten my inner muscles to clamp down on his cock, making him grunt. "Words mean nothing." His mouth lowers to capture mine, kissing me deeply as he moves inside me with short, deep thrusts.

There's a wave building inside me, climbing higher and higher with each stroke of his cock and graze of his teeth. The sound of his hard panes meeting my soft curves mingles with the moans and sighs filling the room.

I run my hands up his solid torso, feeling his muscles ripple with each thrust. My fingernails dig into his broad shoulders as the passion takes over my limbs, scratching the inked skin. Gage's grunts and moans feed into my veins until I'm dizzy from the pleasure.

His lips are everywhere, latching onto every inch of skin he can reach. He sucks on the side of my neck as he explores me. His left arm supports his weight while his right hand grabs greedy handfuls of my ass, thigh, fleshy waist, and palms my breast to fondle it roughly.

The wave grows stronger, the current threatening to steal me into the undertow as he plunges into me so hard and deep I struggle to take air into my lungs. I'm getting so close. He can feel it.

"You want to come, don't you?" He reaches between us to rub my clit, making me tremble against him. "You want to come all over my cock."

"Don't play with me," I warn him. I swear if he decides to stop now, I'll gut him like a fish. I'm sure he can read it all over my face, and he grins down at me—a smile of deep satisfaction, his movements never faltering.

"I like playing with you, little devil. But not about this, because I like pleasing you so much more." His hand on my clit gives a sharp smack against my swollen flesh—once, then twice—and it's all I need.

"I'm coming," I cry. "Oh yes, Gage." The floodgates open, and the tsunami pounds through me until there's no chance of survival. I writhe against him, his name leaving my lips over and over as the pleasure carries me away.

"That's right, Menace. You're coming for *me*." His eyes are fixated on my face as I fall apart around his cock, and it's his undoing. Gage is at the point of no return, his grunts growing louder and heavier as he pistons in and out of me. "Fuck, Jill."

His dark eyes never leave my face as he explodes inside me, pumping roughly through the power of his own release. His arms shake above me, growls turning into guttural groans. He slams into me once, twice, three more times as he rides out his climax before he finally stills inside me. His arm gives out, and he collapses on top of me, completely spent.

Laying crushed beneath this tattoo god, I can't wrap my head around what just happened between us. I've never come so hard in my fucking life—it's almost as if he read a manual on exactly what to do to my body to maximize my pleasure. But this wasn't practiced or calculated. It was instinctual. He didn't need an instruction manual because he read *me* and knew exactly what I needed. And he sure as hell gave it to me.

Goddamn.

Neither of us move for several long seconds as we recover enough to regain brain function, our panting and sighing the only sounds filling the room. I can feel the erratic beating of Gage's heart against my chest, and I know he can feel mine. Gage's nose presses into my hair with a deep inhale, nipping lightly at the sensitive spot where my neck meets my shoulder, then soothing it with his tongue.

"I knew it." His deep voice vibrates in his chest and into my bones. "Fucking you is the reason I'm on this earth." When he lifts his head to look down at me, the gratified look on his face tugs at my soul and threatens to steal it.

What am I supposed to say to that?

When he leans down to capture my lips with his, I'm relieved. It's not often I'm at a loss for words, but I can't seem to scrape together a full sentence. The man has thoroughly fucked my brains out, leaving nothing but mush.

Our mouths move together in a languid kiss, this one more slow and sensual than before. He brushes a strand of dark hair away from my cheek before cupping my face. Pulling back to look down at me, his gaze is intense and his tone turns contemplative. "The plans I have for you, Jillian Hart."

That snaps me out of it.

"The only plans I have are to go home and shower you off me before my dinner plans." I finally got my voice back. Gage smiles at my words like he finds them flattering.

"No amount of showering will ever wash me off of you, little devil. I'm permanent." He pulls out of me, leaving a satisfying ache. When I move to get up, his hold on my jaw turns possessive. "Threaten to let another man touch you again, and I won't let you come," he says, and I know he means it. Defiance trickles through me, and I narrow my eyes at him.

"Bold of you to assume you'll ever get the chance." I'm bluffing, we both know it. But I can't let him have the last word. He chuckles darkly, like I'm a child who's in way over her head. But he lets me get up anyway.

Gage remains lounging on the couch when I stand, and I feel his eyes on me as I reach up to run a hand through my tangled hair—I hate to think what my bangs look like right now. When I turn my back to him, he reaches out to grab a handful of my ass before giving it a smack and watching it jiggle. "Soon, I'm going to be inside this gorgeous ass of yours."

I bend down to pick my clothes up off the floor, looking at him over my shoulder. There's no denying this will happen again. His big dick energy actually matches his cock —and he knows how to use it. But I'm not about to stroke his ego.

"You're a decent fuck, Gage. Don't ruin it with your mouth."

"That's *exactly* what I'm going to do." The dark promise in his voice sends a shiver through me. "I'm going to ruin you with my mouth. And my fingers and my cock."

I slip on my shirt before stepping into my shorts and tugging them up my legs. It takes a few bouncing hops to get the fabric over my hips and ass so I can button them. I grab my shoes and bra off the floor before heading towards the door.

"I'm leaving," I say over my shoulder. "Don't follow me." I spare him one last glance as I reach for the doorknob.

He lays on the sofa completely naked, his gorgeous tattooed body on full display. The wicked expression on his face makes it look as if Satan himself is planning to make me his queen of the underworld. Our eyes clash in a silent conversation. Flicking the lock, I yank the door open and strut out.

It doesn't matter where I go. He's always following.

CHAPTER EIGHT

GAGE

Her outfit is for me.

The strapless black top that leaves Jill's entire chest, neck, and shoulders bared to the world, covered in hickeys and bite marks, is all for me. Yesterday I finally got to fuck her. Today, Jill stood in front of her mirror, saw my marks, and made a choice. She got dressed knowing that everyone who looked at her would see that she'd been marked.

By me.

Gratification—dark and insatiable—courses through me, making my cock stiffen. Whether she wore this outfit because of me or to spite me, I don't give a shit. Either way, Jill woke up, looked in the mirror, and thought of me. It was the marks made by my mouth that forced a decision.

Even if it was just a few minutes, I occupied her mind, planting seeds of permanence. It won't be long before I've invaded her subconscious so thoroughly there will be no chance of eradication.

And thinking about me deserves to be rewarded.

Those marks on her skin will fade and heal. I plan on

replacing them as often as I can, but I'm going to give her something that won't fade. Something more permanent. One day, very soon, she'll wear my ring on her perfect finger and carry my last name as a symbol of our undying devotion.

Shifting back in my chair, I grip my hard dick through my jeans and watch the live video playing on my computer screen. Jill stands in the women's dressing room, chatting with one of the other bartenders, Angelina.

Hiding cameras in the women's dressing room, according to Messer, is sick and perverted. "Watching all those girls get undressed when they don't know they're being watched is messed up," he says. But I don't give a single fuck about those women. I'm not watching them, just her. And I'll do whatever it takes to keep my eyes on Jill.

My eyes trace the way her full lips move while she talks, the supple curve of her cheeks when she smiles. The bruises caused by my mouth decorate her smooth, plump, tan skin, disappearing under her top—but I know they don't stop there. Under the fabric are more marks made by my teeth, lips, and tongue. Her heavy round breasts, the dip of her fleshy waist, the delectable crease where the soft curve of her stomach meets her full, voluptuous hips. All marked by me.

The memory of how she tastes, how her tender flesh felt between my teeth, has my grip tightening painfully on my boner. I unbutton my pants and pull down my boxers to let my erection spring free just as Angelina walks out of the dressing room.

Now it's just us—just me and my Jill.

Jill opens her locker, making me grip myself again in anticipation. I squeeze the head of my cock when she pauses, and I know she sees it. She reaches into the locker and pulls out the long black velvet box with the card. She looks around as if whoever left that gift for her might still be lurking somewhere in the room.

As if I might be watching.

Her eyes scan the room, unwittingly making eye contact with my hidden camera. For a short, glorious moment, she looks right at me. Those gorgeous green eyes of hers gazing into mine like she can see me. I groan, giving my cock a few rough pumps as the lust whips through me.

When she turns back to look at the card, I swear I can read her lips as she reads it to herself.

Wear this until my hand can take its place.

xoxo, Gage

I didn't have to sign the card for her to know who it's from, but I did anyway.

When Jill lifts the lid and sees the diamond choker necklace sitting inside, her eyes widen slightly, and I can't help but smile. Her fingers run over the sparkling gems like she can't believe they're real. There's a small moment of hesitation and I know she's considering her options.

Does she put on the necklace and give me what I want? Or refuse the gift because I'm the one who gave it to her? The idea of either outcome has me stroking myself, the desire too much to resist. Either way, I have her mind, right now in this moment. She has to make a decision.

A decision about *me*.

I can see the moment she mentally says 'fuck it' with a shrug and the purse of her lips as she pulls the jewelry out of the box. Watching her clasp the necklace around her throat has my adrenaline spiking.

Stroking my cock faster and harder, Jill turns back towards the camera with my diamonds sparkling around her neck. She looks so damn pretty it hurts.

Will she wear it for me the next time I fuck her? I imagine what it will be like to feel those diamonds when my hand is wrapped around her throat again. How those gorgeous green eyes will gaze up at me, glittering like jewels that put those diamonds to shame, as I destroy her perfect pussy with my cock. Breasts bouncing, thick thighs wrapped around me, and her juicy ass moving with every thrust. Her fuckable full lips parting on a loud moan as radiant ecstasy takes over her face.

Every muscle tenses sharply and I let out a heavy moan as my release barrels through me like a semi-truck, pleasure claiming my limbs and hot ropes of cum shooting out of my cock until I'm spent. With heavy-lidded eyes, I track the woman on the screen as I catch my breath.

I'm not a religious man, but watching Jill come is as close as I'll ever get to heaven. She's the salvation to my damnation, and I will worship at her altar in every lifetime.

CHAPTER NINE

GAGE

"Welcome to Inferno, the hottest nightclub in Chicago." I spread my arms out and grin against the urge to sneer at the words coming out of my mouth.

I sound like a fucking infomercial.

Catering to clients with deep pockets is part of my job as the club owner—a necessary evil. But that doesn't mean I have to like it. I'm not about to kiss their ass, either.

"Very nice," Richie says, looking around. He's the cardholder of the group, an oil tycoon, so that makes him the man my staff needs to keep particularly happy. His ice-blue eyes scan the club, taking special notice of the bottle girls as they walk past. I wave one of them over, a leggy brunette with massive fake tits.

"The high rollers are on the way to their table. Bring their bottles in five minutes with the top three," I instruct, referring to the bottle girls Richie ranked as his top three when he reserved the table. "And get Jill from behind the bar. I want her on service too."

If I have to spend the night pretending to like these

asshats, I'm going to make sure I have Jill within reach while I'm at it.

The girl nods and strides away to follow my orders. I turn back to the group with a grin. "Alright, let's get this party started."

"Hell yeah!" Richie's guest, Warner, exclaims. His enthusiasm tells me he's got shallow pockets. He's just here for the ride. His gaudy outfit screams of a man without money, begging for people to think otherwise.

I lead them through the club, pointing out the guest DJ who has the crowd hyped, and the two different bars. My eyes scan the staff behind the counter serving drinks for a glimpse of dark chocolate hair, but come up short.

She must already be getting changed. *Good.*

Up in the Executive Lounge, the six men spread out on the sofa. Within five minutes, four bottle girls appear with large bottles of champagne and tequila reposado, sparklers blazing. They pump the bottles to the thrumming music, swiveling their hips and shimmying their chests. My eyes scan them briefly before losing any and all interest.

Jill's not one of them.

She must still be getting dressed. I know she likes to make an entrance.

Lounging on the sofa as the party begins, I watch the chaos unfold around me. But my participation doesn't start a second before my party favor walks through the door.

Jill struts in like a force to be reckoned with, wearing a sparkly black mini-dress that flashes the lace garters at the tops of her sheer black thigh-high stockings. My mouth waters at the sight of her, my cock stirring to life at the first glimpse. The diamonds sparkling around her neck have me shifting myself in my pants.

She immediately joins the other girls, introducing

herself to the guests with her man-killer smile, and sliding behind the bar to make their mixed drink requests. Her eyes connect with every other pair in the room except mine. Her gaze evades me so completely it's glaringly obvious that she's making a point not to look at me.

A smile tugs at my lips as jealousy itches through me. I need her attention like an addict jonesing for a hit. Like being pulled by gravity, I follow her behind the bar as she starts mixing a drink. I lean in, caging her against the counter with my arms as I slide in behind her. My chest presses against her back, her luscious ass against my groin.

"My necklace looks really fucking good on you," I murmur in her ear. I feel the shiver that runs down her spine and smile against her hair. Each breath fills me with the scent of her perfume—something deep, complex, and intoxicating.

Just like her.

"I'm not the type of girl to say no to diamonds, even if they are from psychopath stalkers." Despite the way her ass is pressing against me and how her breathing has quickened, her tone remains nonchalant.

I want to change that.

"I prefer the term sociopath," I say smoothly, taking one of my hands from the counter to wrap around her waist. My palm flattens on the soft curve of her lower stomach, my fingertip pressing dangerously close to her pretty pussy. I can almost feel the heat of her through the material of her dress.

"And I prefer not to talk to you."

"I can think of a few activities we can do that don't require talking," I say, unashamed of the hunger in my voice. When the temptation proves too much, I inch my hand down until my middle finger is rubbing her right where I want her. Jill sighs, her hips rolling ever so slightly to chase the friction we both desperately want.

"Hmm, I'd prefer an activity that doesn't include you." The retort leaves her sharp tongue easily, but I know my Jill better than that. Her body can't lie to me.

"You're such a pretty liar."

Pulling my hand away, I turn her to face me. My erection presses against her stomach—hot, heavy, and aching for her. I stare down at her and grin at the way her pupils dilate when she looks at me. I know mine are probably big as fucking saucers right now. I'm so turned on.

"Forgive my debt, and maybe I'll change my mind."

The spark of defiance in her eyes—the unrelenting need to defy our connection when it serves her purpose—is breathtaking.

Letting the humor drop from my face, I give her a glimpse behind the mask at my soul-deep desire for her. "Not a chance in hell, little devil."

Jill's eyes dance between mine as if she's looking for a tell. She won't find one, because I'm not fucking bluffing. We stare at each other, locked in our connection, for a long moment. Then, as if her mind finally caught up with her, I watch as Jill's walls rise firmly back into place. And just like that, the menace is back.

"Then it looks like I won't be wasting any more time with you tonight. I need to focus on getting other men to open their wallets for me." She looks down to make a show of adjusting the neckline of her dress, tugging it down a fraction to bring my attention to her incredible cleavage. "Have a good night. I know I will."

"Go make your money, but don't waste your energy. You're gonna need it later when you're staying late to clean the bar."

Her eyes narrow into a withering glare that would easily cut any other man at the knees. "Bite me."

"Don't threaten me with a good time, Menace," I murmur before stepping back and rounding the counter. Jill finishes making the mixed drinks while I watch. I see someone join me at the bar in my peripheral vision, but I don't tear my eyes away from her.

When Jill finally walks out from behind the bar—passing by me without a second glance and obviously fuming—I bite back a grin at the knowledge she's going to be spending the rest of the night angry.

And she'll be thinking about *me*.

"Fuck," Warner groans beside me, stepping back and craning his neck to check out Jill's gorgeous ass. "The big girl is sexy. Might take her home tonight and split her fat ass open with my dick."

Darkness swells inside of me, and I have the urge to rip his eyeballs from his skull and ram them down his throat.

I tip my head back and drain the contents of my glass before slamming it on the bar to get his attention. I shake my head slowly.

"No." I pull up the hem of my t-shirt and wipe my mouth, flashing him the handgun I have tucked into the waist of my jeans—one that now has a full clip with his name on it. "No, you're not."

Warner's eyes clock the weapon, and the way his arrogant smirk instantly disappears feeds the potent animosity brewing inside me. Letting my shirt fall back into place, I lean my elbows back against the counter to take a casual stance. Cocking my head to one side, I slide my gaze to him —expression as calm as still water.

His face pales considerably, his shoulders stiffening as he gulps his drink. His eyes dart around briefly, searching for anyone who might've seen it too, someone to come to his rescue. But there's no escaping this. "Hey, I—I uh," he stammers. "I didn't realize she was—"

"*Mine.*"

My tone offers the word, but my eyes state it. He nods quickly before lowering his eyes to the glass in his hand.

"I'm just gonna go back over there," he mumbles, tipping his head towards the table with the other partiers.

"You do that."

I watch as he scurries away like the little cockroach he is, satisfied when he doesn't even glance in Jill's direction as he rejoins his idiot friends.

CHAPTER TEN

JILL

Everyone is gone, and yet here I am playing barback.

Again.

The private party didn't end until three in the morning when the drunken guests were ushered into their waiting cars, and two of the bottle girls climbed into the back seat to continue the party at their hotel. All of the other girls left an hour ago, leaving me to clean up the wreck the party left behind.

Gage sat on the sofa watching me clean, collect glasses from around the lounge, and pick up empty bottles. When I moved to the bar to clean the counter and wash the glasses, he followed me like a shadow. He's currently standing just over my shoulder while I work, so close I can feel the heat radiating from his chest on my back.

"*Shit.*" The remnants of a champagne glass spill onto the hand towel I'm reaching for, covering it in sticky liquid.

"Here." A tattooed hand enters my line of sight with a clean rag. I snatch the cloth and spin to face him.

"Don't you have anything better to do right now?"

"Nothing's better than this."

Huffing out a deep breath, I force myself to accept there's no getting out of this. And it sucks, but things could be a lot worse. I could be stuck with one of Jonas' gross old clients instead of this devastating man who makes my imagination run wild with every glance. I don't have to like it, but there are definitely things I can use to my advantage.

"You're a tattoo artist," I say, picking up a glass to polish.

"One of the best." Gage states, inching closer.

"If you own a tattoo shop, what are you doing with Inferno?"

I take a step back, my shoulder bumping into the doorway to the stairwell.

"Jonas got cocky and lost, he couldn't hold onto this place. But I won't make the same brainless mistake. That's the thing about power; you have to know your limits. I only take what I can keep."

"So you take people's misfortune and twist them around their necks until they hang in a noose of their own making. That's pathetic." My tone is sharp, hoping to cause lasting damage. I place the now-spotless glass on the counter, tossing the rag down next to it.

Gage's chuckle speaks to his security, completely unfazed. The deep tone resonates through my bones as he raises his arms to lean over me in the doorway. My eyes catch on the way his biceps stretch the material of his T-shirt. "Nice try, little devil. I quite like having you tied to my strings."

"If you think you have any real hold on me, you're dumber than I thought you were,"

"Don't kid yourself, pretty girl. We both know exactly what kind of hold you like from me."

"Gage, baby. My pussy really likes your cock, so I use it." I allow my breasts to rub against his chest, my head lifting to inch closer to his lips. "But don't think for a second that it would keep me from skinning you alive if I got the chance."

I've never seen a gaze so ravenous as his eyes sweep over me with heated intent. A wicked smile slowly appears on his face that makes my pussy clench.

"I know. That's exactly why I plan to keep you." His arms drop from the doorway to crowd me, stepping forward until I'm walking backward into the private VIP stairway. Gage kicks the door closed behind us, and we're swallowed in darkness.

Shadows dance across the angles of Gage's face as the red lights flicker. His hand circles my throat as his body pins me against the wall, a delicious darkness in his gaze. "You're the perfect woman, Jill. Made just for me to worship." His grip tightens on my throat, adding more pressure and promises of domination. "But I'm going to fuck you like the monster you think I am. I'm going to use and abuse every inch of this masterpiece of a body—until you can't remember your own name, and mine is the only one coming from your fuckable lips like a dirty prayer."

His words barely register past the waves of need pounding over me. I've been love bombed before, lavish praise from a man isn't new to me. But Gage is next level—his intensity is as alarming as it is intoxicating. Even if I wanted to believe him, I'm not buying what he's trying to sell me. He doesn't really know me, how can he know if I'm his perfect woman?

A man will tell you whatever they think you want to hear in order to fuck you, but he's wasting his breath. I'm already going to let him fuck me.

My heart pounds in my chest, pumping pure lust through my veins as my pussy throbs. Every inch of my body is on fire, itching for a relief that only he can give me. He looks tempted to kiss me, but he doesn't.

"Now," Gage says, winding a lock of my hair around his fist and using it to pull my head back. "Get on your knees and open that pretty mouth for me."

The urge to defy him—to refuse and remain in control—flickers through my mind. But I'm so fucking turned on I lower to my knees instead. Gage makes quick work of unzipping his pants and pulling out his erection. His big cock stands proud—thick and veiny and waiting for my mouth. Large tattooed hands thread through my hair, fisting until my scalp stings.

As soon as I part my lips, he's sliding his length into my mouth until he hits the back of my throat with a groan. His already stiff cock hardens even more as he watches himself move between my lips. My jaw loosens to accommodate his girth, my tongue licking along the raised veins up and down his length.

Holding me by my hair, Gage slowly withdraws until he's almost out of my mouth. My lips remain wrapped around the broad crown, circling just beneath the sensitive tip. When he pushes back in, it's quick and powerful.

I meet his gaze as he pumps in and out of my lips, his pace picking up speed until he's roughly fucking my mouth. His eyes remain locked on mine.

"Your mouth was made for my cock. Look at it, taking me so well." His fist tightens in my hair—the pain sharpening my senses. "Such a pretty little whore on your knees for me."

Lust pours through me until I'm dripping with it. My thighs clench together against the pulsing between them.

"Take it all the way into your throat, just like that," he growls, forcing himself to the back of my throat. "You like having my big cock in your mouth, don't you?"

I nod against him, and his head tilts back with a groan. His jaw tightens as my tongue circles his length, and I'm being pulled off of him.

I gaze up at him, eyes tearing and fully turned on. He gazes down at me for a moment but can't handle it for too long.

"Stand up." I stand and let him lead me down a few stairs. "Bend over for me." Kneeling on the stairs with my ass in the air, Gage flips up my dress and mutters a curse.

"Goddamn, you're killing me with this lacy little underwear." His voice is rough with desire as he palms my ass cheeks before wrenching my panties to the side. Looking over my shoulder, Gage's dark gaze is haunting as his hands punish my clothing for standing between him and my skin. Then he's lining himself up with my drenched pussy.

My cry of pleasure echoes in the stairwell when he pushes into me, stretching and filling me. I'm so aroused and hypersensitive, I can feel every ridge and vein as he pulls out and pushes back in even deeper. He slams in and out of me, pushing so deep he bottoms out every time. My back arches against the bliss he ignites, and it's not long before I'm teetering on the edge of oblivion.

With a primal grunt, Gage changes his angle, stroking a spot that has me seeing stars. My orgasm steals my breath when it hits, and I'm flying through the air. I let out a breathless cry, my pussy clenching around his cock as my orgasm ripples through my entire body.

I've barely returned to earth before Gage is pulling out of me, and turning me to face him. "Open up for me,

Menace." As soon as my lips part, his cock is between them. With two pumps, his entire body quakes with his release. His jaw clenches with a resonating groan, eyes locked with mine as his climax overcomes him. Hot cum shoots down my throat and fills my mouth, and he rasps, "let me see it."

I open my mouth and stick out my tongue, and he cups my face. The animalistic look of unbridled passion on his face makes me feel powerful. I'm his undoing. "Now swallow, we can't be making a mess in the stairwell."

Closing my mouth and swallowing is a gift I'm bestowing on him, and the look in his eyes tells me he knows that.

"Not even my wildest fantasies could've created you." His grip on my face tightens as we catch our breath. His thumbs swipe the edges of my lips like they'll fix the mess that is my makeup right now. "Come home with me."

I look up at him in consideration, my brain fighting through the fog as my body comes down from the high of orgasm. I could go home with him, go a few more rounds with him. But that would mean willingly giving him full access to me.

"My shift is over." I pull out of his embrace and stand. Gage watches me adjust my dress and put distance between us, physically and emotionally. "I'm gonna go."

Gage stays at the top of the stairs as I start my descent. When I make it to the first floor, he calls after me before I open the door.

"See you tomorrow, little devil." I glance up at him, the red light casting shadows across his haunting expression. "And every day after that."

CHAPTER ELEVEN

JILL

"Angelina?" Walking into the club for my shift, I look at the other bartender prepping her kit behind the bar—the bar I'm supposed to be working at. "What are you doing here?"

"Working..." she responds, flashing me a confused look. "I'm on the schedule."

That can't be right because I'm on the schedule tonight. Or at least I was last time I checked two days ago.

"Since when?" I'm getting irritated now. I wouldn't have gotten ready and come all the way here tonight if I didn't have to. Someone in management fucked up.

"Since yesterday." Angelina pulls out her phone and shows me a picture that she took of the schedule. To add insult to injury, my name's been crossed out for tonight, and Angelina's name has been written in pen beside it. "Sorry, girl. I thought you knew, or else I would have sent you a text."

"It's not your fault," I assure her, my eyes scanning the area for the night manager. "Have you seen Miranda? I have a few choice words for her."

"She said something about a broken locker in the dressing room." Angelina waves her hand towards the employee door. "Good luck."

"I'm not the one who's going to need it."

She laughs behind me, but I'm already moving. Stalking through the club, I skirt around barbacks and servers prepping the club for opening, on a mission.

I find Miranda in the women's dressing room with one of the bouncers, Jax. She's supervising while he uses a screwdriver to jimmy open one of the lockers that's been jammed for almost a week now. She raises her hands in submission when she sees me coming in hot.

"Don't start with me," she says defensively. Jax looks over to flash me a dimpled grin as he checks me out, his bulging biceps intentionally flexing.

"Looking good, Jill," Jax comments. I flash him a wink before crossing my arms over my chest and leveling a glare at Miranda.

"Then who should I start with, Miranda? Because someone decided to do arts and crafts on the schedule next to my name. Why the hell am I here?" Miranda's shoulders go up helplessly as she searches for words.

"I don't know, honestly. When I made the schedule, you were on it, and I didn't change it." She gestures to the door. "And if it wasn't me, there's only one other person who could've done it. So I suggest you go ask him."

Gage.

I narrow my eyes at her, agitation bubbling inside me at the knowledge that the man who watches my every move is now manipulating my work schedule. He's so desperate to insert himself into my life he's no longer happy showing up wherever I am—he now wants to choose where I show up and when. And he has the power to.

I don't like being manipulated.

"Fine," I concede, earning a small relieved sigh from the woman currently under my deadly stare. Turning on my heel, I storm into the hallway towards the owner's office back behind the VIP booths. I enter without knocking, letting the door swing open until it hits the wall with a bang.

Gage sits behind the desk, leaning back in his chair with an arrogant smirk on his infuriatingly handsome face. He knew I was coming.

"Fuck, you're hot when you're angry," he states, eyes raking over me hungrily. "I would've changed the schedule a lot sooner if I knew that meant you'd be in my office looking like this."

I narrow my eyes at him as I saunter closer. Placing my palms flat on his desk with a smack, I lean forward to stare him down. I don't give a damn that he can see straight down my minidress. In fact, I prefer it.

"You fucked around with my work schedule to make me angry?" I challenge, my anger undeniable. Gage cocks his head to one side and takes his time looking at me like he's memorizing the image.

"It's definitely a perk," he answers, running his tongue across his bottom lip before biting it with a smile. The movement is so small, but it makes my heart stutter, and I hate that it's so damn sexy. My body comes to life under his gaze, the mostly healed marks he left on me aching to be remade. "But that's not why you were taken off the schedule. I have other plans for you tonight."

I stand and place my hands on my hips, my pointed gaze demanding. "You better start talking, or you're about to watch my sweet ass walk back out the door and go home."

"You'll be serving a private party."

"You pulled me from behind the bar on the busiest night of the week to do VIP bottle service?"

"Poker," he corrects me, making my stomach drop—I have a visceral reaction to that word after what happened with my brother. "I'm hosting a private poker game tonight. You'll be serving drinks."

He changed my regular bartending shift so I can serve him and his asshole buddies alcohol while they piss away amounts of money that could save and ruin lives? A humorless laugh escapes my lips. "No."

"It's not a request, Jill." Sitting forward in his chair, his smile turns vicious. "This is the part where I remind you that you don't have a choice—I say, you do. Go grab your kit and meet me outside. If you're not in the parking lot in fifteen minutes, I'm coming in after you."

White-hot anger flashes inside of me. There are a million words on the tip of my tongue, ready to lash out and eviscerate him. But my temper turns Gage on, and knowing that he'll get off on it stops me. Instead, I take a silent, calming breath and hammer him with a sweetly acidic smile.

"Yes sir." The heat in his eyes means my choice of words did nothing to put him off, so I continue. "Any excuse to flirt with a room full of men with money."

With that, I turn and saunter out of the room.

I wait until it's been exactly sixteen minutes before I step out of the club into the parking lot with my bartender kit in my designer leather backpack. Gage is waiting for me like I knew he would be, standing like he does when he watches me—relaxed and settled like he has all the time in the world. He's leaning against his motorcycle, muscular arms crossed. He straightens when

I approach, his gaze taking stock of my bottle service heels.

Since I'd been planning on standing behind the bar all night, I'd worn a comfortable pair of my worn-in Dunks. But a high-stakes poker game calls for some sexy nude pumps—these are my money-making heels.

"Another thirty seconds, and I would've had to hunt you down. I was almost looking forward to it. My night could use a little excitement," he says, stepping close until we're chest to chest. Even in my heels, he's a few inches taller than me, and our lips are always just a breath away from each other.

"Pity," I respond, feigning a sympathetic pout that makes him smile. He lifts a helmet and slips it over my head, adjusting the strap to make sure it's secure before putting on his own. His eyes gaze into mine intensely for a long moment, smoldering at me, before he snaps down my face shield. Climbing onto the bike, he holds out his hand for me to join him.

"Come here, baby."

I obey and step closer, allowing him to guide me onto the seat behind him. Pressing my chest to his back, he pulls my arms to wrap around his waist.

"I ride hard and fast. You better hold on tight."

"I've heard that before," I shoot back. The sound of his laugh is cut off when he starts the engine. The powerful machine roars to life, rumbling and revving beneath us. My grip on him tightens instinctively when the engine revs again, and we're whipping out of the parking lot.

We roar through the city, heading further downtown. The summer night air whips around us. There's something about being on the back of a motorcycle on a summer evening that feels like flying. The power of the machine vibrates through my body, making me grin from ear to ear as I hug Gage's muscular frame. Even with my helmet, the fresh air is charged with something that tastes like freedom.

The cityscape blurs past—skyscrapers and historic buildings—until we approach a familiar gate. Passing through, we enter The Raven's circular drive. The grand entrance of the luxury hotel greets me like an old frenemy, offering a warm hug of grandeur with a backhanded slap of mockery.

Gage pulls up to the entrance before cutting the engine. Pulling off his helmet and running his hand over his short hair, he climbs off the bike. Helping me off, he unclips the strap of my helmet and lifts it off my head. I gaze up at him as he fixes my mussed hair, his strong tattooed fingers gentle against my face.

"This is all just a ploy to get me into a hotel room, isn't it?" I murmur.

His hands linger on my cheeks, his lips twitching with a smirk. One of his hands trails down my cheek to grip beneath my jaw, pulling me in with a possessive hand on my throat. His lips meet mine in a kiss so deep and sensual I can feel it all the way down to my toes.

"We both know I don't need a ploy to get you into a hotel room," he murmurs against my lips. "Now, come upstairs." Handing both helmets to the valet, Gage leads me into the hotel with a hand on the nape of my neck.

The interior is decorated in the art deco style—dark, rich tones, detailed line work, and bold gold fixtures. Geometric chandeliers hang from the high ceilings, and symmetrical woodwork adds a modern feel. The front desk sits in the center of the lobby, with the hotel bar to the right. A grand staircase leads to a landing with three elevators before splitting to either side and wrapping around the massive chandelier.

I've walked through this lobby a million times, and being back feels like taking a cyanide pill coated in sugar. Up until Tommy's disappearance, when Jonas and those goons had basically kicked down my door to repay my brother's debt, I spent my nights mixing drinks behind the bar in the hotel restaurant. Lana still works here as a concierge—it's where we met. And I fucking miss it.

Working at The Raven bar was the best job I ever had. Lana's convinced she could get my job back for me if and when the time comes. If anyone could, it's Lana.

As the concierge, Lana has a lot of powerful people in her back pocket. She has solid connections everywhere in this city: retail, entertainment, clubbing, banking, arms dealing—you name it. She even knows the owner of this hotel, Matteo Manici, *intimately*.

Matteo is one of the highest-ranking members of the mafia here in Chicago, but I'm not supposed to know that. Lana's hooked up with him a few times. I guess he has a thing for blonde bombshells.

He's also one of those asshats who'd crawl on his hands and knees for a fat woman in the bedroom, then refuse to be seen with her in public. So Lana uses him like a tool in her belt.

Damn, I miss this place.

Focus, Jill.

Walking up the stairs and stepping into an empty elevator, I focus on being in the moment. Gage reaches out his free hand to press the button for the thirty-fourth floor, and the reflective doors slide closed, caging us in the elegant mirrored box.

Gage stares at me in the mirror as we begin the ascent,

his eyes touching every part of me. The heat of his hand on the back of my neck burns as hot as his gaze, heating my blood. Standing with him against my back feels like standing in front of an electric fence. The air between us is charged until the sparks are practically flying, and my body is humming.

"Damn." His deep voice washes over me, sending goosebumps across my skin. "I've never liked elevators before now."

"Whoever put mirrors in here was a perv," I mutter, though I don't hate being under his gaze.

"I should find out who it was and send them a fruit basket," he counters. I sigh and roll my eyes, making him smile. Nothing I say or do seems to put him off in the slightest. The meaner I am to him, the deeper his obsession with me takes root.

He wants me. He *always* wants me. If I don't keep my signals firmly set to red, he'll take any and every opportunity to pounce—and I'd let him. As much as I'd love for him to fuck me against these mirrors, I need to make it through this night feeling in control. For as long as I can, at least.

If this elevator doesn't hurry the fuck up, I swear.

His fingers start to massage my neck, his eyes tracing the curve of my shoulder down to check out my ass. The elevator slows to a stop at floor thirty-four. "Fifty-two seconds," Gage says as the doors slide open smoothly. "I can do a lot to you in fifty-two seconds."

"Only if I let you," I reply flatly before stepping out into the hallway.

I don't know where we're going, so I allow him to guide me to the right and down the long, rich, green hallway. This floor is all suites, so we only pass a few doors before stopping at room thirty-four-oh-six, the Onyx Suite.

Gage doesn't pause to knock before pulling out a keycard to unlock the door. He ushers me into the suite and closes the door behind us. The suite is one of the largest and most opulent in the hotel. The walls are a rich black color with intricate gold framework and ornate sconces. The arched floor-to-ceiling windows bathe the spacious room with the light of the setting sun. Geometric chandeliers hang from the high ceilings, illuminating the detailed crown molding and wall paneling. The sitting area, full kitchen, and dining room are all furnished with high-end decor in creams and bronze.

The entire building screams *wealth*. Even the sage-infused air feels expensive.

Anders is waiting in the living room of the suite while staff set up the poker table and wet bar. Gage leads me to the sofa where he sits and reaches for me—no doubt wanting me to sit in his lap. I sidestep him and opt for an armchair instead as his eyes burn a hole in my profile.

"Jill, nice to see you." Anders' grin is wide and knowing.

"Hi, Anders. I would say I'm happy to be here, but I'm not a liar." I lean back, folding my arms over my chest and crossing one leg over the other. Gage and Anders discuss the group of players coming to the poker night while I sulk.

I move to the wet bar and prep for drinks as the other guests arrive. First is Grecko Vladinski, an older Russian man with salt and pepper hair and a severe expression etched on his weathered face. Completely unimpressed, he barely glances at me when he comes over to the bar and orders a double vodka.

Next to arrive are Dane Presley and Brent Wrenfield. Dane saunters in with his ginger mustache and his brightly colored tattoos. I see the moment he registers my presence and beelines over to where I stand at the bar. Leaning against the counter to invade my personal space, he orders a whiskey sour. Luckily more men enter the suite before he can attempt any conversation.

I hadn't recognized him when I first saw him that night in the VIP lounge, because we'd never met. But I know who Dane is, I've heard his name countless times from my brother, Tommy. They were gambling buddies, Dane was always calling Tommy to invite him to the casinos and poker tournaments.

I don't like that.

I recognize Brent Wrendfield from a Forbes cover featuring the top tech moguls. He's dressed more like a dad at a superstore TV sale than a mogul though—his graphic T-shirt is definitely over ten years old. He orders a craft beer with a fresh lime wedge.

Dallin Feldman is a preppy, blond playboy who is definitely throwing his trust fund around. He struts into the suite and calls the set up 'cozy'—his condescension clear. Gage is quick to call out the fact Dallin recently lost his yacht in the Maldives at their last 'cozy' night in, and I have to hide my grin when the playboy's smirk falls from his face. He orders a Negroni.

The last man saunters in wearing cowboy boots that I can tell aren't for show. He introduces himself as John Wilder. With his black button-up shirt tucked into belted wranglers, he looks like a wealthy rancher who isn't afraid to get his hands dirty. He strolls over and orders a scotch on the rocks with a Texan drawl before kicking back in a seat at the poker table.

The men all gather around the table, and the cards are dealt. As soon as Gage is seated, I feel his eyes on me. I'm here to work, and something in the way his attention rains down on me says he has no intention of letting me forget it.

CHAPTER TWELVE
JILL

The rustle of cards is slightly muffled as the fancy poker table meticulously shuffles the deck before the hands are dealt. I watch from the bar, but the game hasn't even gone around everyone at the table before Gage is beckoning for me. Again.

"Jill, my whiskey is a little warm. Why don't you freshen it up for me." Lifting his glass, he dangles it between his fingers. He soaks up my glare like a tropical plant in the sun, his eyes tracking me as I walk over.

Of course his whiskey is warm, he ordered it room temperature.

Asshole.

Gage hasn't gone a full ten minutes without telling me to do something. I've been waiting on him hand and foot since the night started. Every few minutes he needs something that requires me to walk over to him and give him the opportunity to touch me.

It's hot and infuriating as fuck.

"Here you go, gorgeous," he murmurs, his hand caressing mine when I reach for the offered glass. When I turn to walk away, his hand snakes around my hips to halt my movements. He crooks his finger at me until I bend down to his level while seated, but not before rolling my eyes.

"Before you go, tell me how many I should discard." I can smell his rich cologne, swirling with the scent of the expensive cigar smoke and vintage liquor. The combination thrums through my veins until I want to lean in closer and spikes my heart rate like a warning that I shouldn't.

But, God, I want to.

"Forget it. I'm not playing your hand for you."

"Just give me a number."

"Two." I toss a random number out so he'll release me before I'm too dizzy to walk away.

"You heard her. Give me two." Gage tosses two cards down on the table to discard before Brent deals him two new ones.

After pouring Gage's drink into a new chilled glass, I make intentional eye contact with him as I place it on the table in front of him before strutting away.

They go around the table, tossing chips into the pot—a few thousand here, ten grand there. Despite my best efforts not to pay attention, I can't help but watch as it comes down to John, Anders, and Gage. When Gage goes all in, Anders decides to fold.

Then there were two.

"You're looking pretty cocky there for someone who doesn't have any cards to stand on," John drawls with the rough voice of a weathered rancher.

"Lay your cards down. We'll see who's still standing," Gage replies nonchalantly. My trained eyes move over every visible inch of him in search of a tell, a sign that he's bluffing. But I don't see anything, not a single goosebump or twitch of an eyelid.

Either Gage has an ungodly good poker face, or he's not bluffing.

When the hands are shown, I have my answer. Or do I?

"*God-fucking-dammit*," John rumbles, shoving his losing cards away. A slow, devilish smile spreads across Gage's face as he reaches for his new collection of pretty poker chips.

Dane, Anders, Grecko, John, and Dallin request more drinks, and I start loading a tray. I make it all the way around the table and hand off the last drink on the tray when he says my name.

I turn to see Gage point to his lap. "You're my good luck charm. Come sit." Every set of male eyes is on me, and I can feel the pressure of their stares. They're a formidable group, but none compare to the intensity from the man speaking.

"You believe in luck?" I challenge, raising my brows. I barely survived being cheek-to-cheek with Gage. There's no way I can sit on his lap. If I don't wither and die, I'll burst into flames.

"I believe in results," he replies coolly, gesturing to the stack of poker chips in front of him. "The chips don't lie." His eyes keep me locked in, the resolve in his voice leaving no room for argument.

I'm sitting on his lap whether I want to or not.

"Alright." I put the bottle down and step closer, stopping just out of reach. "I sit on your lap, and I get to keep my poker night tips." A round of chuckles breaks out across the table.

"Are you negotiating with me, little devil?" Gage asks, his head tilting, voice eerily calm.

"You want this ass on your lap? I want my tips." I'm not

backing down. Gage's eyes move over me slowly, his gaze touching me intimately in his perusal. His attention makes my heart race and my nerves stand on end, feeling like I'm in the sights of a heat-seeking missile.

I can take it. I like to play with fire.

"There are a lot of places I want that gorgeous ass," Gage responds, the rest of the men whooping around me. Their eyes are still on me, but it only fuels my confidence. A devilish grin slowly spreads across Gage's face, and adrenaline spikes through me. A rabbit staring down a wolf, hoping for a good chase. "Alright, you keep the money."

Crossing my arms over my chest and cocking my hip, I narrow my eyes at him warily. I don't trust him as far as I can throw him, and if I'm going to be sitting on Gage's lap, I'm getting something out of it. He meets my gaze without flinching. Kicking back in his chair, he holds one hand out to me and pats his lap with the other. The look I cut him with promises pain and suffering if he's lying, but he simply smirks.

Motherfucker.

As soon as I step close enough, Gage's hand snags mine and pulls until I'm all but falling onto his lap. His muscular legs feel solid beneath me, denim rough against my bare thighs. The heady scent of leather, cognac, and tobacco envelops me as his hands grip my hips to shift me right where he wants me. My insides are liquifying, every nerve igniting under his touch. One of his hands snakes around to palm my thigh, giving it a possessive squeeze, his fingers just inches from my needy pussy. The other reaches forward to pick up the cards he laid face down on the table. He discards two cards and has John deal him two more.

"I can feel my luck changing already." His nose grazes

the shell of my ear, his voice low and heavy with meaning. "I bet you can feel it too."

"So far, all I feel is unsatisfied."

His cock is hardening beneath me, making me throb with desire. I shift slightly, pressing my ass against him in search of friction to alleviate the pressure building between my thighs. His hand on my waist pulls me closer and slides beneath the hem of my dress.

I have the undivided attention of every man in this room. Grecko looks bored, and I know he's simply watching because I'm his only source of entertainment while he puffs on his stinky cigar. Dane, Brent, and Dallin watch silently, cards mostly forgotten, as their eyes search for movement where the table blocks their view of Gage's hand below my waist. John and Anders are gazing at me intently, but their eyes remain on my face, no doubt soaking in the arousal and need I'm emoting with each breath.

I feel the attention pouring down on me like the warmth of the sun on my skin, fueling the lust building inside me. Gage can feel it too, his hand finding my lace panties.

"This round is just getting started, Jill. It's all about timing. You don't want to give yourself up too soon." His fingers stroke me through the thin fabric, already soaked through. I let out a sigh, growing desperate. If he doesn't finish what he's started, he'll pay dearly—one way or another, I'm going to make a mess on his lap tonight.

"Let's see what we have here." Gage's voice washes over me, drenching me with promises of devastation. Pushing aside my panties, his wicked fingers find my pussy as his other hand lifts the cards up closer to show me.

"What do you think of this hand?" he asks, showing me his cards—a royal flush. Dipping his fingers into my wetness, he brushes his fingertips expertly across my swollen flesh. He circles my clit once, twice, three times—teasing me before he pushes two thick fingers inside me. I arch against him, seeking more. "Pretty good, isn't it?"

"Yes," I breathe. He pumps in and out of me once before withdrawing almost completely, his thumb relentless in its assault on my nerves.

Now we're finally getting somewhere.

Pleasure sparks inside me, growing and spreading like wildfire. Desire bleeds through my body until it's pumping through every vein, and my head is swimming.

"It's not always about what cards you're dealt. It's what you do with them." He's teasing me now, pushing just the tips of his fingers inside me to the first knuckle before slowly withdrawing, pushing in further very gradually each time. Too gradually.

"So do something with them." I move my hips to meet his fingers, moaning when he grants my request by driving his fingers into me to the hilt and finding a magical rhythm that makes me delirious.

"Do you think anyone else here has a hand as good as mine, little devil?" His voice is deep and rough with hunger. My eyes drift closed as my body begins to float, one of my arms reaching up behind me to anchor against his shoulder while the other hand grips the edge of the table for dear life.

I want more, need more.

As if reading my mind, he gives it to me. Keeping his pace steady, his hand shifts to push deeper as he slams into me harder, the heel of his hand slapping against my sensitive clit. He's earned some honesty from me, so I give it to him. "No."

"What should I do with this amazing hand, hmm? Fold

or go all in?" His fingers curl inside me, touching the spot that has stars flashing behind my eyes like lightning.

"Oh fuck," I moan, gasping and rocking against him. This man is the devil with the way he completely possesses every inch of my body.

"That's not an answer." He's as desperate for my release as I am. "Tell me."

"All in," I pant. "Now." The sound of his chuckle, raspy and deep, almost pushes me over the edge.

"Such a greedy girl." He rewards me with three fingers, filling and stretching me as he strokes the spot deep inside that has my breath stuttering. "You're dripping down my hand, soaking my lap. Let's see how wet I can get this perfect, needy pussy."

The sounds of my breathy pants and moans fill the room shamelessly. Gage's breath in my ear grows harsh as he finger fucks me into oblivion, his big cock hot and hard as a steel rod against my ass. Pleasure radiates through me, building and growing like an electrical storm, ready to take out everything in its path. Then his fingers pull out of me to roughly pinch my swollen clit, and the bite of pain sparks inside me like a detonator.

Euphoria explodes through me, every nerve firing all at once. My back arches with the force of it, my body completely overwhelmed. Gage's cards lay forgotten on the table as he holds me close while my orgasm rips through me.

"Gage," I moan his name over and over again, a chorus of pants and sighs leaving me as I'm consumed by blinding pleasure. "Oh, god." I struggle for breath, writhing against him. My mind is completely blank, and my thoughts are finally silenced as my body processes the bliss that's over-taken my limbs. Slowly, the tension fades, and I melt back against his chest, completely spent. A deep, cleansing breath enters and exits my lungs through my parted lips.

"Holy fuck," someone mutters from across the table, but I'm not sure who.

"That was the hottest fucking thing I've ever witnessed," Gage murmurs deeply into my ear after a minute. Pulling out of me, he replaces my panties and tugs my dress back down. Lifting his hand up past my face, I can see his hand glistening with my arousal before he sticks his fingers into his mouth to suck me off of them with a groan. "So fucking sweet."

"How do I get a taste?" Dallin asks, licking his lips. Gage tenses against me, his tone darkening.

"You know better than to ask me to share, Feldman." A thrill runs through me at the danger in his voice. "Now, let's hurry this game up before I get mad, and no one can walk away from this table." That seems to shut the other men up, and they continue the game. Anders sweetens the pot, and Dallin folds with a string of curses.

As soon as I think my legs will support me again, I attempt to stand up. But Gage isn't having that. He holds me on his lap easily, his rock-hard erection pressed between my ass cheeks. "Not so fast, sweetheart. You're not done here."

"Now that you've shown us what you got," Gage says, taking his cards off the table. "Lay them down, boys." Each of the men starts showing their hands—Grecko playing three of a kind that has Brent, Anders, and John folding. Dane lays down a full house, beating out the old man, but his hand isn't good enough. Gage plays his royal flush, winning the entire pot worth almost a hundred grand.

"Your time's up," I say, pulling his hands off me to climb off his lap. "I've given you more than enough luck for one night." Stepping away from the man doing his best to claim my soul, my eyes don't miss the wet mark on his lap where I came all over him.

So far, Gage has made me come harder than I ever have before. I'll die before I admit it to him—no one but Lana gets to know. But it's the reason I let him anywhere near me instead of gutting him like the other men who've tried to get away with shit.

They fucked around and found out.

Gage's ability to play my body until I've reached unbelievable heights of pleasure has given him access to me that looks past a lot of the shit he tries to pull. And as long as the orgasms outweigh the urge to slit him open, I'll keep using him to get off.

"That was quite the show you just gave my boys." As Gage's eyes move over me, I can practically see the images of what he wants to do to my body flash through his mind. "You really worked for your tip."

"I do love it when the tip is big." I move my gaze until it lands on Dane. "I hope you don't disappoint me, Dane." With that, I saunter off to the wet bar.

I busy myself with cleaning up the bar while the men play another hand. John and Grecko get into it about the difference between equity and 'being liquid', and Dane tries to strike up conversation with me from across the room— something Gage shuts down immediately.

Scooping ice into a shaker, I add gin and a small splash of vermouth before I put on the top and give it a good shake. Pulling out a chilled martini glass, I pour the cold liquid into the glass and add a lemon twist. Lifting the rim to my lips and taking a sip, my tongue welcomes the taste of the dirty martini.

Drinking on the job as a bartender is a big no-no,

though most people in the service industry sneak drinks regularly. Making myself a martini right in front of the man who owns both the club I work at and me would be considered a daring move. But I'm not making a statement. I simply don't give a shit. It's been a long night, and I need a stiff drink.

And there's no leaving this job.

My body alerts me to Gage's presence before he speaks. I can sense him coming to stand closely behind me, and my entire being prickles with awareness. His energy shrouds us like a storm cloud, tension radiating from his powerful body.

"You're wasting your time with Dane." His voice is low, the rough undertone of anger is fucking sexy. "He can't give you what you need."

Picking up my glass, I turn around to face him and tilt my head up to meet his gaze. A sharp edge to his calm demeanor—almost indiscernible—transforms his handsome face from cool to lethal.

I like it.

"What Dane can or can't give me isn't something you need to concern yourself with." Pressing the cool glass to my lips, I take a sip.

I don't want anything to do with Dane. In fact, Dane is one of the reasons my brother ever moved from making smaller bets at casino tables to the high-stakes games that first drowned him, then sucked the life out of him. My brother's gambling addiction started at fifteen with the discovery of online poker. He'd been able to keep his head above water until he met Dane Presley. Dane raised the stakes, and Tommy ultimately couldn't pay the price.

Gage is a very jealous man, that much is clear. He's a loaded weapon that will be useful when pointed in the right direction. So I'll give Dane some attention—I'll even let him flirt with me. He'll pay for his sins soon enough, and I won't have to lift a finger for this one.

"You like games, little devil. But I've never lost a hand." He lifts his fingers to his nose and inhales deeply to prove his point, letting the breath out with a deep growl. "I can still smell you on my fingers, so filthy and eager. I bet your needy little pussy is still dripping for me, throbbing for my cock to fill it." He takes another step forward, tilting his head and running his eyes over my body. "You'd like that, wouldn't you? I should claim your pussy right here, and now—rip that hot dress off your sexy body and fuck you right here on the bar until you pass out from the pleasure."

My entire body throbs, aching for him. He's right. I want his cock to slam balls deep into me until I'm falling apart. My pussy pulsates at the thought of it, my clit swollen and desperate as lust spears through me. I'm so fucking turned on, it's ridiculous. I know he can see it in the way my breathing changes and how my pupils dilate. "I'll pass. I already got what I wanted from you tonight."

"Seems like you need a reminder about who you belong to."

"You can pay for my attention, but you can't buy my interest." I lean up to press a soft, chaste kiss to his lips. "You want me? Earn me. So far, I'm not impressed."

Gage stares down at me, his dark eyes so intense that I allow myself to get caught in them briefly. Being under his gaze fuels me, filling my battery and reaffirming my position. It's a reminder.

He may hold all the power, but I'm the one in control.

"Hey, doll, get me another scotch," John calls from the table. "If I'm not going to win tonight, I might as well be good and drunk."

"Coming right up," I call without breaking eye contact. I place my hand on Gage's solid chest, letting it run down his muscled torso until it reaches where his heavy cross falls. I wrap my fingers around the cold metal and give it a tug, pulling him in closer. Gage watches me without blinking, his eyes laser-focused with a desire so potent I can practically taste it. Tilting my head up and leaning in, he does the same. But before his mouth meets mine, I bring my waiting glass to my lips to toss back the last of the cocktail.

"Duty calls." I let go of his cross and give it a pat. "I wouldn't want to get in trouble with my job."

Gage chuckles, the sound rich and terrifying. My breath hitches when his hand wraps around my throat beneath my jaw, and I'm being pulled flush against his chest. My free hand presses against him in an attempt to steady myself. The smile on his face is one of dark satisfaction when his lips lower to claim mine. He kisses me soundly—with sweet, sultry give and rough, hungry take.

After a long moment, he finally pulls back just enough to look at me, the smile returning to his face like we're in on the same joke. "Little devil, you're nothing but trouble. And I'm made for chaos."

CHAPTER THIRTEEN

JILL

Walking through the door of *Stained Heart Tattoos* a week later, my eyes move around the space. It's a nice place, nicer than I was expecting.

"Hi, can I help you?" Despite the tattoos covering the plus-size woman at the reception desk, her smile is as bright as her pink hair. There's something about her that radiates sunshine.

"I made an appointment to get a tattoo," I say, looking past the reception desk. "My name is Jill."

Her eyes move from the computer screen to really look at me, making me pause. I'm about to ask her if something's up, but then she smiles.

"Jill's a pretty name. It suits you," she says, clicking at the computer. "I'm Stevie. I'll have you follow me."

I follow her past the front desk to the workstations. Two men and a woman lie on tattoo chairs while artists ink their skin with needles. Dane sits at a workstation in the far back corner, sketching at a desk.

"Welcome to the chapel." Stevie gestures around with

her arm. I'm not surprised by the amount of black in the interior design. With sleek black walls and expensive-looking equipment, the historic building adds an air of charm enhanced with modern fixtures. The stained glass windows that rise several stories to the cathedral ceilings are stunning showstoppers in the otherwise monochromatic interior, adding both color and light to the space.

My eyes catch on the images laid into the stained glass windows—an angel holding a bleeding heart in his hand, a woman in biblical garb weeping, a horse geared for battle—they're beautiful. I can see why Gage kept them.

"I'm not built for church, so I hope this is as close as I get," I scoff. Narrow wooden pews and organized religion are two things I have no interest in. Stevie laughs at that, nodding to two of the other tattoo artists. One is stocky and tan, with thick black hair styled in Viking braids. The other is bald, with tattoos covering his head up to his hairline and large green gauges in both ears.

"You're definitely built for worship, Angel. I'd join you in the confessional any day," the Viking says. I roll my eyes as he makes a show of checking me out. He's not unattractive. In fact, he's kinda hot, but looking at him does nothing for me. Stevie swings out her hand to roughly knock him upside the head.

"Shut up, Saint. Your pedo 'stache is bad enough. No one wants to go into the booths with you."

He reaches up to touch the little line of hair on his top lip before shooting an accusing look on the bald man tattooing a woman in the next chair over. "That's it, I'm shaving this damn thing."

The bald guy looks up from his work to shake his head. "Not unless you wanna pay up. You've got two more weeks, Nacho Libre."

"Dammit," Saint groans. "I'm never playing pool with you again, Orion."

The bald guy—Orion, I assume—snorts at that.

"God, I can't wait for Vanessa to come back from L.A. I'm so sick of these whiney little boys," Stevie says, flashing me an apologetic look. Saint grins and opens his mouth, obviously about to say something else to me, but Stevie cuts him off before he gets the chance. "Seriously, Saint, don't even bother. This is Jill."

The silence that falls over the room is startling.

Needles stop, conversations halt—no one even breathes too heavily. I look around at all of them, my eyes narrowing in confusion. Saint looks at Stevie and gestures to me. "As in *Jill* Jill? Gage's Jill?"

Stevie nods, crossing her arms over her chest with a satisfied smile at how the man deflates. This time, when Saint's eyes move over me, it's with reverence. He nods a few times in understanding, "Ok, yeah, I get it."

"It's just Jill," I state firmly. Irritation itches through me like a heat flash at the implication I'm something that belongs to Gage. I don't belong to anyone, debt or no debt.

Speak of the Devil.

Like the mention of his name summoned him from the underworld, Gage strides into the chapel through the dark doorway in the back corner.

"Well, well, well, look who we have here," his deep voice sends a thrill through me and makes my pussy throb. He's wearing a black tank top that shows off his bulging tattooed biceps, strong forearms, and large, rough hands to perfection. He runs his tongue across his bottom lip before he bites it as he looks me over from head to toe.

He's way too hot for his own good. And mine.

"To what do I owe this pleasure?" he asks, striding closer.

"I have an appointment to get a tattoo," I say. "My first one."

"You never forget your first."

"It won't be the first virginity I lose in a church." It's the truth. I've come full circle—though I didn't *come* in that church when I was sixteen.

I'm sure there's some irony in there somewhere.

"Tell me what you want." Those words coming out of Gage's mouth could bring any woman to her knees—but I'm here for a reason, and not even Gage and his wicked mouth will distract me.

At least not until later.

"I want a martini glass," I say, hooking my thumb in the waistband of my mini skirt and pulling it down to show the expanse of skin above my pussy where my thigh meets my stomach. "Here." I turn around and flip up the hem of my skirt to show my ass swallowing my thong. "Or maybe here, I haven't decided." All eyes are on me when I look over my shoulder. After they've all gotten a good look, I drop the fabric back into place and turn back around to face them.

"Come with me," Gage says deeply, his eyes hungry to get started.

"Oh, I didn't make myself clear. My appointment isn't with you." My eyes slide over to Dane, who now stands in the group. "You'll take good care of me. Right, Dane?"

"Fuck yeah," Dane mutters before clearing his throat. "I mean, yeah, I can do that for you."

Gage's jaw clenches as his gaze cuts between me and the other man, his eyes promising pain and suffering. After a breath, he leans his head back, running his tongue across the edge of his teeth, and grins—the smile of a serial killer making plans for his next victim.

"Go ahead. I hope he gives you an experience you won't forget," he says, the violence residing in his tone chilling the room by several degrees. "*I* won't."

It's a promise. A death note.

Everyone in the room freezes—everyone except me. I walk towards him, completely at ease. Stopping only a foot from him, I look over at Dane. "Lead the way."

The fact that Dane moves shows just how stupid he really is. Everyone else in this building, including the ones only here for tattoos, can tell that Gage is deadly. And he isn't bluffing. I know it—in fact, I'm counting on it. And Dane's sealing his own fate right now.

No wonder he's such a shitty gambler. He doesn't know how to read a room.

I follow Dane into one of the confessional booths along the back wall. Turning around, I make eye contact with Gage as Dane reaches for the curtain. Gage's dark eyes bore into me. His jaw clenched tightly as he stands like a harbinger of death plotting his vengeance. His dark expression is calm as still water, but the anger is rolling off of him in waves as tension crowds the room.

Stevie glances nervously between her boss and me, and I know she can feel it too. I flash Gage a wink just before the heavy black fabric closes and severs our connection.

"Alright," Dane says once it's just the two of us. He rubs his hands together eagerly, his eyes traveling over me. "Come lay down in the chair and let me get a good look at my canvas."

I refrain from rolling my eyes as I recline on the large black leather tattoo chair. He sits on a rolling stool next to the chair, leaning in close as I tug down the waistband of my skirt again to expose the expanse of my bikini line. A gross humming sound comes from Dane's throat as he stares at my bare skin, his hands running across the smooth surface.

"You shaved for me," he murmurs in a way that makes my skin crawl.

"I'm waxed," I respond flatly. He's not special, and I don't like him thinking he is. But he still grins at that—and for a split second, I consider torching this whole plan and just stabbing this creep myself.

Using Gage's sociopathic tendencies to exact my revenge on this weasel was a good plan, and it'll definitely work. By the look on Gage's face when the curtain was closing, I wouldn't be surprised if he set Dane on fire right here in the shop. This asshole's suffering will be delicious, and it's the only reason I'll put up with this cockroach touching me long enough for this tattoo.

Dane sketches up a simple design of a black and white martini glass made of clean, delicate lines to stencil onto my skin. The sting of the tattoo needle is thrilling, making me wish different hands were holding the ink gun— wicked, tattooed hands adorned with silver rings.

The whole process takes under an hour, though it feels so much longer. The sounds of the tattoo shop behind the curtain are the only distraction that keeps me from crawling out of my skin until Dane finally leans back.

"Alright, you're done," he announces, handing me a hand-held mirror. "And it looks pretty good if I do say so myself."

I might not be a tattoo expert, but even I can tell he did a mediocre job on a very simple design. For the amount of time his hands were on my body, you'd think he was tattooing something with more detail. But despite the uneven line work and unsaturated black, I couldn't care less about the tattoo. It's served its purpose.

"Great," I say simply, which he takes as a compliment. He grins at me, leaning closer. He opens his mouth again, probably to do something stupid like ask me out, but he doesn't get the chance.

"Dane, your next appointment is here," Stevie says, her head appearing around the side of the curtain. Her eyes connect with mine, and I have to bite back a smile. She's here to rescue me.

"I'll be out in a few minutes," Dane replies, completely missing our silent conversation, his eyes still on me.

"Her appointment was supposed to start ten minutes ago, and she's got a schedule to keep. Now quit dragging ass and get out here." Stevie's insistent tone makes it clear she's not going to let him brush her off. Dane rolls his eyes but still shoves his stool back and stands up to acquiesce. Clearly Stevie's the one running the show around here.

I like her.

Taking the opportunity to escape, I follow when Stevie ducks out of the curtain. Pulling back the fabric, I come face to face with Death himself. Gage looms just on the other side of the curtain, every muscle in his incredible body radiating with tension. His sexy jawline is sharp as a knife as he clenches his teeth against his anger.

I look up at him, forcing my body to remain at ease while he stares me down. His attention sets me on fire, every inch of me lighting up under his gaze.

"You're very eager to see it, huh?" I tug down my skirt to show him the ink now permanently etched into my skin. "Do you like it?" I ask, raising my brows expectantly. Gage barely glances at the damn thing, his fury swirling around him like a dark cloud.

"Do you?" he counters, his deep voice rough and edged with violence. The sound makes my heart race and my pulse jump.

"You were right. It was an experience I'll never forget." I lean up and press a sensual kiss to his jaw. "I thought of you the entire time." I step back before he has a chance to get a hold of me. Just then, Dane steps out of the booth, skirting around us.

His timing couldn't be more perfect.

Gage's eyes land on Dane like a vulture eyeing roadkill. The malice sharpening his gaze sends a thrill through me, lust heating my blood until I'm wet and throbbing for him. But instead of leaning closer like my body is begging me to, I take another step back.

"I've gotta go," I announce, bringing his attention back to me. "I wouldn't want to disrupt your day at work." Seeing that he's about to reach out and stop me, I evade his grasp to saunter through the chapel towards the front desk.

When I pull out my wallet to pay, Stevie flashes me a look that says she's not sure what's going on, but she approves. She announces my total and accepts my credit card, her eyes glancing past me every once in a while. I don't have to look to know what's happening behind me.

"Here you go," Stevie hands me my receipt, an entertained smile tugging on her lips. "Please come again soon."

"Oh, I definitely will." I flash her a bright smile. "Bye, Stevie." With that, I strut out the door, leaving the chaos I designed in my wake. Stepping outside, I breathe in the fresh summer air and slide on my sunglasses.

Wow, what a beautiful day.

CHAPTER FOURTEEN

GAGE

The sun set a while ago, daylight is long gone—leaving the easy darkness of night. The sounds of the city echo through the buildings and fade into the background as white noise. Even if it weren't so pitch black outside, I wouldn't hesitate for a second.

Footsteps sound in the parking lot with the jingle of keys. Dane approaches where I'm waiting by his car. Even though he doesn't see me coming, I know he senses me.

But not until it's too late.

Stepping up behind him, I don't even allow him to turn around and look at me before I strike. Clamping my hand on the back of his head, I smash his face down onto the side of his car, hard enough to knock him unconscious and break his nose in the process.

Whistling to myself, I lean down to hoist him over my shoulder in a fireman's hold and head towards the back door into my office.

The entire building is now empty, Dane was the last one here. I let him leave for the night—let him clean up his station and lock up the shop through the main doors—like it was just a normal night for two reasons. One, it's better for me that the cameras saw him leave for alibi reasons. And two, because I want him to feel the full weight of terror when I give him what's coming for him.

He spent the last three days looking over his shoulder for me, keeping one eye on the door at all times. I watched on the security cameras as he glanced around every ten seconds and jumped at every little sound. His paranoia was satisfying, so I let it build until he drowned in it. And just when he thought he was safe, that he got away with it—here the fuck I am.

There aren't any cameras in my office, not ones that anyone has access to. The surveillance for my office is kept hidden on a separate server that only I have access to for confidentiality reasons. Anders handles the rest of the security for my business, but my office is off-limits. My clients value their privacy, and so do I.

Carrying Dane into my office, I lock the door behind me before I drop him onto my tattoo chair. The plastic sheeting covering the leather crinkles under his weight as I strap his arms onto the armrests and secure his ankles down. Reaching into my tattoo station, I grab a pair of black disposable gloves and pull them on with a snap.

The metallic chink of my knife sounds in the silence as I flip the blade open. Being none too gentle, I begin cutting and ripping the clothing off his body until he lies naked and pathetic. I sneer at the tattoos scattered over his body. They're tacky and ugly as fuck.

The blood dripping from his bashed nose gets me excited. Adrenaline courses through me, and the anticipation swells. This fucker is about to feel pain like he's never experienced before.

I'm going to enjoy this.

If I were a patient man, I would sit and wait for him to wake up on his own. But I'm not. So instead, I decide to give him a little wake-up call.

I light one of the cigars I stole from his workstation. The end sparks to life, embers flaring as it starts to burn. The smoke burns my nostrils, and I scowl at the damn thing. Of course this bastard would like this rank shit.

It's noxious and disgusting, just like him.

Standing over him, I take the tip of the cigar and press the burning end to his skin. A thrill races through my veins at how his flesh singes in a near-perfect circle. Dane's eyes pop open with a pained yelp, his gaze looking around frantically at his surroundings. When his eyes land on me, they bulge in fear.

So fucking satisfying.

"Gage, what—" he struggles against his restraints, looking down at his naked body. I can see when panic sets in. "No, *no, no, no.*"

"You knew this was coming," I say calmly, sucking on the gross cigar to keep the spark alive. I blow the smoke out into his face, making him cough. "You've known me long enough to know what you were asking for. Hell, you were practically begging for it. So, here we are."

"Is this about Jill?" Her name on his unworthy lips makes my temper rage.

"Say her name again, and I'll cut your fucking tongue out." The cigar presses into the eye of his gypsy woman tattoo, making him howl. I press it down a little too hard and leave it on a little too long. When I lift it, the melted flesh is charred, with blood springing to the surface.

Oops.

"I didn't touch her, man. I barely even looked at her. I swear."

"You never could tell a decent lie. Apparently, not even to save your own life."

"This is crazy, Gage." He attempts a laugh and a reassuring smile. "C'mon, you know me."

Walking around the chair, my tongue runs over my top teeth in contempt. Watching his body move on the chair as he fights against his restraints has the anger boiling hotter inside me, fueling my rage. I picture Jill lying behind the curtain with his talentless fingers all over her. All over what's only for me. What's *mine*.

"Exactly, I know you. I know what kind of a scum-sucking rat you really are. A greedy little opportunist who never knows when to quit." I lean in closer. "Your grabby little hands are always reaching for what's not yours to touch. This time, you went too far."

He's right-handed, so I grab his left. He resists my hold, but it's useless. His hand trembles in mine, and I soak in the racing of his pulse. Lifting up his pinky, I turn to look him in the eye. "Did this finger touch her?"

He starts to shake his head frantically in a lie of self-preservation. We're way past that.

Dane tattoos with his right hand, so his left hand would be the one used to wipe and manipulate the canvas—my Jill. Every finger on this hand has touched her.

A malicious smile crosses my face, and he stills. "Go ahead. Lie to me."

He pales considerably, the blood draining from his face. I wouldn't be surprised if he pisses himself right on my chair.

"Okay, it touched her." Before the words have even left his mouth I snap his pinky with enough force to shatter the bone. Dane yells, his breathing becoming erratic. He huffs his breaths through clenched teeth against the pain. His agony itches through my blood like a drug.

I'm just getting started.

Lifting up his ring finger, I cock my head to one side.

"Did this finger touch her?" I ask, earning a groan. He hesitates but doesn't give any excuses or lies this time. Finally, he nods. That finger gets snapped too—twice.

Finger by finger, I ask which ones touched my Jill. Soon, his entire left hand is mangled and swollen, all five fingers rendered completely useless. Then I move to his right hand. Only three of those five fingers are spared—the ones that only held the tattoo gun.

Snot and tears run down Dane's face, mixing with the blood trailing from his nose as he cries. Staring down at him, I don't feel an ounce of remorse or sympathy, just malice.

"Nothing else touched her, I swear. Nothing," he blubbers, but I don't believe him. My eyes trail down his body to his limp dick.

His *tiny* limp dick.

"You touched yourself, didn't you?" After Jill left with her tattoo, Dane disappeared for a good twenty minutes. "Touching her made you hard. Being so close to her pussy and tits, feeling the softness of her against your hands, made you hard as a fucking rock. You were so turned on that you went to the bathroom after she left, and you jerked yourself off, imagining it was her. Didn't you?"

"I don't know what you want me to say. She's hot. I couldn't help it." His stammering grates against my self-restraint. "I couldn't help myself."

"Did you rub her?" I ask, my voice shaking as I fight to stay in control.

"What?"

"Did you rub your erection against my Jill while she was in your chair?" I say the words slowly, the deadly intent swirling through me so powerful I can taste it.

"I—I didn't mean to. I was reaching for something and —" His entire body is trembling as I fist his balls in my hand, squeezing them tightly.

"Say it." My knife chinks open, ready to spill blood. His response has me seeing red, all control leaving my body as my demons take hold of me.

"Yes. My boner touched her, but—*ahhh*!" His words trail off into screams of agony, raw and unfiltered, as my knife saws the testicles from his body. His wrinkly ball sack is tossed to the floor at my feet. Blood spills over the plastic-covered chair onto the tarps covering the floor. Dane's body jerks, his back arching, as his eyes roll back in his head. Losing consciousness, his body goes limp.

Power pulses through me, addicting and euphoric. I feel vindicated as gratification rolls over me and settles into my bones.

I don't know what made him faint—the blood loss or the pain. I don't give a shit. I'll patch him up with a few rough stitches and a bandage around his shriveled junk. Letting him bleed out would defeat the whole purpose. I won't kill him—letting him live is so much better.

Dane will live the rest of his life not able to fully use his hands to create the art he's dedicated himself to. He'll never get an erection thinking of my Jill again or at all. Most importantly, he'll never lay another finger on my girl.

No one will.

CHAPTER FIFTEEN

GAGE

Cutting the rumbling engine of my motorcycle does nothing to quiet the energy coursing through me. Parking is tight, so I walk the block and a half with powerful strides until I see the building come into view.

She left her fucking blinds open.

Jill stands in her living room in full view of where I stand on the street, looking into her apartment. She's looking into the full-length mirror she has set up in the corner of her living room, admiring herself from different angles in a sexy new black lace bodysuit.

Her ample body is fucking banging, perfectly show-cased by how the lace cuts high on her full hips, and her generous ass swallows the thong back. This must be a new work outfit. She's a showstopper. Even with a skirt or shorts on top, every man in the city will be bricked up the moment they lay eyes on her. They can look all they want, can desire her all they want.

They'll never get the chance to touch.

Jill disappears into her room for a few minutes, and I

consider rounding the side of the building to her French doors. But when she emerges after a few minutes, my entire body stands at attention—especially my cock.

She's wearing a red mesh lingerie set, the tiny little thong sitting high on her hips, covering nothing but a tiny triangle between her legs. The scarlet bra top has lust ripping the air from my lungs. The underwire cups her big tits perfectly with a big satin bow tied across the front to keep them in. All it will take is the tug on a ribbon to have her nipple in my mouth. I'll unwrap her like the gift she is.

My cock is so hard it almost hurts.

Pulling out my cell phone, I dial her number. I watch her grab the phone and answer it without looking to see who's calling.

"Hello?" Even distracted, her sultry voice is alluring.

"You better be wearing that for me," I say deeply, reaching down to adjust the raging boner in my pants. She freezes and looks around her apartment like I might be standing right behind her.

Soon, I will be.

"Maybe, maybe not." The way she smiles into the phone, a playful smile that spells trouble, has me taking a step closer to her window.

"No one else will ever get the chance to see you in it."

"I don't know, we'll have to see. Won't we?"

"I'll make sure of it."

"Oh, will you?" She's teasing me, and her taunting has me making a beeline to the door of her building. "And how do you plan on doing that?"

"Let me in, little devil."

"What are you, the big bad wolf?" she asks as I stalk towards her front door. I could go around back, but I don't need to give away those secrets—yet.

"If you don't open the door, I'll huff, and I'll puff and find my own way in." Either way, I'm going to devour her. There's a moment of silence on the line, and for a split second, I wonder if I'm going to have to use the side entrance after all. But then I hear the slide of her chain and the click of the deadbolt on the other side of the door.

As soon as the doorknob turns, I'm crowding the door. I storm into the apartment, meeting a stunned Jill standing just inside the entryway with the phone still pressed to her ear. I pluck the phone from her hand, drop it on the entryway table to my left, and kick the door shut behind me.

Jill gazes up at me with those striking green eyes of hers, full lips parted. I take a step towards her, and she takes a responding step back, making me grin. She wants to play? I'm up for a little chase.

"You look—" My eyes travel over every inch of her in the little red set. She looks even better up close, my mouth is watering, and my dick aches. "Edible."

"What are you doing here?" The question falls flat as she takes another small step backward. Her gorgeous pupils are dilated, and the way her breathing changes tells me just how turned on she is. When I rip those little panties off her, her pussy will be drenched for me.

"I'm here for you." Pulling off my leather jacket, I toss it onto the floor beside me. "And you opened the door."

She's gonna run.

Jill turns on her heel and darts across her kitchen. A primal sound rumbles in my chest as I run after her. I let her stay a step ahead of me for a second just so I can watch how her ass bounces. It only takes a few strides before I'm right on top of her.

A strong hand around her throat tows her body towards

me until I can pin her between the wall and her kitchen counter. She stares up at me, her breasts pressing against the big red bow with every excited breath, just begging for me to set them free.

When I lower my head to kiss her, her hand rears back to slap me across the face. Hard. My head whips to the side, completely taken by surprise, just as her favorite switch-blade clicks open. When I turn back to look down at her, I feel the cold metal where she's pressing the sharp tip to my throat.

I gaze down at her, a smile spreading across my face as she drags the sharp edge across my skin, both teasing and threatening. "A knife," I'm so fucking turned on. "You don't have to flirt with me, Menace. I'm right here."

"You're everywhere," she says.

I'm everywhere she is.

"And I always will be. You were created just for me, Jill. There's no escaping me, escaping *this*."

"Who says I'm trying to escape?" She drops the knife, letting it clatter onto the floor, before wrapping her arms around my neck to pull me down for a kiss. Our mouths clash, lips devouring each other greedily, furiously.

I thread one of my hands through her thick, dark hair, fisting at the scalp and giving it a sharp tug. Jill lets out a breathy little moan that begs for more, driving me wild. My tongue dives into her mouth to invade and conquer, drinking her in like a man dying of thirst.

Our mouths move together, hers letting me take the lead. She allows me to dominate, and her submission buzzes over my skin like a newfound sense of power. Keeping my hand fisting her hair, my other hand moves down her luxe body to slip under the scrap of fabric covering her perfect pussy.

Jill's breathless pants turn to moans as I stroke her, reveling in how drenched she is. All for me. A wave of hunger hits me, and I'm ready to eat. I want to lay Jill out like the feast she is.

Jill's cry of surprise when I turn her around and lift her up onto the kitchen island melts into a moan when my mouth latches onto her neck. Sinking three fingers into her perfect pussy, her hips move to meet my thrusts as I taste her skin. Her every amped breath powers through me like wildfire until I'm nothing but smoke and ash.

Jill's hands claw at my clothing, grabbing and scratching in search of my skin. Her nails dig into me, raking across my naked chest and shoulders until she draws blood. The rough desperation as she marks me has every one of my nerves standing on end until my entire body is electrified.

With the tug of the ribbon, the offensive bow keeping me from Jill's gorgeous heavy breasts falls away. Her perfect dusty rose nipples greet me, begging for my lips until my mouth waters. Leaning forward, I don't hesitate to take a taste. My lips are greedy against her skin—licking, sucking, and biting like I'll never get the chance again.

I feel as the orgasm builds inside her, the walls of her pussy fluttering around my fingers. I want her to come, I need to see her fall apart for me. Then I'll suck every last drop from her gorgeous pussy.

Curving my fingers to touch that magic spot deep inside her, Jill's enchanting eyes roll back in her head. She's so beautiful it hurts to look at her, delirious with pleasure, but I've always been a masochist.

"Gage—" She gasps, sending primal satisfaction coursing through me. I'll never get enough of my name on her delicious lips, especially when she's chanting it like a spell.

"Say it again," I demand.

"Gage, I'm…I'm coming." Jill's body writhes against me as the pleasure overcomes her. Her pussy clamps around my fingers so tightly it makes my cock jump. Her cries as she's tumbling over the edge carry my name over and over. It's music to my fucking ears.

I want more.

Pushing her back on the counter, I pull her hips until her ass is all but hanging off the edge. Dragging the tiny little panties down her legs, they're thrown over my shoulder before I'm diving in between her thighs face first.

A growl vibrates through me as her arousal coats my tongue. She tastes so damn sweet I could get a sugar rush. Her hips buck against my mouth as I taste and explore every delectable inch of her. My lips latch onto her clit, sucking on the swollen bud like it sustains me, making her squirm and sob in ecstasy. Keeping the bundle of nerves in my mouth, I give a low hum—the vibrations make her thighs quake, her hands threading through my hair desperately. When my teeth nip at her swollen flesh, it's all too much.

Jill's back bows off the counter as the euphoria steals her breath. Her hands in my hair fist painfully, egging me on as I ride out her orgasm. I drink her in, savoring the honey as the delicacy it is. My lips don't leave her until she goes limp against the counter. When I finally stand, I can feel her dripping down my chin.

Stepping around the island, I brush the hair from her flushed face before leaning down to kiss her. She moans against my lips softly, and I know she can taste herself on my lips.

"You taste that?" I ask, making her nod against me. "That's how good you taste."

"No wonder you were enjoying yourself so much."

"Almost as much as you were." She turns her head to look at me, eyes bright against the sated expression on her gorgeous features. "I bet you're going to be looking at this counter differently from now on."

"It's making me hungry."

"You want something to eat?" She nods again. "What do you want, pretty girl?"

"There are some snacks in the fridge." Walking over to the fridge, I ignore the rock-hard boner begging for relief against my boxers as I pull out a cheese tray and some chocolate-covered strawberries. Stepping back over to the island, I gently help Jill off the counter before taking a seat on one of the stools.

Jill walks over to her fridge, grabbing a knife on the way over. Opening her freezer, she reaches into the ice bin and pulls out a large chunk of ice made of several cubes melted together. Placing her glass on the counter, she plops the ice on top of the cup before she starts stabbing. The solid mass splinters and breaks until the pieces are small enough to fall into the glass without protest.

Pouring in sparkling water, she adds a packet of electrolytes. Taking the knife, she uses the blade to stir the powder until it's dissolved. Looking over at me, she brings the knife to her mouth and runs the flat of her tongue along the blade to lick off the drops of liquid before taking a sip of her drink.

If I didn't already have a boner the size of a baseball bat for her, that would've had me bricked up immediately.

She's so *fucking* hot.

Walking back across the kitchen, drink in hand, Jill sits

on the stool next to me. She reaches behind her back to unhook the red bra before tossing it on the counter, and when I look at her in question, she simply shrugs. "It served its purpose."

"It definitely did."

"You going to take care of that?" Jill asks, eyeing my erection. As she pops a cube of cheese into her mouth, I can see her considering wrapping her lips around something else instead.

"When I'm ready." And I'm not ready for this to be over yet.

"What'd you do to Dane?" Jill asks curiously, her lips wrapping around a strawberry in a way that heats my blood.

"What I'll do to anyone who touches you. Something he'll never recover from." I swipe a drop of the red berry juice from her full bottom lip with the pad of my thumb. Sticking my finger in my mouth, I suck the juice off with a groan.

"Pity," she says, her tone saying she feels anything but. Her bedroom eyes lock with mine as her expression turns heated. "What're you going to do to me?"

Leaning in, my hand grips beneath her jaw to pull her in closer. "Something you'll never forget." I need to teach her a lesson she'll never want to learn again.

My hand beneath her jaw slides lower to circle her throat, giving it a firm squeeze. Jill's eyes meet mine with a sinful smile and a breathy laugh that has awareness trickling through me.

I hold the power, but I'm not the one in control.

Not by a long shot.

"Take your last bite," I instruct her, allowing her to snag one last square of cheese before I'm hauling her into my arms with a surprised squeal. My steps are large and fuelled with purpose as I take us into the bedroom. I'm not gentle when I toss her onto the bed.

I've been thinking about this from the moment she stepped into the confessional with Dane.

Grabbing her ankle to drag her down the bed, I flip her over onto her stomach and yank her hips up until her sexy dimpled ass is in the air. One of my hands tangles in her hair as I press her face to the mattress, leaning down to growl. "Don't move. Your ass is mine."

Jill lets out a muffled moan, making me fist my already aching cock. I'm hard as fucking steel. Pushing down my boxers, I kick them to the side as my cock springs free. Reaching for the drawer in her bedside table, I find the lube she keeps there. Opening the bottle, I spread Jill's cheeks and let a generous amount pour out onto her dusty pink little hole. She moans when I run my thumb over the entrance, pressing the tip of it inside her briefly before reaching for my cock.

I'll lubricate her, but that's as gentle as I'm going to be.

She let another man touch her glorious body—a body that isn't hers to share. Not anymore.

It's time to remind her who owns it.

Drizzling lubricant into my palm, I run the slickness down my length and toss the bottle back in the drawer. Standing beside the bed with Jill's ass waiting for my cock, I take a moment to soak in the sight. Her delectable asshole glistens at me, begging to be filled, her pretty pussy already dripping and swollen in anticipation.

Bringing my hand up, I give her ass a hard smack, watching how the ample flesh ripples and bounces before grabbing another rough handful. Jill moans loudly beneath me, making lust burn through my veins. She is so goddamn beautiful, her body is pure sin.

Looking down at her—at how deeply perfect she is— has a fresh wave of anger surging through me. Another man put his hands on her, thought he could have her. Dane thought he could sample something that's only for me.

And she fucking let him.

"You did a bad thing, Jill," I say darkly, my voice rumbling deep in my chest. "You let him touch you. You let him put his greedy hands all over this beautiful body. A body that belongs to *me*."

My hand connects with her ass again firmly in another harsh spank, the skin turning pink. "There are no more warnings, Menace. No one else gets to touch you. No one." Pressing the head of my cock to her tight bud, cruelty takes over. There's no patience or gentleness in me as I slam into her with one hard thrust. Jill cries out, her breathing turning heavy as I shove past any resistance her body puts up until I'm balls deep inside her.

Holy fucking shit.

She's so goddamn tight, so hot. My eyes roll back at how good she feels, squeezing the life out of me. "This body doesn't belong to you anymore. It's mine. I decide who gets to touch it, enjoy it. Let someone touch it without my permission again, and I won't hesitate to put a bullet right between his eyes. Then I'll tie you up so you can't even touch yourself."

Pulling out and thrusting into her again, I start moving inside her roughly. Jill's cries are an intoxicating mix of pain and pleasure. My hands sink into her generous thighs for leverage as my cock pistons inside her.

"Oh god, you're so big." Jill all but sobs, her pussy dripping down her thighs. "So fucking deep."

"That's it, take it. Take every inch of my cock with your greedy asshole." Reaching down, I grab a fistful of her hair and pull her up onto all fours. She looks back at me over her shoulder, tortured pleasure overtaking her expression.

Perfection.

"You should see how your gorgeous ass is taking my cock, Menace." I use my grip on her hair to leverage myself even deeper with every thrust. Her lips part, eyes closing, crying my name as her orgasm builds. "Oh, you like that. You like having my cock destroying your asshole. Don't you?"

The desperate cry I get in response isn't good enough. Not nearly. "Say it."

"I like your big cock in my asshole," she gasps, and I can't help but growl. Her ass pushes back to meet me for every stroke, begging for more.

"That's right, heathen. Just like that. Fuck my cock with your tight ass. Ride me." Electricity collects at the base of my spine, building and growing like nothing I've ever felt before. "You want to come so badly, don't you? I can feel just how close you are. Jesus, you're squeezing me like a fucking vice."

"Gage, I'm—" Jill cries, barely able to form a word as I pound into her. "I'm gonna come."

"You haven't learned your lesson, Jill. Who does this flawless body belong to?"

"Gage—"

"Who?"

"*You.*" She's completely breathless now. I can feel her body quaking with the impending orgasm she desperately needs. "It belongs to you."

"That's right. You don't decide when you come. I do," I state darkly. "Ask me nicely."

"I'll kill you," she snaps sharply, biting her lip against the withheld pleasure that continues to grow. I chuckle, I can't help myself. She's so fucking perfect.

"Try again." I slam into her to the hilt and leverage my hips to force myself so deeply inside her that I'm sure she can feel me in her throat. Jill cries out again, her hand fisting in the bedsheets. She doesn't just want to come, she needs to.

And so do I.

Then those pretty words come from her beautiful mouth. "Please let me come, Gage. Pretty please, I need to come."

I love her sharp tongue, but *fuck* I'll do anything if she asks me nicely.

Anything.

Still moving my cock inside her ass, I wrap my arm around to find her swollen clit and give it a firm pinch. "Come for me, little devil."

Like I held a match to a fuse, Jill's entire body bows as her orgasm tears through her like a bomb. Every muscle shakes with the force of it, her asshole clamping around my cock. Her helpless cry of bliss is music to my ears.

"Jill, holy fuck." The words are ripped out of me as my own climax strikes like lightning. The sparks collecting in my balls explode, pleasure whipping through me like a live wire. I move through my release, powering into Jill as I empty into her.

When I finally slow to a stop, I sway on my feet, my grip on her hips tightening to steady myself.

"Damn you, Gage Lawless." Her voice is breathless and soft, her body completely spent and pliable.

"Jesus, Jill, you're exquisite." Pulling out of her, I spread her ass cheeks and watch as my cum drips out of her tight bud, branding her as mine.

Her body is built just for me—every cute dimple, delicious crease, and generous curve divinely designed to take my cock, fill my hands, and sustain my mouth. She couldn't be more devastating, more perfectly tailor-made if she had stepped out of my own fucking fantasies.

Jill is the whole package, and now that I've had her, I'll never crave anything else like I do her. There isn't anything to want with her, she's all I need. All I've ever wanted.

"Don't move, baby."

I walk to the bathroom and grab a washcloth, running it under warm water, before returning to the bedroom. Jill hasn't moved an inch, it doesn't look like she can. Her body is a sated puddle melting right into the mattress. Her eyes are heavy-lidded as they track me, and I can tell she won't last much longer before she passes out.

A deep sense of pride spreads through my chest at the thought.

I wore her out.

With gentle hands, I tenderly clean her up—wiping her clean of her arousal and mine. "You can't stay unless you make breakfast in the morning," she says, the defiance in her voice seeping away as the exhaustion overtakes her.

"I'll make you whatever you want," I inform her. Hell, I'd hire Gordon Ramsay himself to cook her breakfast in bed if she wanted me to.

Reaching up to the head of the bed, I pull back the covers to make room for my Jill. "Come here," I say, helping Jill roll over so I can wrap my arms under her knees and around her back to scoop her up. With one large step, I'm able to lay her down on her pillow and pull the blanket over her.

"Get some rest, you're gonna need it."

"I'm still not sorry," she murmurs, her blinking slowing as sleep threatens to drag her under. She's about to lose that fight.

"Sweet dreams, baby," I say softly, leaning down to press a kiss to her forehead. Her eyes slip closed as she falls into unconsciousness. And just like that, she's completely dead to the world.

Exhaustion creeps into my body, fatigue dragging at my limbs. I need to sleep, and I'll be in bed with Jill wrapped around me very soon. But not yet.

Grabbing my discarded jeans off the floor, I pull my cell phone out of the pocket. Falling heavily onto the vanity chair beside the bed as I press the contact and raise the phone to my ear, my eyes trace Jill's sleeping form while it rings.

"You wanna tell me why you're calling at four in the morning?" Anders answers on the third ring, his voice rough with sleep.

"Dane is out, tell everyone. He doesn't step foot into a game or a casino in this city ever again," I state.

"Shit. What did he do?"

"He touched Jill."

"Alright, he's out," he agrees without hesitation with an adamance that reminds me why he's my best friend. "I'm assuming he doesn't have that hand anymore?"

He knows me so well.

"Not the use of either of them, probably ever again. Unless he figures out how to tattoo with his toes, his career is over," I state, making him chuckle. "Oh, and I cut his balls off."

"Goddamn," Anders mutters in surprise. "You cut his balls off? That's intense."

"Dane's lucky that's all I cut off." The darkness creeps into my voice. "He touched her."

"He had it coming." There's movement on the other side of the line. "I'll start making calls. Do you have footage you need wiped?"

"Nah, I got it covered."

I've done my due diligence to cover my tracks. After today, the grabby little weasel doesn't exist to me, and he's no longer welcome in my city.

Goodbye, Dane Presley.

CHAPTER SIXTEEN

JILL

He's watching me.

Spending the night at Inferno was Lana's idea. Working here isn't my choice, but it's the best club in the city when you're looking to party. Since we know all the bartenders and bouncers, it was easy to get in and be served. Maybe a little over-served, but who's counting?

Not me, I'm drinking for free.

Even in the middle of the crowded club dance floor, and more than a little drunk, I can feel Gage's eyes on me—I've felt them all night. My body hums with awareness as I dance against Lana, the feeling of his attention feeding my growing addiction.

For weeks, Gage has found his way into my life. He's slowly wedged himself closer and deeper into my every day until he's part of the inevitable. He's at my work, on my nights out, and in my apartment. Now he's even been in my bed. I should be bored of him by now, especially since we've had sex multiple times. Usually, I grow tired of a man after spending so much time with him. And yet, I can't seem to get enough of Gage.

He wants my body, that much is clear. And I have no problem with a mutually beneficial physical relationship, especially with someone as sexy as Gage. But there's something else too, something that doesn't feel purely sexual. It's foreign, I can't quite put my finger on it. It's in the way he looks at me, and how he speaks to me. It's the way every one of his words is backed by action.

Despite the chaos of the pulsing club on its busiest night, Gage's presence dominates the room. It doesn't take me more than a few seconds to spot him sitting just off the dancefloor, his muscular tattooed arms crossed, his powerful legs outstretched. He looks irresistible, like a guilty pleasure I want to indulge in. And I'm not one to deny myself a little pleasure.

Lana announces she's going to the bar when I decide to break away. Strutting over to him, my head swims as I bend down. Grabbing a fistful of his shirt, I pull him into a steamy kiss. Our lips move together, hungry and a little sloppy. He's a damn good kisser, I could do this all night.

When the song changes, I pull away to continue dancing. Bracing one hand on his knee, I swivel my hips to bring it down low. When I stand back up, I remain bent at the waist and straighten my legs to stick out my ass before tossing my hair back. The movement throws me off balance as my head swims, and I stumble. Big, strong hands are on me in an instant, holding my waist to stabilize me.

"I love this song." Instead of losing my rhythm, I continue to dance with Gage's hands on my waist.

"Mmmm, so do I." Gage's grip loosens to let me move freely, but he doesn't remove his hands. I lift my mostly-empty drink over my head as I move to the music, tossing my hair from side to side.

"Your feet must be tired, Menace." He leans back and pats his lap. "Come here." I'll admit it's a tempting offer— my feet are killing me, and I'm just tipsy enough to be unsteady in these heels. But if I allow him to reel me in, I won't be able to untangle myself from him until I've had my fill, or he has. I'm not ready to call it a night, and I'm not about to ditch Lana.

"In that weak-ass chair? Don't count on it," I scoff, giving the chair major side-eye. "The chairs in this place can barely handle all of this." I shake my hips to make a point.

There's no way they'll hold up the both of us. And don't get me started on the ones with arms—whoever designed those clearly has something against women who have any junk in the trunk.

"Jill, come take shots with me!" Lana calls. I look over to find her at the shots bar waving me over.

"Hell yeah! I'm coming." I shout with a grin. Turning back, I decide to steal one last kiss. Gage's hands tangle in my hair as our lips move together, our tongues dancing as we devour each other. I pull back when I start to lose my breath, leaning in close to speak in his ear.

"When I'm in bed tonight touching myself, I'll be thinking of you." I lean back and bite my lip with a smile at how his gaze sharpens with hunger. "Have fun watching. I know you will be."

With that, I'm pushing out of his grasp and strutting away from him. I don't have to look back to see if he's still watching—I know he is. The familiar weight of his gaze on me as I cross the dancefloor to the bar is exhilarating.

"Damn, babe. That was hot. Do you need a minute?"

Lana teases, giving me a knowing look. I'm so turned on that if Gage walked over to fuck me on the bar right now, I'd let him. My vibrator is definitely getting some action tonight.

"I need a shot," I declare, reaching for one of the hellfire shots lined up on the counter.

"Cheers to us and the obsessed men who can't get enough." Lana holds out her glass for me to clink before we both toss back the liquor. The fireball scorches all the way down, the cinnamon mixing with jalapeno for an added kick. I squeeze my eyes shut and enjoy the burn—it hurts so good.

"Speaking of men obsessed," I say, making Lana groan. "Were you going to tell me Christos was still in town? I thought he was supposed to leave like a week ago."

"He was. His plans changed, that's all." Lana tries to shrug it off, but I can see right through her. Now, it's my turn to give her a knowing look.

"You mean he changed his plans for *you*," I counter. "Tell me he's not sticking around to try and convince you to sail away with him."

"He can try all he wants. I'm not going," she insists. "I have a life here. I'm not just going to drop everything to spend the summer with a man facing RICO charges."

"Do you want to go? Maybe you should go dark for a little while. You know your job will be there when you get back."

"Christos is fun fling material, but that's where it ends. I'd never marry the guy, he's completely unstable. Besides, there will always be more men to invite me on their yachts. Jewelry and shoes are nice, but they don't replace the little things. I want a man who buys me Ferragamo then helps me take my makeup off before bed after I drank too much at dinner. Until then, I'll let men whose dicks match the size of their bank account wine and dine me."

Lana's definitely more of a romantic than I am. We always joke just how fitting her last name is. While I want turbulent passion and mutual obsession, she craves a love like an iron fist in a velvet glove—someone who will tenderly braid her hair before pulling it.

I want that for her. If anyone deserves to find the love of their life, it's Lana.

"We're not going to settle," I state. "I know there are men who are perfect for the both of us out there, and we'll find them."

"Or, in your case, he'll find you and follow you like a shadow," Lana laughs, making my heart skip a beat. My eyes stray across the club to where Gage sits, exactly where I left him. Our eyes meet just as one of the servers, Rene, leans down to hand him a drink that looks like cognac. His eyes never move from me when he takes the glass and brings it to his lips.

"I don't think perfect is the word I'd use to describe Gage." There are a million other descriptions on the tip of my tongue, but perfect isn't one of them. Lana follows my gaze.

"Jill, that man over there is so perfectly matched to you it's actually a little scary. But you can deny it for a little longer if you want."

"Well, I'm denying it," I say, pulling my eyes away. Gage is a good fuck, but he's a complicated man. And that isn't a web I'm mentally able to handle right now.

Maybe when I'm sober.

"Whatever you say. Do what you want."

Exhaustion washes over me, the aching of my muscles

settling in with the fatigue. I'm drunk, horny, and ready to go to bed. "I want to go home."

"Are you going home with him tonight? It sure looks like he wants you to."

"No, I'm going home to my place, in my own bed." *With my vibrator.*

Walking arm in arm, we make our way through the crowds towards the door. Bouncer Jax holds the door open for us, flashing his dimpled smile and offering to give us a ride—and not in his car. Lana flirts back, but we both walk away with no intention of taking up his offer—tonight, at least.

"Tonight was boring. There were no hot guys to dance with."

"Well, duh," Lana laughs. "That's what happens when the Grim Reaper himself is standing a few feet away looking like he's about to break the neck of any guy who gets too close to you."

"What?"

"You seriously didn't notice Gage following you all night, marking his territory?"

Honestly, no, I didn't. I spent most of the night forcing myself not to think about him or let my eyes look for him. I didn't even notice he spent the night only a few feet away.

"I must've missed that." I bite the tip of my fingernail in an attempt to hide my smile, but it's no use. "What a freak."

"You like it."

"It's pretty hot," I admit with a nod.

"*You're* the freak," Lana laughs as our car pulls up. We both climb in the back, and the driver pulls away from the curb. Lana's apartment is only a block away from mine, so sharing a ride is usually our go-to when she's not staying at a hotel with one of her boy toys.

The car pulls up to my apartment building to drop me off first, and I lean in to kiss my best friend on the cheek. "Text me when you get home so I know I don't have to go on a murder spree," I say, shooting a pointed look at the middle-aged man behind the wheel.

Well, another one. But Lana doesn't know that.

"I will." Despite her obliviousness to my lethal urges, Lana smiles like she knows exactly what I'm capable of.

"Bye, Lovie," I sing as I climb out of the car. I blow her a kiss and give her another little wave before walking up the steps to my building. The car idles at the curb while I pull out my keys and use the fob to unlock the front door. It's not until I've walked into the entryway and closed the door behind me that the car pulls away to take Lana home.

I should hear from her in the next ten minutes that she's home safe. If not, I'm going on the hunt.

The first thing that comes off when I enter my apartment is my bra—right through the neckline of my dress. Shuffling into my bedroom, I kick off my shoes on my way to the bathroom and start taking my makeup off. A text from Lana lights up my phone before I've finished moisturizing.

Laying in my bed, the lust pulsing through me has me shuffling into the kitchen. Opening the fridge, I reach into the crisper drawer and pull out my vibrator. Once back in my room, I let my panties fall down my legs before getting into my bed.

The silicone is cold, fresh from the fridge, and it burns deliciously against my heated flesh. Laying back against my pillows with a loud sigh, I swear I can feel a pair of dark eyes on me. The owner of those eyes is the one touching me, filling me with lust until I'm delirious. His name escapes my lips on a moan as I'm wrecked with pleasure.

"*Gage.*"

CHAPTER SEVENTEEN

JILL

Another day, another shift at work. It's been four days since I've worked—four days since I've seen Gage. That night at the club was a blur. I'm not sure I remember everything that happened. I mostly remember shots, dancing with Lana, and more shots. The one thing I remember vividly is flirting with Gage and how good he tastes when I'm tipsy.

I'm sure Gage has had his eyes on me on my days off, but watching me run errands and relax on the couch isn't enough for him. He summoned me to pull a double shift tonight, making Miranda call me in early to set up the bar. The club is empty, and there won't be anyone here for several hours.

Except Gage. I know he's around here somewhere, watching.

It's just him and me.

My handbag slips as I'm putting it in the locker, causing the contents to spill out onto the floor. I mutter a curse as I bend down to pick them up. Reaching for my lip balm and keys, my eyes snag on the keyring. An extra key has me doing a double take—it's gold, the rest of my keys are silver. Where the hell did this come from? What does it open? Who put it here—

There's only one person who could've done this.

I snap a picture with my phone and send it to Gage.

> What the fuck is this?

My phone dings almost immediately with a response, making me roll my eyes.

> It's a key.

I can just picture the smirk on his face while he's looking at the phone right now.

> I'm not blind, I can see that. A key to what?

> My house.

> And why is it on my keyring?

> Because I put it there.

Frustration and irritation have my grip tightening on my phone, and it dings again.

> You're so hot when you're angry.

I don't bother to look around. I know he has eyes on me —whether it's in person or through the cameras.

> I'm going to kill you. Slowly and painfully.

> I love it when you're mean to me.

>> Why do I have a key to your house?

> Because it's so much harder to fuck you through a locked door.

Another text comes through.

> I'm so hard right now just thinking about you using that key.

>> You're delusional if you think I'm going to use it.

> You will. And I'll be there to reward you when you do.

The last text that comes through is an address, and one click shows me a townhouse in downtown Chicago. His house.

Desire burns through me as I close my locker and walk out of the dressing room. He's not in his office, but I find him sitting at one of the tables just off the empty dance floor on the main floor. The look Gage gives me when I walk up says he was expecting me.

"You need to stop messing with me and my stuff," I say, crossing my arms under my chest and cocking my hip. He smiles and runs his tongue along the bottom of his top teeth as his eyes travel over me.

"Yeah, not gonna happen."

Rolling my eyes to the ceiling like I'm praying for strength, I huff out a deep breath dramatically and look around at the empty club. "You're just sitting here in the silence alone?"

"I just finished meeting with the DJ for next month's event. And now you're here. Come have a seat," Gage instructs, gesturing to his lap. I roll my eyes and place my hands on my hips.

"I already told you, the chairs around here aren't built for bigger bodies."

"Look again, little devil." His words take me by surprise. "There's not a single chair in my club that can't handle all of you. Not anymore."

"You're lying," I say, even as I look at the chair to see that he's not. What used to be flimsy 'chic' chairs that were clearly chosen for aesthetic purposes have been replaced by elegant metal chairs that look as functional as they are pleasing to the eye. They actually look sturdy as hell.

"Call my bluff," he goads with a smirk, knowing that I can't. "I'm not having anything in my club, or anywhere else, that isn't designed for you, Jill. You're gonna have to think of another excuse if you want to avoid me, and I don't plan on making it easy for you. Now come here."

He reaches to snag my hand and starts to reel me in, and I let him. His eyes gazing into mine show the passion and desire that his nonchalant expression doesn't. Once I reach him, I lift one leg over his, then the other, my arms wrapping around his neck until I'm straddling his lap. I lean in close to press my chest against his, our lips just centimeters apart. His hands plant firmly on my ass, pressing me even closer.

"Happy?" I breathe. His eyes roam my features like he's already memorized them, and he's simply refreshing his memory. The look on his face answers my question before he does.

"Very."

He replaced every single chair in this entire club—for *me*. All because I made one comment. The thought has warmth rushing through me as a small knot forms in my stomach. I wait for him to mention the catch, or how I now owe him something in return. But it never comes.

Tommy would've told me exactly how much the new chairs cost, hinting that I cost him all that money—even if it was all his own idea. There were always string tied to everything.

Thinking back to when I was eighteen, I snuck out to meet up with my older brother and some of his friends. Tommy said the only way I was allowed to hangout with them was if I got them some beer. So I flirted with an old man outside a liquor store to buy a six-pack for me.

When I arrived at the overlook where Tommy and his friends always hung out, one of his friends, Trevor, was very excited to see me—too excited. He kept getting closer, trying to touch me. When he leaned in to kiss me, I'd pushed him off and decided I wanted to go home.

Tommy had rushed after me, trying to coax me to stay. That's when I knew something was up.

"What's going on?" I asked him, arms crossed.

"I lost a bet." The way he said it had my eyes narrowing.

"What does that have to do with me?"

"Trevor lent me the money, with one condition," Tommy winces as he continues. "He gets to makeout with you."

"What?" The word leaves my mouth sounding more like an accusation than a question. "What the hell, Tommy?"

"I know, I'm sorry. I needed the money." Seeing that I'm about to walk away, he grabs my arm. "But you've said Trevor is cute, right? So kissing him will be no big deal. Come on, Jillybean."

I had stared at my degenerate brother for a moment, his big green eyes pleading with me. Trevor was a decent looking guy, so kissing him wouldn't be the end of the world—under different circumstances, I probably would've been excited about it. So, I relented.

"Fine. But don't ever try to pull this shit on me again. Next time I'm not going to rescue you."

So I'd kissed Trevor— it was terrible and sloppy, and he tried to grope me in the process.

But that wasn't the last time Tommy roped me in to save his ass, not even close.

"What are you thinking about?" Gage's question pulls me out of my memories and my focus lands back on the man holding me. I pause for a moment to really look at him.

Taking advantage of my up close and personal view, my eyes run over the details of him. How the perpetual five o'clock shadow across his angular jaw adds a rough edge to his gorgeous face. That his dark brown eyes carry flecks of mocha and onyx in them, and how intricate the ink that covers him all the way up to his chin really is. "Your tattoos are beautiful."

"So are you."

"You sure lay it on thick, don't you?"

"You like how thick I am. Or do I need to remind you?"

"Can we have a normal conversation for like five minutes before you turn into a horn dog?"

"We can try, but no promises."

"Why tattoos? With your skill, you could've been an artist."

"I am an artist. My work is recognized around the world. The canvas I've mastered is one of the most challenging. The human body is a beautiful and fragile thing, and I turn it into a masterpiece."

"Is that why you've covered yourself in ink? To become a masterpiece?"

"Let's be honest, I was a masterpiece without the ink. Now I'm a god."

"Is that the purpose of all these?" I lightly trace some of the designs decorating the skin of his sternum with my fingertips.

"Tattoos don't always need to serve a purpose. Sometimes, they're a desire. Secrets, stories, dreams. All of them walking around for the world to see."

"You seem very passionate about this. I like it."

"You like when I'm passionate about other things, too."

"Four minutes," I announce. "You lasted four whole minutes without talking about sex."

"Let's try again. I have really good stamina, let me show you exactly how long I can really go."

"Hmm, fifteen seconds. You finished before we even got started. I have to say, I'm very disappointed."

"Third time's the charm." His gaze on me turns more serious. "Tell me about your family."

"You want to have this conversation right now?" I look down pointedly at how we're sitting. Gage simply tilts his head as he waits. "Let's go back to talking about sex."

"No," he replies deeply. He's clearly not going to drop this.

"There's nothing to tell." I shrug. "Now that Tommy's gone, I don't have one."

"Your parents?"

"They're both dead." His insistent gaze doesn't falter, so I relent. "My dad was a drunk. Some might have called him a functioning alcoholic. I don't remember a time I was with my dad when he didn't have a drink in his hand or alcohol on his breath. When he mixed his liquor, he got mean."

"And your mom?"

"She was a broken woman and his biggest enabler. She never spoke up unless it was to make excuses for him. She cooked, cleaned, and taught me that women are meant to be seen, not heard. I don't take after her, clearly."

"How did they die?"

"A car accident." Bitterness twists in my gut. I hate telling this story. Sensing my discomfort, Gage's arms tighten around me to pull me in closer as I continue. "My mom went to go track my dad down at the bar and take him home. They got into a huge fight, and my dad took the keys from her. He was plastered and pissed. When he got like that, he liked to drive really fast just to scare us. When he lost control, he hit another car head-on. All three of them were pronounced dead on the scene: my mom, my dad, and the other driver."

Wendy Corwin, the other driver, was a forty-six-year-old single mother of a pre-teen daughter. My dad created three orphans that night.

"How old were you?"

"You already know all of this," I point out. "I know you know it."

"Tell me anyway."

"I was nineteen. My parents didn't have much, but I inherited a few thousand dollars that I put towards community college and bartending classes."

"What about Tommy?"

"What do you think?" I scoff. "Tommy's share of the inheritance was down a slot machine within hours of the check being cashed. He was about to finish trade school to become a welder, just like my dad." Dad had insisted it was the only appropriate profession for a real man. And with how much of a screw-up Tommy was, following in Dad's footsteps was the only option to prove himself. If there's anything my brother cared about more than a bet, it was my dad's approval.

My brother and I weren't super close before the accident. But losing both our parents in one night forced us together. Only having each other to lean on forged a new bond—one where I was the rock, and Tommy was the sand that shifted around it. We were dysfunctional, but we had each other. Until we didn't.

Now it's just me.

Sensing my darkening thoughts, Gage's eyes read me like a book. "And then your brother disappeared." I nod.

"And somehow, I got strung up in his noose." I look at him pointedly, but there's not an ounce of apology in his expression. Only intense interest and deep-seated possession.

I hate how much I like it.

"I prefer my diamonds around your neck. Or my hands." And now we're back to talking about sex. The subject change is a relief, which I suspect was his intent. The rattle of fresh ice being poured into the cooler behind the bar sounds in the background, announcing the arrival of a barback. It's time to get ready for my shift.

"Are you just going to sit here and hold me on your lap all night?

"If I want to."

"I have things to do."

"I better be at the top of that list."

"You wish." I roll my eyes, but Gage's arms flex around me.

"Yes, I do."

"I'm getting up now. And you're going to let me." This time, when I pull away from him, he lets me. His hands linger on my hips when I stand, giving them a greedy squeeze before I step out of his reach. If there's one thing this man knows how to do, it's get me wet in the middle of the club.

Walking away with his eyes on me, I know I'm in for a tough night. There's nothing worse than being forced to serve drinks all night in drenched panties, knowing the tattoo god who's always just a few feet away would rail you to the point of no return.

I'm screwed. But not in the way I wish I were.

CHAPTER EIGHTEEN

JILL

"**G**age isn't here" are the first words out of Stevie's mouth when I step foot inside *Stained Heart Tattoos*. It's like she saw me coming from a mile away.

"Why do you assume that's why I'm here?" I play dumb, but she sees right through me.

"Give me some credit," she laughs. Letting out a deep breath, I relent.

"Okay, fine, that's why I'm here," I admit, making her grin in triumph. "Where is he?"

"He's on a ride with the Saints. A voicemail or text is your best bet if you want to tell him something. He doesn't check his phone when he's on the road."

"The Saints?" I ask, confused. "As in, the Chained Saints?" Since when is Gage part of the most notorious motorcycle gang in Chicago? How has that never come up before.

Stevie nods, reading the question written all over my face. "His parents and brother are members, so he likes to ride with them when he can."

His parents? His brother?

Her response has me realizing I don't actually know that much about Gage. He seems to know every detail about me, always desperate to learn more. But what do I actually know about him? His history, family—all secrets to me.

Normally I wouldn't care—I don't usually bother to get to know my fuck buddies that well. It usually ruins it for me. But something about this revelation doesn't sit well with me. I want to know the answers to the questions swirling in my head right now.

I want to know Gage.

I don't have time for this right now.

Forcing myself back into the present, I smile at the woman in front of me.

"Ok, thanks, Stevie." Walking out of *Stained Heart Tattoos*, I pull out my phone and pull up Gage's number. Buttering him up in person was plan A, but since he's not here, I'll have to make do with the alternative.

The phone rings three times, and I'm expecting to leave a voicemail when the line picks up. The sound of rumbling engines coming through the phone does nothing to drown out Gage's deep voice. "I like seeing your name show up on my phone."

"Stevie said you're on a ride."

"I am." A motorcycle engine revs as if to prove his point. "We pulled over."

"You had the entire Chained Saints Motorcycle Club pull over on the highway so you could answer the phone?"

"You called, so I answered," he says, making my heart flutter. "Are you missing me, little devil? You wanted to hear my voice, didn't you? Or is there something else you miss?"

"You're right, there is something I'm missing," I say

seductively, toying with him. "My shift today. I won't be at work."

"Why's that?" His tone sobers.

"I have something else to do," I add a little false sweetness to my voice. "Enjoy your ride." With that, I hang up.

The drive over to the Medical Examiner building is torture and not the fun kind. Every mile I get closer adds to the ball of lead in my stomach. Pulling into the parking lot of the drab industrial building, my GPS announces that I've arrived at my destination. I park in a spot and slump back against my seat with a heavy breath.

The Medical Examiner's office is a large, daunting concrete atrocity. The idea of walking in there is depressing in itself, but the potential of what I might find once I'm in there has my stomach in knots.

Tommy.

Not knowing what happened to my brother feels like Chinese water torture—a constant picking in the back of my mind that's slowly tearing a hole through my psyche. I force myself to suck in a deep breath and let it out heavily as I pull myself together.

Ready or not, here I fucking go.

Pushing open the door, I climb out of the vehicle, ready for war. I'm mentally bracing myself for any outcome, but I'm not sure it's actually working.

"What are we doing here? You have a fetish for men with tags on their toes?" The deep voice that speaks just over my shoulder sends a shiver down my spine. I turn to look at Gage, where he stands leaning against my car.

Damn, I must really be in my own head if I didn't notice him walk up.

I roll my eyes, but the look I flash him doesn't carry its usual lethal sharpness. "*I'm* here because I got a call from the Medical Examiner. There's a John Doe that matches my brother's description. They want me to see if I can identify him."

The chances of this unidentified man being my missing brother are basically zero, but knowing that doesn't diminish the gut-wrenching fact that there's still a sliver of a chance that it is him.

"Is that so?" Gage's tone sounds as skeptical as I feel. He gazes at me for a moment, reading the nerves written all over my face, then gives a short nod. "Alright, let's go see a body."

The fact that I allow him to take me by the hand and lead me toward the building without protest or retort tells him just how rattled I am. He gazes down at me intently when I check in at reception, his eyes burning a hole through my already cracking psyche while we stand in the bleak waiting room.

Gage's dark eyes don't stray from me for a single second —even when the medical examiner, Dr. Maynard, comes to show me back to the post-mortem examination room. The white-haired British gentleman glances nervously at the man looming behind me like he's death himself, finally come to claim his soul.

The exam room is depressing and sterile—with sad linoleum floors, harsh fluorescent lighting, and cold steel equipment. There's a large metal table in the center of the room where a body lies covered in a white sheet. The knot of dread in my stomach tightens with every step I take until I'm standing right beside the table.

"He was found in a ditch along the highway, we suspect a hit-and-run. There's a lot of swelling, especially in the face, which might make him hard to identify. Dental and DNA have been collected, but the labs are always backed up, so those results could take a while," Dr. Maynard says, his posh accent softening his delivery. "John Doe is a white male, early to mid-thirties, six feet tall, dark brown hair, green eyes."

Anxiety wraps around me like a noose when he reaches for the top of the sheet, my heart threatening to pound right out of my chest as I struggle to remember to breathe. The doctor pauses for a moment to look at me, and my entire body tenses. "Ready?"

Am I ready? What kind of question is that?

What if it's him? My brother—my older screw-up brother who constantly let me down—could be lying dead under this sheet. His cold, lifeless body could be lying on this table. Alone and unclaimed. He was a bastard, but he didn't deserve to be mowed down, run over, and left for dead.

This could be Tommy.

Then, at least, I'll finally know what happened to him. That's what I want, right? Answers? If I have to walk out of this godforsaken dump without some sort of closure, I'm going to lose my shit.

I hesitate.

It's only for a moment, but the silence rings through the room, making the seconds feel like minutes. A strong hand at my side reaches for mine, intertwining our fingers with a reassuring squeeze. I don't have to look at the tattooed hand giving me comfort to know it belongs to the man at my back, his gaze burning a hole through my temple. I'm tempted to look at him, but if I meet his all-seeing eyes, I might not be able to hold it together. I'm barely keeping my shit together as it is.

"I'm ready," I say finally, the steadiness in my voice belying the turmoil wracking through my entire being. The older man lifts the sheet and folds it down, revealing the disfigured remains of a man to his collarbone.

A toxic cocktail of relief and disappointment washes over me at the sight of the man—a complete stranger. His hair is about the right length and color, and the damage to his face should make it impossible to know for sure. But something in my gut tells me I'm not looking at Tommy.

"It's not him," Gage says, too quietly to be talking to anyone but me.

"Do you have his personal effects?" I ask, dragging my eyes away from the body to address the Medical Examiner. Dr. Maynard nods and walks over to a bin sitting on the desk against the back wall. Pulling out a large plastic bag, he walks over to give me a better look.

My eyes scan the contents of the clear evidence bag, my focus bouncing from each of the personal items. A handful of change, a tarnished gold ring, a used tissue, and a pair of broken sunglasses.

"It's not him," I state, certain.

"Are you sure?" Dr. Maynard asks, encouraging me to take another look. But I nod.

"I'm sure. This isn't my brother."

There's no paperwork to sign, and I don't bother with pleasantries before I'm charging out of the godforsaken room in search of air.

I need oxygen.

Walking out of the suffocating building and stepping outside, I feel like I can finally breathe again. My feet carry me purposefully through the door and towards my car, my body needing to be in motion with all of the emotions I'm keeping barely contained.

Gage keeps pace with me easily, I can feel him right

behind me. His presence is both intrusive and annoyingly comforting, which grates on my already fraying nerves.

My head is spinning with so many unanswered questions and so many *what-ifs*.

Another dead end, another useless lead. I know law enforcement's interest in my brother's case is going to dry up, and probably soon. This failed experiment just used up some of my goodwill with the city, and I'm leaving empty-handed. No death certificate, no body.

No hope.

It's fucking maddening.

"It wasn't Tommy," I mutter to myself, shaking my head.

"No, it wasn't." Gage's deep voice has me halting mid-step to look at him. His dark gaze clashes with mine, holding me captive.

"How did you know?" I think back to what he said back in the exam room. He'd never met Tommy before, so how would he know it wasn't him?

"You. I saw it in your eyes," he replies. "What were you looking for in his belongings?"

I turn back around to continue my stomp back to my car. I have to keep moving, or I'll go crazy. "My brother wears a gold bracelet. It's this tacky Cuban link monstrosity that he never takes off. It has a pair-of-aces charm on it. Tommy's convinced it's good luck, he calls it 'the ace up his sleeve.' He hasn't been without it since he won the damn thing in his first real poker game." I let out a humorless laugh. "On his very few good days, it was the reason for his winning streak. On all the other days, it was his ticket out of a slump."

"You didn't get answers today, but you will someday." I whirl on him, all but colliding with his chest from his proximity. All of the emotions building inside me have come to a head, my eyes blazing like a volcano on the brink of eruption.

"Those are just words, Gage. Not everyone gets pretty answers tied up in a bow. In fact, most of the time, you're left with nothing but the possibilities of what should've been while living with everything that isn't." I push on his solid chest, only to find him movable as a mountain. He takes a small step back to give me some room, his eyes never leaving mine. "The reality is, this is all I'll ever get—maybes and *some days*."

I'm not going to keep getting my hopes up just to be let down over and over again. I can't. It's like my brother is still in my life with the way I'm being jerked around. Nothing but disappointments and frauds—like father like son.

"I have to get out of here." I reach for my car door but pause before I get in. "I'm going to Lana's. Since I know you're gonna be following me." Sliding behind the wheel, I peel out of the parking lot and make my way through the city to the one person I really need right now.

My best friend.

"I know, baby. I was looking forward to seeing you tonight, too, but my friend really needs me. We can go out another night." Lana coos into the phone, looking at me and rolling her eyes at the needy man on the other end of the phone. She smiles at whatever he says next. "Yes, it's Jill. You remember Jill, right? She's having a family emergency, and I need to be here for her right now."

She's already been here for several hours with me. I arrived at her apartment a complete mess. We talked about what happened at the Medical Examiner's office today, and I cried. By the time we moved on to other, less dark and twisty, topics Lana decided to cancel the date she had planned with a music producer we met a few weeks ago. I told her it wasn't necessary, but she insisted. And not so secretly, I'm happy about that decision. We're gonna make tonight a full-on girl's night sleepover.

"Oh, thank you, baby. Are you sure? You're so sweet." She flashes me a wink, making a smile tug at my lips. "Yes, I'll call you tomorrow. Bye, handsome." Lana ends the call and drops her phone on the counter before pulling me into another hug.

"He's having *Carbone* delivered to us," she says, making me laugh. If anyone can get a guy to send food from one of the nicest restaurants in the city after canceling a date last minute, it's Lana. "Okay, now that that's done—let's get comfy and open a bottle of wine."

I follow her into her bedroom and head straight to her dresser. Pulling out a pair of her cozy pajama sets, I start to change. "What, no Christos tonight?" I ask, pulling the little shorts up. Lana reaches into her drawer, pulls out some silk pajamas, and starts to undress.

"Nope." When she doesn't explain, I flash her a look that says I can read her like a book.

"Care to elaborate?" I ask knowingly. Lana tries to shrug it off, but she knows me better than that.

"He's been on edge about some business deals and has to sort out a few things for the next couple of days. I figured it was better to give him some space and stay out of it."

"Is he putting you in danger?" I ask, scooping my hair up into a messy bun on top of my head.

"No," she says none too convincingly. I narrow my eyes at her.

"Are you sure about that?"

"Please, Jill. With the guys we date, are we ever not in a little danger?" She has a point. "I'm not with Christos, so his mess won't touch me. Besides, with your guy around, it's like we have our own security detail. He's probably parked outside right now, watching the building."

That's also true. He followed me all the way here, the sound of his sexy motorcycle echoing in the distance at every turn. If he's not still outside right now, chances are he has eyes on me somehow. He's always watching.

When did that become a comfort?

"Okay, the only talk of boys we're gonna be doing for the rest of the night is when we send in our dinner order," Lana declares, pushing her hair out of her face with a headband. I follow her back out into the kitchen, where she opens a bottle of wine. "Now, what do we want to eat?"

CHAPTER NINETEEN
GAGE

Striding into the dressing room, I feel like my body is being drawn by a magnet. Jill is standing just inside the door like I knew she would be. The sight of her settles my raging soul, and a small weight is lifted off my chest.

She's been avoiding me since the day at the medical examiner's office last week, not that she would admit it. But I've noticed how she edges away from me, how she's the first to break eye contact. I tried to corner her earlier behind the bar, but she muttered something before using one of the servers dropping a glass as a distraction to make her escape.

She thinks one emotional afternoon looking for her brother was a sign of weakness, and she doesn't like that I was the one who saw her crack. But I don't see it that way. All I saw was a strong woman trying to find the answers she needs.

Looking for her brother has been weighing on her, and the stress of it shows more everyday. I'm tempted to ease her mind, but I know she's better off not knowing the truth.

At least not yet. Her brother was a leech, sucking the life out of her. She deserves a life free of him.

But that doesn't stop her from having questions. She might not have gotten them the other day, but I liked being there anyway. I want to be there to hold her hand next time too, and I plan to be.

"What are you doing in here?" Jill asks flatly. "Did you miss the part of the sign on the door that says *women's* dressing room?"

"You said you wanted to fuck." I spread my arms out and gesture to my body. "Here I am."

"What I said was 'fuck off.' But nice try." Her sharp words make me grin. "While you're here, make yourself useful and zip me up."

I step forward, breathing in her sensual perfume. Taking hold of her open dress, I grasp the zipper where it sits halfway up. My hands itch with the desire to yank the little piece of metal down with so much force that the dress tears in two. Instead, I drag my fingers along the curve of her ass and spine as I close the dress.

"What exactly am I zipping this up for?" *Or who.*

"I have a date." Her response has my expression darkening. She looks at me over her shoulder, her eyes looking pointedly at my crotch, feigning a pitying expression. "But have fun taking care of your *little* problem."

She turns to leave the room, but I'm faster. My hands grab her by the waist, leg kicking the door closed with a bang. I use my hold on her to slam her against the wall, and my body follows. Her full breasts press against me with every amped breath, every one of her soft curves molded against my hard panes. She looks up at me with those enchanting eyes, making my possessive tendencies surge.

"Another man touching you isn't good for his health," I

inform her, darkness rumbling beneath my voice in a very unveiled threat. Jill's expression remains unbothered, but her eyes on me heat. Her eyes pull from mine to briefly glance at my lips, and I'm sure she's going to kiss me.

Do it, kiss me.

Instead, she gives me a smile that settles into my chest and makes my cock twitch—one full of dark promises. "That's not something you need to worry yourself with," she says, piquing my interest.

I'll see about that.

Jill pushes against my chest just hard enough to side-step out of my grasp. The sultry look she flashes me over her shoulder before walking out the door has me striding to my office.

Clicking open the security footage, I track her movements through the halls on my monitor while I pull my Ruger out of my desk drawer and check the clip. I watch Jill move through the club towards the front door while I tuck the handgun behind my back into the waistband of my pants and pull my shirt over it. Even in a hurry and pixelated on a screen, Jill looks infuriatingly good in her little black dress. Grabbing my keys off the desk, I'm on the move.

It was raining earlier, so I didn't take my bike to the club. I drove my Yukon, which gave me an advantage. Jill might be listening for my motorcycle, but she won't be looking for my car. She's going to lead me straight to the sack of shit that's going to lose his hands if he even thinks about touching her.

Vince fucking Rossi.

The edges of my vision turn red at the sight of the loan shark's ugly face.

I followed Jill to an upscale restaurant, where she found a seat at the bar. After fifteen minutes, I was beginning to think she'd lied to me—that there wasn't another man after all. But then Vince showed up.

He walks up to where Jill sits at the bar and doesn't stop until he's leaning so closely over her shoulder that he's practically on top of her. Taken slightly off guard, Jill turns to find Vince's mouth just centimeters from hers. A look of contempt flashes across her face so fast that anyone else would've missed it before her sultry smile—but I didn't. That's when it hits me.

This isn't a date. It's a hit.

Jill isn't going to fuck Vince tonight. She's going to kill him. Adrenaline floods through me at the realization, the excitement seeping into my veins until I'm intoxicated. A grin spreads across my face, and my muscles relax as I ease back against my chair.

This changes everything. Instead of watching some asshat paw my girl and plotting his slow and painful death, I get to watch my Jill do it. And she does it so beautifully.

The entire time they're at the bar, I can't pull my eyes away from Jill. Watching her is like watching a Venus fly trap ensnare its prey, beautiful and seemingly innocent—coaxing and teasing until it's too late. Vince is leering at her like a kid in a fucking candy store, ready to indulge until he's made himself sick—not that I can blame the sucker. Jill is magnetic. She knows when to lean in, flash a smile and a seductive glance, and when to pull back to play coy.

When she stands from the bar before she's even finished her second drink, Vince follows eagerly, crowding behind her with his hands on her waist that have my lips twitching in disdain. If Vince weren't a dead man walking, I'd already have him pinned against the wall with my 40mm jammed against the hard-on he has for my girl.

Instead, I follow in the shadows as Jill leads him out of the restaurant and into the parking lot. Walking past the cars, Vince trails along behind Jill as she pulls him by the hand around the building. Being in heels doesn't seem to slow my girl down at all as she struts through an alleyway toward an abandoned building that's currently waiting to be made into new condos.

Demolition day is tomorrow.

My clever girl.

Before they enter, Vince loses his nerve for a second. His steps falter and he pulls his hand from hers as he opens his mouth to protest. But Jill looks back at him with that devilish smile, and he's pulled right back in. She might not know that I'm here with her, but that look on her face is just for me.

Her dark soul singing to mine.

I need that shit on repeat.

Vince follows Jill through the door, looking like he's about to get away with murder—the fucking idiot. He's about to get what's coming to him, and I have a front-row seat.

It's pitch black inside the building, with only the city lights outside filtering through the broken windows and holes in the walls. The structure has been stripped to its studs, with debris scattered across the cement floor. The sound of sexy heels clicking against the floor echoes through the empty space, allowing me to move in silence.

Placing myself behind a half-demoed wall, I admire the way Jill's black dress moves with her dramatic curves when she finally slows to a stop—she's fine as hell. Vince looks around at the dump and says something to her, making her smile up at him in excitement. Unlike Vince, I'm smart enough to know what that smile means. But the dumbass takes it as an invitation.

Vince doesn't see the blade, but I do. The light glints off the metal at her side, bringing my body to life. A thrill runs through me in anticipation, my cock standing at attention.

The loan shark takes another step closer to her, completely oblivious that he's inching closer to his death. Undoing the zipper of my jeans, I shove down my pants to grip my throbbing cock. Lust pours over me, hot as molten lava that melts into my bones.

If only I could hear her voice from where I'm standing.

Jill waits for Vince to make his move before she makes hers. He closes the distance between them, lunging at her like a man who has the upper hand. Jill uses that in her favor, leveraging his own weight against him to impale his body on the blade.

She's gotten stronger since the last one.

Goddamn, she's the most incredible creature to ever walk this planet.

Just like the others, Vince is taken completely off guard. His eyes bulge in shock as he stumbles backward, the blade now covered in his blood. He looks down at her hand, then at his stab wound—the blood soaking his white shirt.

I pump my rock-hard cock, biting back a groan at the sensation.

When the shock on Vince's face wears off, anger replaces it. The malicious intent in his eyes is clear, making me tense.

He gears up to attack, but Jill works fast. She lashes out with her blade, slicing his cheekbone. Vince rears back, pressing his hand to his face and his fingers coming away covered in blood. Jill uses his moment of distraction to plunge the knife upwards into his torso.

The strangled wheezing sound Vince lets out tells me she hit her target: the lungs. Vince folds over like a lawn chair and collapses onto the ground, coughing and gulping. Jill stands over him, blood dripping down her lovely arm like an angel of death.

The fire in her eyes burns so brightly it steals my breath. The exhilaration on her face, so pure and powerful, has my hand all but strangling my erection. The friction is building, my eyes unable to move from the divine figure standing over her fallen victim.

Jill steps forward and crouches down next to Vince's convulsing body. With the way she looks at him as she murmurs something—boldly and with absolute control—I can tell she doesn't plan on toying with him for too long, not like Jonas.

With Jonas, she took her time, letting him die slowly as she savored the sweetness of the moment. This time will be hard and fast, exactly how she likes to be fucked. And just like last time, we'll both get off from it.

Vince lets out a short, garbled cry as Jill plunges her blade straight into his heart. She presses all of her weight onto the knife until it's to the hilt. Vince stills beneath her, his wheezing breaths and tortured grunts of pain dissipating into complete silence.

Heat flares through me, every nerve in my body firing all at once as hot cum shoots from my cock onto my hand. The pleasure is white hot, whipping through my limbs. My jaw clenches from the intensity of it, a silenced groan building in my chest coming out as a harsh, shuttered breath.

Jill doesn't move for a long moment, just gazing down

at the now-lifeless asshole. His dead, unseeing eyes stare up at her in return. She mutters something, a smile ghosting her lips when she reaches into her neckline and pulls out a tiny vial. Crouching down, she runs the container along the blood streaming from the slice on Vince's cheek to collect a few drops.

Holding a vial up to the light, Jill speaks again—this time loud enough for me to hear. "For someone so ugly, you have some very pretty blood." The sardonic tone in her voice has my cock beginning to stiffen all over again. She's so fucking sexy when she's being cruel. "Rest in misery, cockroach."

With those last words, she stands and walks away. I watch her until she's out of sight, listening to the click of her heels until her footsteps have completely disappeared. Putting my dick away and pulling out my phone, I track Jill's location until she's safely in her apartment. Only once I know I'm alone do I emerge from the shadows.

Seeing Jill's handiwork up close and personal is like looking at a work of art. The stab wounds are both painful and precise, meant to inflict intense suffering right before the end. The fact that she took this ugly brute of a man who was twice her size down so easily and without hesitation fills me with pride.

My Jill is a powerful little thing.

I grin as I look down at the blood coating him and picture just how stunning the color of it will look on Jill's full lips.

Leaving the body here was reckless, but I expect nothing less from my girl. Now that she's finished with him, she's ready to move on with her life. And I'll make sure she can, just like I did with that cock-sucker Jonas.

Jonas' body was easy to get rid of—now he's nothing

but a pile of dust at a crematorium. She got lucky with Carter when the cops assumed his death was a random attack.

A happy tune whistles from my lips as I begin to scrub the scene of anything that can be tied to Jill. Disposing of the body won't be too difficult—there's a building around the block with an incinerator big enough to fit this fucker. Soon, he'll be nothing but smoke and ash, and Jill will be free to live without the ghost of her vengeance coming back to hound her.

I'm the only shadow allowed to haunt Jillian Hart.

And I'll never let her go.

CHAPTER TWENTY

JILL

My knuckles turn white against the death grip on the phone pressed to my ear. Hours—and days—of follow-up calls, sitting on hold just to get a full voicemail box. Getting the same run-around by receptionists and other drones—all just to lead to this conversation.

"Cold? How can it be cold? Tommy's only been missing for a few months," I demand, my anger wishing it could reach through the phone and strangle the detective on the other end.

"Listen, Miss Hart," Detective Condescending says. "We've followed procedure to the letter, but with no leads, there's nothing more we can do. According to the Coroner's report, the amount of blood at the scene is enough to assume your brother is deceased. And with the circles your brother ran in, finding a body isn't a common occurrence. We can't dedicate more manpower or hours to this case unless we're provided with more evidence."

"So you're not even going to be looking anymore?" My

tone is sharp and bitter, but I don't give a fuck to try and sound pleasant. The time for pleasantries is over.

"Unless something new comes up, our hands are tied. Sorry, Miss Hart." My phone beeps in my ear to indicate the call has ended. He hung up on me.

Motherfucker.

I pace back and forth for over an hour, his words running through my head on a loop, making me angrier each time—*cold case...no leads...your brother is deceased...our hands are tied...Miss Hart.* I hate when they call me that—*Miss Hart*—like I'm some sweet kindergarten teacher in a romance novel.

Snatching my purse off my kitchen counter and my keys from the bowl on the entryway table, I storm out of my apartment. Slamming my car door shut, I rev the engine a few times before whipping out of the parking garage into the summer night and weaving through traffic. My hands tighten on the steering wheel until my fingers ache, my heartbeat matching my racing mind.

By the time I pull up to the curb, my head is such a mess there's no going back. My breathing quickens as emotions crash over me, potent and crushing. I climb out from behind the wheel and slam the door shut. My car alarm beeps behind me as I flash the keyfob over my shoulder, stomping up the steps to the front door. The keys in my hands jingle irritatingly as I slip the shiny metal into the lock and turn it easily.

As the door opens, my control fractures.

I want to rage, and I want to crumble. I want to charge into the bar with a bat and start swinging until there's nothing left but rubble with no chance of repair. Nothing but pieces left shattered and broken—just like my family, just like my life.

Just like me.

Turmoil builds inside me as I close the door behind me until I'm practically shaking.

"Whoever you are—you better have a damn good reason to be here right now, or I'll enjoy putting a bullet in your head," a deep voice rumbles as a switch is flipped and light floods the room. Gage stands at the edge of the large kitchen, shirtless and deadly, his gun pointed right at my head. I watch the realization settle over him, his eyes lowering to the key in my hand.

"Well, well, well, look who's here." He smirks, lowering his gun and tucking it into the back of the sweatpants hanging low on his hips as he saunters towards me. "I knew you'd be here before too long. You couldn't wait to use that key, could you?"

I tighten my grip on the key when my hand starts to tremble, emotion overwhelming me like a dark cloud as I stare at him. Moisture wells up in my eyes, blurring my vision. A sob escapes me as the first tear rolls down my cheek.

All teasing and humor vanishes off Gage's face in the blink of an eye. He eats the distance between us in a few large strides, pulling me into his arms without hesitation. I melt into him as his body envelops me. Wrapped in his embrace, the floodgates open, and I fall apart.

We stand there in silence for a while as I cry into his chest. After a few minutes, he pulls back just enough to look down at my face, his hand cupping my cheek to lift my eyes to meet his. The anger in his expression builds with each tear that falls down my face.

"Who do I need to kill?" There's a rough, demanding edge beneath his low voice. I gaze up at him, my mouth opening then closing without a sound. He wants to know what happened, but I can't talk about it right now. If I start explaining before I get my emotions under control, this city will never recover from the damage of my inevitable rampage.

Sensing my wrath surging has his own rising. His darkness is brewing just below the surface, itching to be unleashed. He starts to reach one arm around his back for his gun, but I stop him by wrapping my arm around his waist to halt his movement.

"Just hold me," I say pitifully. He leans down to press his lips against mine, kissing me softly.

"I *am* going to hold you—I'm going to hold you, hug you, and kiss you until the smile is back on your face. Then I'm going to hunt down the reason for your tears and laugh while I destroy it." Desire rolls over me at the passion behind his words. I lean up to recapture his lips, my tongue tangling with his.

"Not tonight," I say against his lips. I slide my arms around to clasp behind his neck as he reaches down to pick me up and support me by my thighs, wrapping them around his waist. I bury my head into his neck as he carries me through the house.

Entering the bedroom, he lowers me onto the bed. When he moves to straighten, I use my arms around his neck to pull him closer, kissing him again. Gage's mouth moves with mine, letting me take the lead as I channel all of my anger and frustration. My nails dig into his skin, clawing and scratching at his neck and shoulders. The emotions swirling through me, potent and dark, pour into him—and he takes it all, gladly, hungrily, and begging for more.

When I finally fall back, my arms letting go to land on the bed beside my head, Gage doesn't let up. His lips trail across my face, peppering kisses along my jaw, cheeks, and the tip of my nose. His strong fingers work to unbutton my pants as his mouth moves across my chest, nipping and licking my cleavage. He climbs off the bed to kneel in front of me.

Taking great care, Gage pulls off my shoes and presses kisses to the inside of my ankles, his teeth sinking into my flesh with love bites that send arousal shooting through me. His mouth moves up my legs, paying special attention to my thighs. When he hooks his thumbs into the waistband of my pants to drag them down my legs until they fall to the floor, his mouth follows its path. Once he reaches my toes, he makes his way back up.

"Gage," I say, hating how my voice shakes. Luckily, I don't have to say anything else. He just knows.

"It's time for bed, baby," he murmurs, pulling back the covers for me to climb under, wearing only my t-shirt and panties. After putting his gun on his nightstand and switching off the light, he climbs into the bed and wraps himself around me. He lets out a gratified sigh and presses a kiss on the top of my head. We lay together in silence for a while, but it doesn't last long.

A strong hand slips under my jaw, tilting my head up until I meet his dark gaze. The city lights filtering through the parted blinds cast deep shadows across his angular face, enhancing all of his beautiful, sharp edges. He's a mercenary eager to do my bidding.

"I need you to talk to me, baby. Tell me what happened." It's a plea and a command. His thumb strokes my jaw tenderly, coaxing me to comply.

"The police called," I say finally, forcing the emotion back enough to get the words out. "About Tommy."

Gage remains silent as he listens and waits for me to

continue, the ticking of his jaw the only reaction to my words. "Apparently, they think that the amount of blood at his apartment means that my brother is dead. They say they don't have any more leads, and the case is now cold. He's assumed dead, and they won't be looking for him anymore. They're giving up on him." I let out a humorless laugh as a fresh wave of anger hits me. "I guess a gambling junkie with a perpetual losing streak and a habit of running from his debts isn't at the top of their priority list."

I shake my head, blinking past the tears of frustration streaming down my face freely. "He's dead—I know it, you know it, the fucking cops know it. I didn't expect them to come to his rescue. But the least they could do was find his body. Give me something to bury, something to say goodbye to. He wasn't much of a brother, but he's all that I had. He was my family. They might not think Tommy deserves closure, but I sure as hell do."

"You'll get your closure." It's more than an assurance. It's a promise. "One way or another." His dark words settle some of the animosity swirling inside me. I can't help but lean up to press a lingering kiss on his lips.

"Get some rest, pretty girl. Tomorrow's a new day to make the world fall to your feet." He brushes the hair out of my face, cupping my cheeks and gently brushing the tears away with the pads of his thumbs. I nod against his hands.

When he lets go and wraps his arms around me, I lay my head on his chest and settle in. The steady beating of his heart is calming, our rhythms syncing. "Goodnight, Reaper," I whisper.

This is where I belong.

CHAPTER TWENTY-ONE
GAGE

I sense her before I open my eyes—can feel the weight of her lush body against mine. The scent of her cherry blossom shampoo fills my lungs with each breath as my nose presses deeper into her hair. I want this smell to be bottled in an oxygen tank, so it's the only thing I ever have to breathe. The only sound she makes is the soft inhale and exhale as she sleeps. Our bodies are tangled together—hers supple and soft against my hard angles as she lays on my shoulder. When feeling her isn't enough, I open my eyes.

There she is.

Waking up to see Jill in my bed feels like the universe finally makes sense. She's mine, whether she wants to admit it to herself or not. After fantasizing what it would be like to have Jill be the first thing I see when I open my eyes in the morning, the real thing is *so* much fucking better. It's unreal.

She's unreal.

There's nothing more beautiful than Jill when she's fired up and blazing through the world, but there's something about watching her sleep. She's peaceful, innocent, and delicate—but not weak, never weak.

I like looking at her this closely. I can lay here and count every one of her long, dark eyelashes. I can trace the pout of her full parted lips and feel how many breaths pass through them. I can see the tiny heart-shaped freckle on her left, makeup-free cheek.

This is where she belongs—in my home, in my bed, in my arms. Soon, we'll be lying in *our* home, in *our* bed. We can live here if she likes this house. If she wants to live somewhere else, I'll buy her whatever house she wants—a penthouse, a townhouse, a mansion in Winnetka. Hell, I'll even buy her a permanent residence in The Raven so she can hang out with Lana all day. It might take me a few hands of poker, but I'll give Jill her every whim. My girl loves to live life on her whims.

Jill's eyes haven't opened yet when she murmurs, "I can feel you staring."

"You're stunning. It's easy to stare," I respond, unrepentant. Her lashes flutter slightly before she opens those haunting green eyes of hers and fixes them on me. Having her eyes on me makes me feel like the most powerful man in the world.

I fucking like it.

"Good morning, gorgeous." I press a kiss to her forehead.

"Oh yeah? What's so great about it?" she grumbles, making me bite back a smile. She's grumpy this morning, and it's fucking adorable. Last night took a lot out of her. I can see the shadows of fatigue under her eyes.

"I'm waking up next to you. I'd say that makes it a pretty good morning," I state with a smirk.

"Yeah, well. Last night was..." She trails off, not sure

what else to say. I wait patiently for her to continue, but she doesn't like my attentive expression. Her eyes narrow at me slightly as she flashes me a look. All vulnerability from last night has vanished with the sunrise. "I'm fine."

"I know you are." It's the truth. Her breakdown, needed or not, was out of character for her, and she's fighting the need to be back in control.

She doesn't like when she shows vulnerability, but I do. I like that she came to *me*, cried to *me*. I was the one she wanted in her most vulnerable state, the one she needed. I like her needing me. I plan on keeping it that way.

She wants control, I'll give it to her.

"Forget about that," I say, rolling over until she's on top of me. The raging erection I've had since she climbed into my bed presses between her legs as she straddles me, making her gasp. "Say good morning to me properly, and I'll cook you breakfast."

Jill looks down at me with a sexy smile that drives me crazy, rocking her full hips against me to have my cock rub against her clit. Even through her panties and my sweats, I can feel the heat of her. "Oh really? What will you cook for me?"

She reaches for the hem of her little t-shirt and pulls it over her head, letting her full breasts spill free. My eyes zero in on them, my brain short-circuiting momentarily. "Anything you fucking want," I rasp, grabbing onto her hips. I'll give her anything she wants. My fingers sink into the flesh as I hold on for dear life, reveling in the full weight of her pressing down on me. I want to feel all of her slamming down on my cock.

"Mmmm, I like the sound of that," she hums, the spark in her eyes so breathtaking I almost nut on the spot. Then she reaches down to run her hand over my length through my pants, and it takes everything in me not to buck off the bed.

Goddamn.

Jill toys with me through the material for a torturous moment until my hands are clamped so hard on her hips I'm sure they'll leave bruises—something we're both happy about. Finally, she pulls my pants down to let my cock spring free. A bead of precum glistens at the top, more than ready to be inside her hot little pussy.

She wraps a hand around the head of my rock-hard cock, running a finger over the slit to spread the precum around the broad tip before pumping a hand down my shaft. My teeth clench as I fight against the urge to take over and fuck the shit out of her. But my patience only lasts so long.

"Inside you. Now." There's no mistaking the desperation in my voice, and it makes her smile. She scootches back onto my legs and leans forward. Her smile turns devious as she lowers to lick the tip of my cock.

"Like this?" Her lips wrap around me, and my shaft disappears into her hot mouth, those big green eyes gazing up at me like a siren. My hands fist the sheets at my sides until my knuckles turn white.

Christ.

Her tongue swirls around the sensitive tip before sucking the soul right out of my body. My hands clamp onto her head and thread through her hair, fisting to pull her head up. If she doesn't stop, this is going to be over a lot faster than either of us wants. Jill releases the crown with a *pop*, the sinful smile returning to her full lips.

She's trying to kill me.

But, fuck, that smile gives me life.

"Oh, I'm sorry." She feigns remorse as she crawls

forward and rises up on her knees. Wrapping her hand around my erection, she guides it between her thick thighs. Tugging her panties to the side, she lowers herself to slide in just the tip. She's already so wet and swollen for me. "I didn't even say it, did I?"

Leaning forward to brace herself on my chest, she lowers until she's fully seated and filled to the hilt. I release a groan—her tight, perfect pussy gripping me like a vice. She lets out a breathy moan, her next words said with a sigh. "Good morning."

The unexpected knock at my door around noon has irritation bubbling inside me. This is only the third time I've convinced Jill to stay over after the night she showed up crying last week, and I don't like our time being interrupted. The last thing I need is her getting spooked and pulling away from me again.

After trying to ignore the unwelcome visitor, the knocking turns more persistent until they're all but trying to kick the door down. Keeping my loaded gun tucked into the waistband of my jeans, I leave Jill in my room to go handle whoever's disrupting our morning.

The banging persists until I turn the deadbolt and yank the door open. A hand with long red fingernails remains raised mid-knock, almost at my eye level. I look down the hand to meet determined brown eyes.

"Finally," the older woman says, pulling her hand back and gesturing to me wildly. "Don't just stand there. Let us in." My eyes move past her teased black hair to the older man standing silently behind her. He stares at me quietly, his thick, dark brows in a perpetual scowl.

"What are you two doing here?" I look back at the stubborn woman still staring at me expectantly. Connie Lawless lifts her brows, threatening to push past me if I don't step aside.

"I want to meet her," my mom states. I look over her head at my dad again, but his stern expression remains as he nods to his wife.

"She wants to meet her," he says simply.

"I want to meet her," my mom repeats.

"What makes you think she's here right now?"

"Woman's intuition."

"How do you even know—" My words cut off as it occurs to me. *Stevie*. "I'm going to fucking fire her," I growl.

"Are you going to step aside? Or do I have to find my own way in?"

Seeing that neither of them is going to give this up, I exhale a heavy breath through my nose and step aside to let them in. My parents enter the house, and I make sure to herd them into the living room. I wouldn't put it past my mom to go room to room until she's tracked Jill down.

"Wait here," I say, pointing to the couch. Dad sits on the couch and leans back to get comfortable, but Mom remains standing. She crosses her arms and raises her brows at me.

"Why, so you can sneak her out the back?" she accuses. I throw her a dirty look.

"What am I, fifteen?" I retort. "I'll go get her. She's not exactly expecting to meet my parents today." I just barely convinced Jill to spend time with me. She's probably going to skin me alive when she finds out they're here right now.

Fuck.

"Just hurry up. I need to see what's so special about this woman."

"You better watch yourself," I warn, turning to leave the room.

"Relax, I'm not going to hurt her or anything," my mom says behind me.

"I can't promise the same from Jill," I say over my shoulder as I walk towards the hallway. My mom laughs at that, her raspy voice cracking.

"I like the sound of her already."

Walking back to the bedroom feels like I'm walking into the lion's den. Jill's in the ensuite bathroom, putting on her makeup. Sensing my presence in the doorway, she glances over at me before returning her focus to her reflection.

"Was someone at the door?" she asks distractedly, her gorgeous ass sticking out as she leans over the counter to get closer to the mirror while swiping on her mascara.

"Yeah." I let out a heavy breath and steel myself. "They're here to meet you."

"Meet *me*?" Her hand pauses mid-swipe, and she straightens, her tone turning suspicious. "Who?"

"My parents." Those stunning green eyes of hers widen slightly in surprise, anger sparking in her gaze as her tone turns accusing.

"*Your parents?* Your parents." She gestures to her bare legs. "I'm not wearing pants, Gage."

She doesn't have a single pair of pants at my place, just her dress from last night and the t-shirt she brought to sleep in. I glance down at Jill's shapely long legs and how her oversized shirt stops high on her thick thighs. Her bare legs are nothing compared to how my parents have seen other women in the past.

Flashback to when I was nineteen, and they walked into my apartment while I was balls-deep in some blonde chick because I wasn't answering their calls. My mom had offered the girl—I

don't even remember her name—a hair tie and said she liked
her boob job while I was still inside her.

At least this time they fucking knocked.

"They don't give a shit about that." Her eyes narrow. "I'll make it up to you, baby. I promise."

"We'll talk about this later."

A smile spreads across my face as she straightens her shoulders and struts past me down the hallway toward the living room. I follow behind her, grinning from ear to ear.

Walking into a room with my parents, or even just one of them, isn't for the weak. *Intimidating* isn't a strong enough word to describe the experience, or so I've been told.

Jill doesn't hesitate before striding into the living room. My mom is standing by the fireplace, looking at the pictures I have on the mantle. Dad is still sitting on the couch, arms crossed, as he watches my mom snoop around.

"Gage says you're here to meet me." Jill's voice catches my parent's attention. "I'm Jill."

"This is my mom, Connie, and that's my dad, Dwayne."

"So you're the woman my son is obsessed with." I cut my mom with a look, but she shrugs it off. "What? Are you not?" She looks back at Jill. "Let me have a look at you."

"You're seeing more of me than I usually show total strangers." The look Jill flashes me says I'm in for a world of hurt later and it shoots straight to my cock. When my parents leave, I'm going to fuck that anger right out of her. Or better yet, I'm going to have her fuck me using all of that rage.

"Oh please, your outfit is practically PG compared to the things I've seen. And you've got good legs, pants are over-rated." My mom waves it off. I walk over to the sectional and sit down on the sofa before reaching out to grab Jill's hips. My fingers sink into her thighs as I pull her onto my lap. She glances back at me, her eyes sharp as she considers whether or not she's going to stay where I put her. I just smile and tighten my hold on her.

Watching Jill talk to my parents has pride swelling inside me. Not only does she hold her own against tornado Connie, but they're laughing together. She even gets my dad—always so stoic and serious—to crack a smile.

My parents spend the entire afternoon at my place, overstaying their welcome like usual. After a few hours, Jill excuses herself to go get her things so she can leave to get ready for work tonight.

After tugging on her dress from last night, Jill tries to slip out while I'm distracted by my mom trying to rearrange my kitchen cabinets. Ignoring the dishes spread on the counter, I don't let her escape so easily. When I catch up to her, she's almost at her car with her keys in her hand.

"Not so fast." I snag her by the waist, pressing her up against her car. "Don't think you can sneak away from me, little devil."

"You better get back in there before Connie decides to go through your room," she says, nodding to the house behind me.

"I don't know why you keep trying to deny what's so obvious." My eyes hold hers, refusing to be the first to look away. She meets my gaze head-on, unafraid.

"What's obvious?"

"Us," I state. "We belong together, Jill." She raises her brows in feigned confusion.

"Do we?"

"Yes."

"You want to convince me?" I nod. "Give it your best shot, Lawless. Show me what you've got." With that, she climbs into her car and drives away. I watch until her car disappears around the corner.

Her words of challenge spark something inside me. She has no idea who she's dealing with. Jill expects me to just try and fuck her into submission. The thought has occurred to me, but I'm not nearly dumb enough to think that's all it would take to get around my girl's stubbornness.

She wants to see what I've got? I'll show her exactly what I'm capable of.

And I'm going to savor it.

CHAPTER TWENTY-TWO

JILL

I sense their presence over my shoulder before I see them.

Someone's here in my room with me.

Walking into my apartment after a shift has never been ominous before. I work nights more often than not, and I've never been afraid of the dark. But now that it's just me and someone lurking in the darkness, alarm bells are going off in my brain.

Trying to remain relaxed, I slowly slide my hand under my pillow. Dread settles in my stomach like a ball of lead when I'm met with nothing but cool fabric.

"Looking for this?" The deep voice is punctuated by the metallic sound of my switchblade springing open. "You should find a better place to hide it. Under your pillow is very predictable."

I turn to face Gage, where he sits on my vanity chair in the corner of my bedroom.

"What are you doing here?"

"You told me to show you what I've got."

"So you decided to break into my apartment?" I ask,

unimpressed. He shakes his head with a smirk, his intense eyes smoldering at me.

"I've been in this apartment every single night for the past five months." His head tilts, dark eyes glittering. "Tonight, I let you see me."

There's no way.

So many small moments flood my brain—all those mornings I woke up swearing I could smell him in my room, the way painkillers and water were always waiting for me on the nightstand, waking up with a clean face without remembering taking my makeup off. I knew I was giving my drunken-self too much credit.

"You're lying," I say without conviction, doubt taking over.

"You keep your vibrator in the fridge, there's a sparkly taser in your third dresser drawer, and you keep your stash of poker tips in the vent behind your vanity." Gage's eyes burn into mine, reaching into my body to steal my soul. And this time, they catch a hold. "The first thing you do when you get home after a night out is take off your bra. You sleep like the dead. Once your head hits the pillow, nothing can wake you—a tornado, a fire alarm, not even having your makeup taken off."

Every word that leaves his mouth has a thrill running through me, my mind racing as I process. He's been here. There's no denying it, as much as I want to. When I was awake, Gage was always in the corner of my eye and in the back of my mind. While I was sleeping, he was in my living room and my kitchen. He was in my bedroom.

I want him in me.

The image of him standing over me, nothing but a dark shadow, while I slept, has arousal pooling between my legs. How his unrelenting eyes must have touched every part of me while I was completely oblivious, unconscious. Did he touch himself while he watched me? Did he touch me?

God, I want him to touch me.

What does he want from me?

He holds up the knife and takes a step forward—my responding step back has me pressing against the wall. "What were you planning on doing with this, little devil? Bleed me dry like the others?"

His question has the blood freezing in my veins. This feels like a trap, I'm not admitting to anything. "I don't know what you're talking about."

"I should be insulted that you lump me in with those scum-suckers." Holding the blade up to the light, he gazes at it thoughtfully. "But the look on your face when you sank this blade into them was the most beautiful thing I've ever seen—you're a fucking goddess. If letting you cut me open means I get to put that look on your face, then don't stop cutting until my heart can no longer pump blood for you to spill. And take your time so I can enjoy it."

The oxygen is being sucked out of the room with every syllable that passes through his lips until I'm light-headed.

He saw me.

Eyes widening slightly in surprise, my lips part to inhale a short gasp at his confession. His heavy attention lowers to my mouth.

"I like your lipstick. This color is going to look beautiful smeared on my cock. Who is it?" He leans closer. "Jonas?" Swiping his thumb down my bottom lip to smear it, he tilts his head thoughtfully. "No, Vince."

My eyelids flutter at the revelation, adrenaline and desire flooding through me. "You know about that?"

"I know everything." The longing in his gaze slices through me until I can hardly take it.

He sees me.

"Why are you telling me all this? Why now?" I ask, shaking my head. It doesn't make sense. I can't wrap my head around it. I can't trust it.

"You wanted to see what I've got, so I'm showing my hand."

"What game are you playing, Gage?"

This time, he doesn't smile at the sharp, threatening edge in my voice. The sober expression remains on his devastating face, silencing any skepticism picking in my brain. His eyes hold mine in a passionate connection that even death couldn't sever.

"No more games, Jill," he says, and I feel it so deeply in my chest it almost hurts. The discomfort is delicious. "There's no life without you, and I'm done wasting time pretending there is. My dark soul's found its match. I'm here to collect."

"Soulmates?" The word leaves my mouth softly and it tastes good on my tongue.

"Soulmates, twin flames, my other half—call it what you want. We're created for each other. I knew it the moment I laid eyes on you." His hand circles my throat as he inches closer until we're chest to chest. I know he can feel my heartbeat thrumming against his fingertips. "Tell me you feel it."

"I—" My brain is short-circuiting as it spins, races, trying to process what's happening. Emotions swirl through me—panic, excitement, lust, elation, doubt—until I'm not sure which one will catch hold.

Gage has challenged me, has matched me at every turn. He's proven to be my equal in every aspect of my life. He takes everything I throw at him eagerly, giving it right back to me and begging for more. The darkness twisting inside him matches mine, edge for edge, like pieces of shrapnel born from the same catastrophe.

Desire has never been a question; I want him, and he's very clearly always wanted me—*needed* me. And at some point, I started needing him and there's no going back.

But is that enough? Can I trust this?

Trust *him*?

Gage waits in complete silence for me to speak, not moving a single muscle. I open my mouth to respond. Unsure of what will come out, I let my instincts take over.

"I feel it." The statement rings in the silence, the truth of it rippling through me until it settles in my bones.

I'm his, and he's mine.

I feel it.

Twin flames.

"Now tell me you're mine."

"You're mine," I smart, making him grin. His grip tightens on my throat, pulling me in closer and liquifying my insides.

"I am." His deep voice washes over me, his dark gaze piercing the soul that's now entwined with his. "Until the heavens crumble and there are no more lives to be lived."

When did this happen? When did he become the lifeblood coursing through my veins?

Leaning up, my lips clash with his. The need is too strong. I can't help myself—I don't want to. Gage devours me like it's his life's mission to take as much pleasure from me as he gives.

And he gives so generously.

Lifting up my dress, the mesh panties are torn from my body without a second thought. His grip around my throat tightens possessively as his other hand strokes my greedy pussy. I'm so fucking wet right now—my arousal drips down my legs, coating his hand as he toys with me. I moan against him, needing more as my hips shift in search of his wicked fingers.

Gage's tongue dives in to dominate my mouth as his fingers give me what I want. Three fingers plunge into me, stealing my breath against his hold. He swallows my moans, my breathing turning heavy as he curls one of the fingers inside me as they pump in and out to stroke that spot deep inside me that ignites every nerve ending in my body.

The pleasure is building, threatening to swallow me whole until I'm nothing but a memory. Feeling the wave building inside me, Gage pulls back to look down at me. My eyes open to lock on his, gasping against the pleasure slicing through my body. And as I reach the peak, the strong fingers around my throat tighten to restrict my air until the edges of my vision blur and my head is dizzy.

And I'm falling.

The orgasm washes over me, and I'm dragged into the undertow. Every nerve ending fires at once, a sequence of fireworks burning hot and bright. My body is reeling, completely overtaken as I surrender to the bliss. My hand necklace stifles every gasp and moan that passes through my lips.

Gage soaks it all in like he'll never get enough—every moan, every shudder, every panted breath. His focus remains locked on me, the object of his every desire, eyes ablaze and muscles taut. As the orgasm fades, his hand on my throat loosens, and I can't help but miss the pressure of it as I drag in the air greedily. My body melts between the wall behind me and the wall of muscles keeping me upright.

Gage doesn't hesitate to take full advantage of my

pliance while I recover. He reaches for the hem of my dress and tugs it over my head before tossing it behind him, completely forgotten. Next goes my bra, leaving me completely naked.

"Fucking hell," he growls, shaking his head. "I will never get tired of looking at you."

"I want to see more of you," I demand, some of my strength returning as I reach for his clothes. Gage's hands work with mine to shed his clothes as I push us away from the wall and toward the bed. He stalks backward until he reaches the bed, shedding his underwear before lowering onto the covers gloriously naked. His body is a work of art, powerful and beautiful. And sinful as hell.

As he scoots back on the bed, I'm following. Climbing onto the bed, I don't stop until I'm straddling him. My throbbing pussy is desperate to be filled by his thick cock as it strains towards me, hard as steel. When I lean forward to kiss Gage, it's in a frenzy. Our lips clash, tongues tangle, and breath mingles. His teeth nip as my lips suck, our hands frantically feeling every inch there is to explore and praise.

Reaching between us, I wrap my hand around the pulsating boner pressing against my stomach. Gage shifts and squirms as I begin to stroke it.

"Keep teasing me like that, and you won't like what happens," Gage warns between clenched teeth. A smirk tugs at my lips, my fingers toying with the sensitive tip as it weeps for me.

"Won't I?" I question, thinking of all the deliciously wicked things he might do to me.

"Inside your pussy." He's lost his patience. All sense of control is gone. "Now." His command sends a new wave of desire crashing over me, and I can't stop from obeying.

I don't want to.

"I'm clean," I sigh, guiding him to my entrance. I don't want to deal with a condom right now. I can't. I need him—bare and raw.

"I'm yours." The meaning behind those two words has me all but swooning. He's clean, and he's mine. All mine.

Sinking down onto his cock until I'm filled to the hilt, nothing between us has my eyes rolling back in my head. Our moans echo in the room as I roll my hips. Bouncing up and down, I build a rhythm that makes my head spin. Gage's hands grasp my waist, guiding me up and down as he mutters praise like a prayer that would make God jealous.

As the friction builds, his desire takes over. Gripping my hips, he powers into me, matching my speed with powerful thrusts until I'm holding on for dear life. Pulling me down to lay on his chest, he leverages his hold to push in deeper. His big cock drills into me so hard and deep there's no escaping the orgasm as it explodes through me.

Nestling into his neck with a loud cry, I shatter into a million pieces. Euphoria drenches me through to my bones, melting me from the inside out. Gage doesn't stop moving, his thrusts hungry and unrelenting as he chases his own release. When it hits, it's cosmic.

Every thick muscle in his powerful body tenses as his bliss hits him like a Mac truck. My name leaves his lips like a Hail Mary as he comes. Each stroke feels deeper as ribbon after ribbon of his hot cum fills me.

When he finally slows to a stop, he holds me there—wrapped around him, chest to chest. Our labored breath matching the racing of our hearts. We stay there, unable to move—unwilling to move—for a long moment. Seconds stretch into minutes as we remain completely and utterly intertwined.

"Where the hell have you been my whole life?" I say finally. And I am a little pissed, because why the fuck didn't he find me earlier.

"Getting ready for when I found you," Gage's murmured words vibrate over me.

"You took your sweet *fucking* time." My sweetening tone softens the sting of my sharp words.

"I'm sorry, baby." I can hear the smile in his voice. He rolls us over until he's leaning over me, brushing my messy hair from my face. When he finally pulls out, I can still feel him inside of me—rooted so deeply that he's a part of my being.

"I'm gonna go get a warm washcloth." He presses a soft kiss against my lips, his muscles tensing as he prepares to get up. But I stop him before he makes it an inch by wrapping my arms around him.

"Don't bother," I say, hitching my leg around his hip. "Something tells me that was only round one for tonight."

"You don't have to convince me, little devil." Falling onto the bed, Gage pulls me against his side. Laying in silence, my brain races to process everything that's happened over the last two hours. And while I'm mentally sorting, a thought occurs to me.

"How do you know? About them?" I ask curiously. He knew about the men I've killed, knew them by name. Gage's eyes lower to meet mine.

"I followed you."

"For how long?" My eyes narrow.

"Longer than you think," he states, unashamed. A smile pulls at my lips as lust swirls inside me at the thought.

"You're a sick freak," I say, fighting my grin. Gage's astute eyes smolder, a smirk crossing his face.

"You're turned on," he points out. I don't deny it. There's no reason to.

"You watched me kill them?"

"Yes." The admission comes out so nonchalant. It's like he's been expecting this entire conversation. "Watching you makes me hard."

"How hard?"

"That look on your face," he groans, shaking his head. "I came every time."

Reaching over him to grab the knife off the nightstand, I lift it up. "You liked watching me cut them with this?" He nods. The urge to use the blade in my hand to draw his blood is suddenly overwhelming, and I know he sees it written all over my face.

"Do it. I know you want to." Gage bites his bottom lip and smiles as I open the knife. The metal gleams in the light, dangerously beautiful. Dragging the knife across his decorated skin, my eyes trace the way the flesh slices beneath the blade. Blood springs to the surface of the two-inch incision, creating a dark pool against his darkened chest.

"That look, right there. *Jesus Christ*." His deep groan vibrates beneath me. I can feel Gage's eyes on me as I run the pad of my finger over the wound and lift it up to the light. The deep red liquid coats my finger, vibrant and beautiful. Pressing my pointer finger to my thumb, I rub my fingertips together to get a better look at the pure crimson against my skin. It's the prettiest color red I've ever seen— deep, rich, and all mine.

"It's so pretty."

"I'm going to look so fucking good on you."
"You already do."

CHAPTER TWENTY-THREE

JILL

Before I open my eyes, I hear it—the buzzing. What is that? The sound is so familiar, but my sleep-addled brain can't quite place it. Pressure pushes on my lower stomach, accompanied by a slight sting. I shift against the discomfort, but something is holding me in place.

"Hold still, baby. I'm almost done." The sound of Gage's voice has me opening my eyes and lifting my head off the pillow. Gage kneels over me with one hand pressed against my hip and a tool in the other. He's dragging the tool across the skin of my bikini line. Is that a tattoo gun?

Son of a bitch.

"Are you tattooing me right now?" I ask, my voice rough with sleep. I'm still waking up, but the tell-tale stinging proves this isn't a dream.

"You really do sleep through just about anything," Gage marvels with a smirk, his eyes focused intently on the skin he's coloring with ink.

"What the hell are you doing?" I demand, trying to figure out what he's up to. All I can see is that he's tattooing over my new martini tattoo before he's gently but firmly pushing me back down.

"I'm fixing it."

"You're fixing it," I repeat, both demanding and bewildered. What the fuck is happening right now?

"That rat, Dane, couldn't even get something as simple as a martini right. I can't believe I let him work at my shop for so long. Your skin deserves better than his shitty work." Gage's words are edged with disgust. He wipes the excess ink from my skin and leans back to look over his handiwork. "A work of art."

"You really think highly of yourself, don't you?" I ask, barely refraining from rolling my eyes. Gage's eyes move from my skin to meet mine, pinning me where I lay.

"Not the tattoo," he rumbles. "You."

Warmth floods through me from head to toe, pooling between my legs. "Are you done?" I ask. The look in his eyes tells me he'll never be done with me. "With the tattoo."

"See for yourself." Releasing my hip, he allows me to sit up and climb off the bed. The skin of my abdomen is tender as I walk over to the full-length mirror in my living room.

The skin around my tattoo is freshly pink, adding to the contrast of the black design. The outline of the martini glass has been evened out so the lines are saturated and clean while still remaining delicate. In the glass has been added what looks like clear liquid. Floating in the dry martini is a twist of lemon—my favorite drink order. The shape of the lemon peel makes me lean in to get a better look.

Is that what I think it is?

"Is that a G?" I spin on my heel and stalk back into the bedroom. Gage stands by the bed, cleaning up his equipment. "Did you tattoo a G on me?"

The accusation in my voice does nothing to dissuade Gage's self-satisfied grin. His eyes travel down my body slowly, reveling in every inch until they land heavily on the ink he just branded me with. "I told you I fixed it."

"You tattooed your initials on my body."

"Just the one." His smile turns wolfish—all teeth and heated intent. "For now." As I saunter closer, his head cocks to one side, and his eyes touch every inch of my naked skin. The look in his eyes tells me he's making plans, and it sparks something inside me.

"Don't worry, Menace. Soon, it won't just be just my initials on your body. You'll have my entire last name."

"What if I don't want to change my name?"

"It's not an option."

"And if we break up?"

The air in the room drops several degrees when Gage flashes a predatory smile that's fully vicious and without humor.

"You're a part of me, Jill, and I won't live without you. Ever. There's no breaking up. The second you even *think* about leaving me, I'll have you chained in my basement, where you'll never get the chance."

"Hmm," I feign a contemplative look that has his expression turning vicious, making a teasing smile tug at my lips. "Don't threaten me with a good time."

Stepping outside, it's a beautiful summer day. Following Gage through the garage into the driveway behind his house, I look at the machine standing in the center of the short driveway. I've never been into engines or mufflers. I

couldn't tell you what make or model Gage's motorcycle is
—just that it's big, black, and crazy sexy.

When Gage told me we're going to a barbecue his dad is
holding with the Chained Saints—and that both of his
parents will be there along with his brother, whom I've yet
to meet—it was a hard sell. But then he mentioned the
prime rib, open bar, and Stevie's world-famous fudge bars
to sweeten the pot. I finally agreed under one condition: we
take his bike the long way.

"What are you doing?" I ask when Gage walks back
inside.

"Grabbing your helmet." He calls from the garage.

"I don't need it. Helmets just mess up my makeup and
keep me from feeling the wind in my hair." He emerges
holding a helmet that sparkles black cherry in the sunlight,
a determination in his eyes.

"You're wearing a helmet, Jill," he states. I raise my
brows at him.

"Am I?" I ask, but he doesn't back down.

"Yes, you are. You can be reckless with anyone else's life
but your own." His eyes meet mine with an expression that
dares me to challenge him. "Besides, I'm going to be
messing up your makeup every chance I get." He leans
down to capture my lips in a hot kiss to prove his point.

When he pulls back, he runs his tongue over his bottom
lip to lick off the lipgloss that's transferred, using the pad of
his thumb to swipe a smudge under my bottom lip. He
grins down at me, looking tempted to kiss me again.
Instead, his arms raise and the helmet is being fitted over
my head.

The padding forms to my head like it was made for me,
and the weight of the sturdy shell is satisfying against my

skull. My eyes meet Gage's through the open-face shield as he fastens the helmet in place and tests it with a good tug. Once satisfied, he pauses to look at me, his head tilting as he smiles.

"I've never been more turned on by a helmet in my life," he groans.

"I would hope not." I raise my brows in expectation. "Now, take me on a ride before I don't want it anymore."

Gage smirks as he slides on his own helmet and climbs onto his black motorcycle. When he reaches out a tattooed hand to me, a wave of attraction hits me hard.

Damn, he's so hot it's ungodly.

Climbing onto the machine behind him, he pulls my arms tightly around his waist until I'm fully pressed against his back. Before he turns on the bike, he addresses me over his shoulder. "Don't lie to yourself, Menace. You'll always want this."

With that, he revs the bike to life—the engine roaring and rumbling powerfully beneath us. Reaching up to snap down his face shield, I do the same, and we're pulling out of the driveway and racing through traffic.

The summer air feels so freeing as it whips around us. Every rev of the powerful engine beneath me vibrates through my core as it carries us through the city toward the suburbs. The cityscape dissolves into open spaces and bigger skies as Gage takes us along the water. The world races past us, and I hold on for dear life.

Sweet freedom.

CHAPTER TWENTY-FOUR

JILL

We pull up to the bar, and Gage lines up his motorcycle in a row of other big custom bikes of all different shapes and colors. Gage stands to keep the bike steady while I climb off, then he's resting the machine on the kickstand and getting off to stand in front of me.

"The Halfway House? Doesn't that defeat the whole purpose of a bar?" I ask, looking at the bar as Gage unbuckles my helmet from under my chin. When he lifts it off my head, I can see the damage that's been done to my hair in the reflection of his helmet. His strong tattooed fingers gently fix my part and smooth down my flyaways without me needing to ask.

"We're halfway between two towns. They thought they were being clever," he explains.

Gage pulls off his own helmet and I reach for my purse in the side bag on the bike. Pulling out my lipgloss to reapply, Gage stops me to lean in and steal a bone-melting kiss before my lip product is in the way. I lean into him, letting our lips linger for several long seconds. When I pull back, I use a compact mirror and swipe some black cherry lipgloss across my lips. Gage was smart enough to avoid this stuff, the plumping effect feels like cooling pins and needles on my skin. It's slightly painful but effective.

Beauty is pain.

"You're so beautiful, it's crazy, " Gage says, making me smile. Taking my hand in his to intertwine our fingers, he leads me towards the side of the building. "The Chained Saints clubhouse is around back."

The aroma of meat grilling that fills the air is heavenly as we walk through a side gate into a courtyard. Dwayne stands at a massive grill covered in different cuts of seasoned meats, flipping and seasoning. Between the look on his face and the apron around his neck that reads, 'Your opinion wasn't in my recipe,' I know he means business.

The clubhouse looks like a large converted garage, with the entire back wall made up of rolling doors that open up to the courtyard full of people. Just inside, I can see a bar and several couches. The entire back interior wall is made up of a mural of the Chained Saints logo of angel wings wrapped in metal chains and barbed wire.

Big, burly men in leather are everywhere, with gorgeous women sprinkled in here and there. I recognize a few faces from Gage's tattoo shop, but most of the bikers are complete strangers.

Except one face that looks ridiculously similar to the man next to me. I mean, it seriously could have been stolen right off Gage's head. He approaches with his arms out like he's looking for a hug.

"Gage!" The deep voice calls. "You finally made it, I'm touched. I was beginning to think you were avoiding us."

Gage reaches out to give his doppelganger a one-armed man hug.

"You're so dramatic. I saw you a few weeks ago," Gage argues, drawing me back into his side.

"Connie said you were trying to keep her all to yourself," he says, looking at me. "Hi, I'm Gage's brother Rio."

Standing side by side, Rio and Gage are living proof of the power of genetics. Both are tall—though Rio is about an inch taller—with muscular builds, dark hair, and dark eyes. Even their mannerisms are mirrored in each other as Rio smirks at me. The biggest difference is in the ink they chose to cover their body. While every visible inch of Gage is covered all the way up to his sharp jawline, Rio only has a throat tattoo and one full sleeve on his left arm that extends down the back of his hand.

"You two could be twins," I inform them. Though I doubt it's the first time they've heard it.

"Fraternal maybe," Rio snorts. "I'm much better looking. It's a shame he found you first, you got stuck with this ugly fucker."

Looking between the two brothers, I couldn't disagree more. While Rio is attractive and carries a strong resemblance, he doesn't hold a candle to my Gage.

"Thanks, but if I wanted the generic version, I would've stopped at Walmart," I reply smoothly. Gage looks down at me and grins, his hand on my hip giving me a possessive squeeze.

"Damn, harsh," Rio says, feigning a wounded expression. He turns to his brother and points at me with a laugh. "I like her."

I've decided I like him too. Rio seems fun, if not a little cocky. But I can look past that—just look at his brother.

"Don't just stand there. Get some drinks and start introducing your girl around. Connie's got everyone very curious."

After grabbing some beers from the bar, Gage walks me around to meet some of the members and their girlfriends. Most of them are welcoming, but a few of the women give me side-eye and fake smiles. Feeling me tense as I flash them my own cold look, Gage explains that they're house mice who float around sleeping with bikers, trying to become a member's old lady. Apparently, they get territorial and don't like hot new girls coming in.

I roll my eyes at that. I'm not the least bit interested in sleeping with any of the MC members. I might be a girl's girl, but I have no patience for women who put themselves in competition with other women over men.

"Finally came out of hiding, huh?" Connie says, taking a swig of beer as we walk up to her. Gage rolls his eyes.

"Hello to you too, Mom," he says sarcastically. "With such a warm welcome, I can't believe we didn't come here sooner."

"Hey, I'm allowed to give you shit, it's my right as your mother." Connie's gaze moves to me. "Jill, I almost didn't recognize you with pants on."

"Mom—" Gage says her name as a warning, his eyes cutting to me.

I tilt my head back and laugh, not the least bit offended. Connie is definitely a character, and I love not knowing what's coming out of her mouth next.

"What?" Connie says innocently. "It's a nice change, that's all I'm saying." She turns to address me like it's just us. "Listen, I heard you've decided to stick with my son. That's great and all, but personally I would've held out and made him buy me a car or something. I'm sure he would've done just about anything to have you. Just saying."

"For god's sake," Gage growls as I laugh again.

"I'll have to remember that for next time." I look up at

him, feigning consideration. "Maybe we'll have a big fight later."

"I like the way you think," Connie says with a nod of approval.

"Food's ready!" Dwayne bellows from the grill. "Come grab it while it's hot."

"Finally," Gage mutters, placing his hands on my shoulders to turn me towards the awaiting food. "Let's go. Anything to separate you two, I don't like you plotting against me."

"He's so sensitive. I don't know where I went wrong," Connie sighs with a shrug, flashing me a wink. Gage ushers me towards the food as I laugh, his expression disgruntled. Luckily, he seems to get over our teasing when it's time to load up a massive plate of the most delicious looking barbecue dishes I've ever seen.

Finding a nice grassy spot along the back wall of the courtyard away from the chaos, Gage lets me get settled on the ground before lowering to the grass next to me.

"I should've worn different pants," I mumble, tugging at the constricting waistband of my denim shorts. "These shorts are not meant for sitting." If I were at home or with Lana, I'd just unbutton the damn things to let my belly hang out and call it a day. But I'm not doing that here.

"Come here, baby. Lay down." Gage lifts up the plate and pats his lap. Pivoting my body, I lay on my back with my head resting in his lap. His fingers tenderly bush a tendril of hair away from my face as he gazes down at me. "Better?"

"Better," I confirm. This position is actually very comfortable, and I really like the view.

"Good, now open up." He lifts the fork and guides it to

my opened mouth. The pulled pork melts in my mouth, and I suppress a moan as my eyes basically roll back in my head.

"That is so good, it should be illegal."

"It is, technically." Gage holds up another bite for me. "You can't legally source some of the ingredients for the sauce my dad makes in the US."

"So I'm eating contraband barbecue right now?" I savor the bite in my mouth with a sigh of appreciation. "Somehow that makes it taste better."

"Remind me to learn how to grill," Gage says, watching how my face lights up at the food I'm being fed.

What can I say? It's really that good.

"No complaints from me, especially if your dad is the one teaching you. Learn as many of his secrets as you can." I open my mouth for another bite, and Gage is already waiting with a forkful. He uses the pad of his thumb to swipe a drop of barbeque sauce from the corner of my mouth, before pressing it between my lips for me to suck off. Something that would usually be sexually charged feels surprisingly endearing as we lay here on a summer day enjoying each other's company.

"Are you going to eat some too? That whole plate isn't just for me." I accept a bite of the loaded macaroni and cheese. Goddamn, is every dish at this function ridiculously good?

"I'll eat in a minute," he says, brushing it off. "I'm busy feeding the Menace. I can't make any sudden moves."

I laugh at that, making him grin. "You're funny."

"You're a lot nicer to me when you've been fed," he comments. I can't argue with that. Nothing brings out the Menace in me like low blood sugar and an empty stomach.

"You've cracked the code." I steal a piece of grilled shrimp off the plate and bring it up to his mouth to eat. He lets me feed it to him, pulling the meat out of the shell So I can discard the tail.

"I'm learning every day," he murmurs. "You're my favorite subject, and I plan to be an expert."

"You already know me better than almost anyone." Other than Lana, he probably knows me better than I even know myself at this point. The thought is haunting in its comfort.

"I know, baby." He opens his mouth for another shrimp.

"Why do you insist on calling me that?" I ask, irritation seeping in with my curiosity. The term has always rubbed me the wrong way—like I'm someone who needs to be taken care of. I can stand on my own two feet, I can fend for myself. I definitely don't need to rely on a man to take care of me.

Gage reads me like a book, one of his hands running through my hair in a way that soothes the animosity raging inside me. "Because if anyone is going to be spoiling you, protecting you, and babying you—it's going to be me. And I'll take any chance I get."

His answer has a fire sparking inside me that's foreign and terrifying—because I like it, more than I can admit to myself. Warmth floods through me, bashing against the walls I've built securely around my heart until they fracture.

"When you say things like that, a big part of me desperately wants to believe you." My tone has softened against the uncertainty I feel.

His adoring gaze doesn't falter against mine, and his steadiness rocks me. The men in my life haven't been immovable—just flaky and unreliable. I've never had an anchor to make me feel secure during the storms of life. I've always ridden them out on my own.

"I don't mind that you don't trust me yet. You will." He leans down to kiss me with lips spiced with cajun seasoning. "Take your time, I'm not going anywhere. Ever." We sit there for a moment in our connection, reveling in it.

"I'm thirsty," I murmur softly. An amused smile tugs at his lips at the subject change, his intent eyes smoldering as his hand brushes through my hair.

"Let's get you a drink." He helps me sit up before he stands and offers me a hand to help me off the ground. Walking hand in hand, we stroll back towards the party.

"You don't have a patch," I observe, a question evident in my tone. Gage's leather jacket is clear of the MC patch on all of the other cuts at this party.

"No, I don't," Gage confirms, glancing down at me.

"Why aren't you a member of the Chained Saints like the rest of your family?"

"I was in and out of foster care growing up. That's where I met Anders and Messer—we were in the same group home. After I aged out, I didn't stick around here to join the Saints. Instead, I moved to New York for a tattoo apprenticeship. That's where I started my business and built my client list."

"You were in the system?" That's surprising to me since Gage has both parents in his life, and they seem pretty close. He can sense my confusion.

"Dwayne and Connie Lawless liked to live up to our last name," he explains. "You've met them, they're not exactly subtle." I can't help but laugh at that. His parents are a lot of things, but no one can call them discreet.

"They got caught?" I guess.

"A lot. Shoplifting, arson, grand larceny—you name it. Their sentences kept getting longer and longer with each strike until they both did eight years for stealing an ATM off a street corner when I was fourteen."

"They stole an entire ATM? Why?" I ask with a surprised laugh. Gage nods with a shrug.

"To see if they could."

"Where was your brother during all of this?"

"We were split up. Rio is five years younger than me, so we were put in different homes. We had very different goals growing up—he wanted to be guaranteed a place to belong by becoming a Saint, build on our family legacy. I found my family in Messer and Anders, and we were determined to make names for ourselves."

"So you and your brother weren't close?" I guess.

"Nah, we barely knew each other. We finally reconnected a few years ago when I moved my business back to Chicago." We've reached the doors leading into the clubhouse, but it looks like everyone is headed inside.

"Looks like the party's moving to the bar," Gage says, taking my hand to lead me inside. "Let's get you that drink."

The bar is crowded, but Gage has no problem cutting through the knots of people to an empty corner along the wall. Telling me to wait here, he makes his way over to the bar to order us some drinks.

Standing at the bar while the slammed bartenders scramble to fulfill orders, a blonde head approaches Gage that has me bristling. She's clearly got her sights set on my man, and he lets her get closer than he should—anything within ten feet is too fucking close. And when she strikes up a conversation, he lets her.

The buxom blonde leans closer and closer, every centimeter eating away at my already thin patience. Gage's eyes remain intently on her plastic face—too fucking intently.

"So where's the party going after this?" she asks, fluttering her eyelashes at him. I'll rip every one of those two-hundred-dollar lash extensions off her face right now. And her eyeballs are going next.

"No one said anything about an after party," Gage says nonchalantly.

"Give me your phone number. I'll give you a call when I find one."

"That's not a good idea."

"Then hand me your phone, and I'll give you mine." One of the other girls she came with calls out, beckoning her over. Before she sachets over to her group, she leans forward to give him a look at her cleavage and flashes what I assume is supposed to be her version of bedroom eyes. "I'll be right back."

Tramp.

Grabbing our drinks from the bartender, Gage walks back over to me. He can sense the storm brewing, and I swear the fucker looks excited about it.

"Go ahead. Get her number, flirt away. I'd love to see what happens when you do." I accept the martini and take a sip.

"Are you jealous, little devil?"

"Jealous?" I lean in so close that my lips brush against his as I speak. "Baby, I'm vengeful. You don't want to see what happens when I get jealous."

"You're so fucking hot when you're mad." Gage pushes off the wall, places his drink down on the nearest table, then strides over to stand behind me. One of his hands wraps around my waist to pull me until my back is pressing against his chest. His other wraps possessively around my throat, lifting my chin to bare the skin of my neck to him. "You have nothing to worry about, Jill. I prefer brunettes who play with knives and have a taste for violence."

"I was never worried," I say, my eyes shooting daggers at the tipsy tramp arguing with one of her wasted friends. "But she should be. I don't like bitches who can't take a hint."

I can feel Gage's chuckle rumble through his chest, the rich sound vibrating over my skin. His nose presses through my hair, trailing up my neck to speak into my ear. "I'll just have to make myself clear then. I already belong to someone."

Bottle blondie's eyes meet mine just in time to see Gage press his lips to my neck to taste my skin. His hand on my stomach lowers until his fingers are halfway under the waistband of my jeans. Her eyes widen slightly in surprise, an offended look crossing her face. She tries to hold my piercing gaze, but after a moment, she averts her eyes when it proves too intense. Watching her stomp away has victory trickling through me.

"She's gone," I say when Gage's mouth doesn't let up from its exploration. His teeth catch my earlobe, giving it a little nip.

"There are other women here. If I stop, they won't get the message." He's growing hard against my back as he groans. "I could get lost in you for days and never get bored."

"What are you going to do? Eat my pussy right here in a crowded bar?"

"I would spend a day with my head between your legs on national television without a second thought. I'll gladly get on my knees to show you where I stand."

"Keep talking like that, and I might let you," I say. "But I don't think Connie would approve." Gage chuckles at that.

"My mom would cheer me on, then skin me alive," he says, pulling back to turn me around. I look up at him, my arms wrapping around his neck. "I'm a selfish bastard, I don't feel like sharing you with the world. At least not tonight."

"Oh yeah? So what are you going to do with me tonight?" I ask, my eyes sparking.

"I'm gonna get you into a nice hot bubble bath."

"Mmmm," I hum. "Keep talking."

"Candles, wine, bubbles." A smirk tugs at his lips. "You —naked and covered in suds."

"And what are you going to be doing?" I raise my brows, the ghost of a smile crossing my lips.

"I thought you'd know me by now," he chides. "I'll be watching." The way he gazes at me sends sparks skating across my skin as the air around us turns hazy with our chemistry. My nails play with the nape of his neck, dragging to scratch him—but not hard enough to draw blood. His eyes warm, arousal rippling through his body.

"Take me home," I say.

CHAPTER TWENTY-FIVE

JILL

The first breath after stepping into my apartment after my pilates class tells me he's been here. The lingering scent of his warm cologne and leather fills my lungs, it's delicious.

Gage.

I briefly pause in the entryway to listen and feel—is he still here? I don't sense him, or anyone else, in here with me. So I toss my keys and purse on the entryway table and walk further into the apartment. My eyes scan the living room and kitchen until they land heavily on the kitchen island.

Four black gift boxes sit on the counter, propped against four large vases of blood-red roses. I bite my bottom lip in a smile of excitement as I approach the display, the fluttering of butterflies in my stomach growing stronger as I get closer.

The flower arrangements are gorgeous, professional, and look very expensive. An envelope sits on the counter with my name written in Gage's handwriting. Pulling out the card with a flaming heart on the front, I read the note inside.

'Wear them out for me tonight, and I'll return the favor.
Xoxo Yours'

I reach for the biggest one of the four gift boxes first. Tugging at the black satin ribbon, I lift the top off the box. I peel the white tissue paper to reveal a carefully folded bundle of gorgeous, rich red fabric. Lifting the dress out of the box, the intricate beading on the scarlet bodice glitters in the light. My smile blooms as I hold it up against my body and turn to look at my reflection in the mirror across the room. The designer dress looks tailored to my measurements perfectly.

Of course it is, Gage picked it out for me.

Stalker.

Next comes the second largest box, which unsurprisingly reveals a pair of black Dior open-toed pumps with a black bow on the back along the simple ankle strap. They're both sexy and elegant, with an edgy twist—just like me. The third box is a necklace. The choker is made of clear Swarovski crystals, with strings of red gems that hang down like blood trickling down a throat.

The last gift is the smallest, and it takes my breath away when I open it. A lip duo sits inside the box, one lipstick and one lipgloss. The deep, complex color is so stunning, it's as if it were created just for me—just like the blood it matches.

I pull out the lipstick to look at the color name: Crimson Sin.

Gage.

My phone buzzes in my pocket with an incoming call and I don't have to look to know who's calling before I answer it. Gage's deep voice speaks as soon as I press the device to my ear.

"Goddamn, that smile on your face is worth every penny." I glance around my apartment in an attempt to spot him out of habit, but I don't see anything. Shocker.

"Stop watching me, or I won't wear them. I want you to be surprised."

"I know every inch of your body intimately, and I've been fantasizing about seeing that outfit on you all day, little devil."

"Then I'm sure you'd be pretty disappointed if you never got to see it on me," I say flatly, pushing my point. Gage's chuckle travels through the phone and washes over me like warm honey.

"Be ready at seven o'clock, gorgeous," Gage relents.

"When you open the door, be ready for me."

"Always."

When the door swings open, Gage's body turns to stone. It wouldn't surprise me if the man's heart stopped beating in his chest and the breath stilled in his chest. The only movement comes from his eyes as they run over me from head to toe more than once.

I've spent the last five hours getting ready for our date tonight. I'm moisturized, plucked, primped, waxed, and fully made up—all just for him. The dress fits like my body was the inspiration, and the shoes couldn't make my legs look any sexier if they tried. I kept my eye makeup simple to let my bold red lip be the focus, with some smoked-out liner and lashes in what Lana calls my 'siren eyes.'

I look absolutely irresistible.

"What do you think?" I ask, batting my eyes at him. When he finally moves, his hand runs over his mouth, and he slowly shakes his head.

"I don't like to give Heaven credit." His voice is rough with reverence that bathes me in praise. "But the angels knew what they were doing when they created you." His adoration charges through my body until every nerve ending is firing at once like a hit of the best kind of drug.

With one long stride, he's in front of me, his hands cupping my face. The urge to kiss me is written all over his face, but he refrains for the sake of the glossy, gorgeous red pout on my full lips.

"This color is breathtaking, baby," he murmurs, tilting my head back to bring my lips just inches from his. "It couldn't be more perfect for you."

"Just like the man it came from," I say, resisting my own need to feel his lips against mine. I want to feel every inch of him as he worships every inch of me. The sparks flying between us burn so hot I'm sure I'd be swallowed whole until I was nothing but ash. "You look so good, I don't know how I'll be able to resist you tonight."

And, damn, do I want to be laid to ruin.

"Mmmm." The sound that rumbles through Gage's chest is so deep and guttural that I can't tell if it's a growl or a moan, and it sends arousal pooling between my legs.

"I want you so badly right now I can't think straight." His eyes burn into mine as I watch his internal struggle. It takes a few minutes, but he slowly gets a hold of himself.

"But I'm not going to get ahead of myself. The world deserves to see you in this dress, and I'm going to watch you bring them to their knees until I get to rip it off of you. I'm going to watch your perfect red lips as you talk, smile, and laugh—until I get to kiss the color off of them. And I'm going to appreciate the way those heels make your gorgeous legs, and that perfect ass of yours look until I have them dangling over my shoulders."

The waves of devotion rolling off him beat against me until I'm breathless and practically clinging to him. If he keeps talking like this, we won't be making it out of this apartment for the next several days. "You have such a way with words."

"I can't wait to have my way with *you*." He lets his hands drop from my face like it'll give him a contact high. "*Jesus*. Come on, Gorgeous, if we don't leave now I might decide to chain you up and keep you locked away all for myself."

The drive across town is filled with heated looks and deep conversation. Gage's hand remains firmly on my thigh, his thumb tracing mindless shapes through the delicate fabric of my dress. When he pulls up to what looks like a nondescript utility building, I can't help but be intrigued.

Gage parks and climbs out of the car before rounding to open my door for me. I accept his offered hand and allow him to help me out of the vehicle. When he just can't help himself, he presses a hot kiss to my jaw, his arms wrapping around me. His hands slide from my waist to grab greedy handfuls of my ass.

"You are unreal," he murmurs. "But don't try to seduce me because I'm not bailing on our date."

"God, you're making me so wet right now." There's a breathiness to my voice that has his heated eyes flaring.

"Maybe now isn't the right time to mention I'm not wearing any panties."

"You're nothing but trouble," Gage grates, his voice rough with desire. I smooth my hands down his dress shirt, appreciating the chiseled muscles of his chest.

"You're going to make us late," I remind him, making a growl of frustration resonate in his chest. "And don't act like you don't like it."

Taking him by the hand, I let him lead me into the building.

"What's with this place?" I look around the concrete room the size of a basketball court. Large paper targets line the far back wall, outlined by the silhouette of a person. Gage's hand on my back leads me to one of the booths at the edge of the room opposite the targets.

"It's a shooting range," Gage states like it's obvious because it is obvious.

"I know it's a shooting range," I deadpan. "Why did you bring me here?"

Reaching into the duffle bag that's waiting in one of the booths, he pulls out a handgun. I stare at the weapon as he pulls back the slide to check if there's a round in the chamber. "I'm teaching you how to handle a gun." Walking closer, he places the gun in my hand. I look up at him, intrigued. It's heavy in my hand, made of metal and deadly force.

"You want me to shoot a gun dressed like this?" I ask, cocking a hip to accentuate my figure.

"I've seen what you can do while wearing heels." Gage bites his bottom lip and shakes his head slowly. "I didn't think you could possibly look any better, but the sight of you holding a gun is the sexiest thing I've ever seen."

The shower of praise coming from him tonight already

has me soaked through, and I won't make it another ten seconds if we don't shift gears. I know he can see the change in my demeanor when my eyes narrow at him ever so slightly.

"Are you sure it's a good idea to hand me a loaded gun when you're within shooting range? I thought your instincts were better than that," I say, flashing Gage a flirty smile. The metal of the gun feels so heavy with power against my palm.

"We both know you'll never pull that trigger on me," he replies smugly, his smoldering eyes holding mine.

"You willing to bet your life on that?" I'm only half teasing, and his eyes cut to mine. He regards me for a moment, letting his gaze wander down my body like he has a million times already tonight.

"I don't mind being shot if you're the one pulling the trigger."

"I'll have to remember that." This isn't the first time I've held a gun, but so far, it's my favorite. And I'll admit, those other times, I was only talking a big game. I never actually intended to fire.

"When you shoot, shoot to kill," he says, his large hands guiding my arms into position. "Always assume the gun is loaded. Aim for the head or the heart. A bullet through the brain is the only sure shot. But there are plenty of places to shoot if you want them to suffer."

Strong fingers position my hands on the weapon's grip, his inked hands closing over mine. My skin heats beneath his touch like tiny sparks of electricity. "Keep your finger off the trigger until you're ready to shoot. And always know if your safety is on or off." Tilting the gun, I can see a small switch on the side just under the slide that's labeled *safety*.

The red dot is visible, showing that the weapon is ready to shoot.

"Is it hard to pull the trigger?"

I've never had to pull the trigger, I can't help but wonder how it feels.

"Not hard, but you have to be firm. When you pull the trigger, the gun will push against your hands. Be cautious of the kickback and keep your grip steady."

"Easy." I take his notes, applying the instructions.

"Now take a deep breath," The air in our lungs rushes out in unison. "I'll step back. You aim and shoot the target until you run out of bullets. You want kill shots."

"Ok." I nod against him. With that, he's pulling away from me and takes several steps back to give me room. As he directed, I keep my finger away from the trigger until I've aimed and I'm ready to shoot. Pulling the trigger, a wave of energy trickles down my spine. My grip braces against the kickback, holding the weapon almost steady.

"Damn," I marvel, looking at the weapon in my hands. There's so much freedom in the power this deadly weapon gives me, a hit of dopamine second only to the feeling of a blade. Chasing that feeling, I pull the trigger again in quick succession-—as fast as I can while still taking the time to aim. *The head or the heart.* I feel so unstoppable as the bullets explode from the chamber to pierce my target. The kick of the gun, the solid weight of the metal in my hands, gives me a sense of confidence and control I've only ever felt when taking a life with my bare hands.

Here, in this moment, I'm invincible.

Metal chinks when I reach the end of the magazine, having shot the last loaded bullet. Damn, this is exhilarating. I flip the switch on the side of the booth, and the pulley system has my target racing towards me. Inspecting it, I count the holes in the paper.

"How many bullets were in here?" I ask, turning the pistol over in my hand to get a better look at it. The grip gives no indication of how much ammunition it can hold.

"That one holds seventeen rounds," Gage says behind me.

"Eight out of seventeen isn't bad. I even shot the brain and the heart a few times," I say, pointing to where the ammunition tore through the paper. Three kill shots, as Gage calls them. Two in the head, one in the heart. "I can do better. Got any more of these?" Waving the gun, my eyes search for Gage.

He's standing not two feet behind me, his gaze fixed intensely on me with a passionate expression. The man is searing a hole right through me, turning my insides into molten lava.

"What?" I ask.

"What do you feel right now?"

Pausing for a few seconds, I take stock of what's going on inside me. What *am* I feeling right now?

"I feel..." A smile slowly spreads across my face. "Alive."

He's watching me, those unrelenting eyes of his soaking in my every reaction. Holding out his hand, I place the gun in his palm. His fingers brush against mine, lingering longer than necessary before pulling away.

With the press of a button, the magazine ejects, and he pulls it from the handle. He crouches down to drop the empty clip into the duffle and replace it with a full one. Raising back to his full height, he slams the magazine back into place and chambers a round with a resounding *chink*.

Replacing the target and sending it flying back into place on the far back wall with the others, he steps forward to wrap his arms around me again. "Let's work on your aim, little devil."

The second part of our date is a romantic dinner at *Taste*, one of the best restaurants in the city. When I asked Gage how he managed to get a reservation, he simply smirked and told me he worked some magic because I'm worth it.

Following the hostess through the restaurant to our table with Gage at my side, I can feel the other diners' eyes on us. True to his word, Gage found a way to show me off in this dress, and I've never felt hotter. Having a tall tattoo-god dressed to the nines on my arm completes the look. We're one ridiculously beautiful couple, especially tonight.

Our table is intimately set for two, with a vase of long-stem red roses that are noticeably not on any other table. Gage pulls out my chair before taking his seat across from me. I look at him, surprised when a server shows up out of thin air to place a dirty martini on the table in front of me. Gage simply flashes me a wink that has my stomach doing backflips.

When the server returns to our table, Gage orders for the both of us—a lobster tail and champagne for me, and filet mignon and a vintage cognac for himself. Watching him take charge is so unbelievably attractive. If I were wearing panties, they'd be drenched. Everything this man does is ridiculously attractive, and he looks damn good doing it.

How did I get so lucky? This man showed up in my life unannounced and stole my heart without contest. I'm not sure what I did to be so blessed for a man like Gage to have found me.

"Something's on your mind," Gage observes. "Tell me what it is." I cross my legs under the table, running the side of my foot up and down his leg absentmindedly.

"I want to know how."

"How?" Gage repeats, confused.

"How you knew I was the one you wanted," I clarify. I've never questioned the why—because it's always been so obvious why Gage and I are meant to be. But how Gage was able to find me is something I haven't been able to figure out.

Gage meets my eyes, his passionate gaze holding mine. Something tells me I'll never get used to the depth of our connection.

"The moment I laid eyes on you, it was undeniable. You're mine."

"Where did you first see me?"

"Helix."

It takes a second, but the memory clicks of the night he's talking about.

"You were dancing in a tight little dress," he continues. "I couldn't take my eyes off of you. Then you turned around, and I saw the fire blazing in those breathtaking eyes of yours. Suddenly, everything in my life made sense. Every decision in my life had led me to that moment in that club. To find you." I hold his gaze for a moment, letting his words sink in as I flirt with my eyes.

"It wasn't like that for me," I say, lifting my glass to take a sip of my martini. The balance of the cocktail is impeccable. "The first time I saw you I wanted to fuck you, then I wanted to kill you. In that order."

Gage tilts his head back and laughs at that. "With you, that sounds like a good time."

"Hmmm, play your cards right, and maybe you'll get

lucky," I tease. He looks at me for a moment, the humor in his expression melting into passion.

"You know now," Gage states. "This is real."

The *this* he's referring to is us.

"Without a doubt in my mind," I confirm, lighting a fire in his eyes.

When our meals arrive, we enjoy our food with heated glances and minimal conversation. The mood has shifted, and both of us are determined to end our dinner quickly so we can finish our night at home. As soon as the dessert plates are cleared, Gage offers me his hand and ushers me to the valet, where our car is waiting.

When we enter Gage's house, all taunting and teasing is done—leaving nothing but passion, desire, and adoration. And for the first time since I've met Gage, his touch is gentle as he carries me to his bedroom and makes tender love to me. With the soft praise and reverence he handles me with, there's only one word to describe it.

Worship.

CHAPTER TWENTY-SIX

JILL

Waking up deliciously sore, blissfully happy, and in Gage's strong arms is like nothing I've ever experienced before. This feeling—the soul-deep sense of acceptance and belonging—is so foreign to me. I've never woken up feeling simply grateful and undeniably happy like this before. And looking at the sleeping man responsible fills me with so much love I can't contain it.

I need to mark him.

Rolling over gently, careful not to jostle the bed and disturb Gage, I snag the lipstick out of my purse on the nightstand and turn back to face him. Swiping the color across my mouth, I lean down to press my lips against the inked skin. Looking down at my handiwork, I take in the crimson kiss. Hmm, I really like seeing my mark on Gage's chiseled abdomen. So I lean down to do it again. And again.

Gage's abs tense and ripple under my lips as my mouth travels across his skin—kissing, marking, and licking. I can feel him wake up against me before his eyes open. Reapplying the lipstick, I don't stop my exploration. Gage remains completely still beneath me, but I can sense his gaze when he finally opens his eyes.

"Don't move," I murmur between kisses. "This is going to take a while."

"Take your time." His deep voice rumbles in his chest, rough with sleep. God, he sounds like the devil himself. It makes my heart skip a beat.

"I'm going to need another tube of this color," I say, reapplying for the fifth time. At this rate, I'll be halfway through the tube of lipstick by the time I reach his neck. I pull back and crawl up to press a kiss to his throat, making a growl vibrate through him.

"I'll buy you a whole case," he promises as I pick up one of his hands and kiss the center of his palm to leave the perfect lip print. Then I lift his other hand to do the same. My eyes lock with his as my lips travel up his arm. He watches me through half-lidded eyes, his muscles flexing beneath me.

A buzzing sound next to the bed pulls my focus to the nightstand as Gage's phone vibrates with a phone call. Looking back at Gage, I'm not surprised that he's completely ignoring it. If it's important, they'll call back. And until then, I have his undivided attention.

When the phone goes silent, I lean up to kiss Gage's lips. His mouth drinks me in eagerly, his hands gripping my face like he'll never let me go. The feeling of true belonging —heavy and sweet—settles inside me. Just when he's about to deepen the kiss, the insistent buzzing begins again, making Gage tense beneath me in irritation. But he still doesn't reach for the phone before it stills. When the device starts to vibrate with a third call, I can feel that our quiet morning together is over.

Pulling back from him, I press one last lingering kiss on

his lips. My eyes connect with his to communicate so many feelings before I sit up. Gage's expression is more than irritated when he reaches over to his nightstand to grab the phone. Answering the call, he presses it to his ear.

"What?" he bites the vicious greeting at the person interrupting our peace. He listens to the person on the other line, his eyes averting from me to stare at the ceiling as he pinches the bridge of his nose. "How much did they deliver?"

There's a brief silence as he listens.

"That's not going to cover the first hour. Where's the rest of it? They better have two more trucks on the way right fucking now." He pauses to listen, his expression darkening. "Fine, I'm on my way. With what they're pulling me away from, they better prepare themselves for what's coming for them." His eyes move back to look at me, his eyes longing against his harsh expression.

With a few more short words, he tensely ends the call and drops the phone onto the bed in irritation. When he looks at me, disappointment wars with his anger.

"I have to go to the club. Most of the alcohol for tomorrow's event wasn't delivered, and I have to make a few heads roll."

"I love it when you talk business," I hum. "We should get you cleaned up."

"No, I'm going to wear your marks until I get to have you again." Gage stands from the bed, naked and glorious, and moves to the dresser to pull out some clean clothes to wear. Leaning back against the headboard, I admire how the tattoos on his muscled thighs and firm ass dance and ripple as he pulls on a pair of boxers.

"Well, you're gonna be wearing them for a while because I work tonight."

I take the opportunity to take in every inch of his gorgeous body covered in my marks, happiness buzzing inside my head. By the time Gage pulls a t-shirt over his head, I feel like I could float right off the bed. I bite my lip in appreciation when he turns back to look at me.

"Good thing you know the boss." With three large steps, he's beside the bed.

"Mmmm, I do know him very well," I say, looking up at him through my lashes. Placing one knee on the mattress, he hovers over me as he takes in my body that's naked down to the sheet pooled at my waist. He shakes his head like he can't fathom that I'm actually real, and it lights me up like a Christmas tree.

"I'd say you have him wrapped around your finger." He pulls me in for a steamy kiss. "I want you to stay in my bed just like this for as long as you possibly can."

"And if I get hungry? Am I supposed to cook naked too?"

"I like the sound of that." My expression turns skeptical, and he relents easily. He doesn't want me cooking naked unless he's here to enjoy it in person with me. "I'll have food delivered for you. You can wear a robe when you accept the delivery, but as soon as that door is closed, I want you back just like this."

"You're very bossy."

"You have no idea."

CHAPTER TWENTY-SEVEN

GAGE

The buzz of the tattoo machine thrums through me like a second heartbeat as the ink pierces my skin until it's permanently stained. My eyes focus sharply on all of the little details as I maneuver the needle across my own flesh. Some of the artwork on my body has been created by other talented tattoo artists, but this one is too important. I'm not trusting this one with anyone else, I'm the only one who can do it right.

The deep red ink is the perfect shade—one I spent over an hour crafting, mixing, and perfecting. Out of all the ink covering my body, this is the most meaningful.

The most special.

I can't claim credit for this work of artistry. I was blessed with this perfection, but I intend to preserve it and I refuse to fuck it up.

Every minute I spend with Jill, the urge to tell her the truth grows stronger, but I know she's not ready yet. Once I know I have her, really and fully, to the point of no return— then I can tell her. But until then, I'm not saying fucking a word. It's not a risk I'm willing to take, not when it comes to Jill.

She won't take it easy, that I'm sure of. No matter when or how I tell her, I'm going to feel her wrath. But I'm not going to lose her because of her weasel of a brother. The cops never found a body, just like I knew they wouldn't. They never will. And as painful as it is, Jill is slowly starting to accept the reality of the situation.

She'll never see Tommy again.

Her life has improved so much since he's been out of her life, whether she's recognized it or not. No more late-night phone calls pleading for money for 'just one more game', no more bookies threatening her with violence when a debt hasn't been paid. No more creeps grabbing at her when Tommy shows up to her apartment blackout drunk with some of his gambling buddies.

I know I technically still own her through Tommy's debt. But I stopped taking her money a long time ago. In fact, there's a bank account with three hundred and twenty-five thousand dollars in it with her name on it. She hasn't noticed yet, and I'm not in a hurry to tell her. I'm a selfish bastard who likes when she shows up for her shifts where I can be close to her.

A *ding* sounds across my office as my computer screen lights up. The motion-activated camera in my kitchen detected movement, the feed showing me a look into my house. Jill's wearing an oversized sweatshirt that falls off one shoulder and reaches her mid-thigh, and she's standing in my kitchen with the food delivery.

After leaving Jill at my house this morning, I spent the next several hours tracking down the missing alcohol shipment. I might have had to threaten a few lives and blackmail one of my suppliers, but the missing liquor was secured—and then some. Dealing with those asshats, knowing Jill was lying naked in my bed, made me extra brutal.

Pausing my work, I stand and walk over to the desk for a better look. Leaning forward to brace myself on the wooden surface, my hand lands on a metallic piece of jewelry. Picking it up, the weight of it in my palm feels heavy with meaning—a symbol of my devotion to the woman I would do anything for. It's satisfying. My fingers absentmindedly toy with the charm hanging from the chain as I refocus on the stunning woman in my kitchen.

I watch as she unpacks the meal I ordered from one of her favorite places—some soft pretzel bites, a Santa Fe salad with blackened salmon, a large order of french fries with extra house ranch dressing, and a chocolate lava cake. The smile on her face with each container fuels me, and I can't help but smile too.

She goes for the french fries first, just like I knew she would. My eyes track how she dips the fry into the ranch generously and pops the entire thing into her mouth. I could watch her all day, just like this.

Except...

Reaching into my back pocket, I pull out my phone and type out a quick text.

> Take it off, baby.

Jill's phone vibrates on the counter next to her, and she leans over to read it. She rolls her eyes, expression turning sassy as she moves to pull the sweatshirt off and dramatically drops it on the floor. Standing gloriously naked in my kitchen, she lifts both of her hands in the air with her middle fingers raised to flip me off.

I chuckle deepl, arousal rippling through me, as I walk back over to my station. Picking up the tattoo gun, I finish inking my skin to the view of the curvy angel eating in my kitchen. But watching only lasts for so long.

> Pick it up off the floor.

> Slowly.

Jill reads my messages, shaking her head. But I can see her biting back a smile as she types her response.

Menace:

> Bossy

Tossing her phone down on the counter, she turns away from the camera. Bending at the waist to stick her big sexy ass in the air, she slowly reaches down to grab the sweat-shirt off the floor. When she rises back up, she gives her ass a shake that shoots straight to my cock, and tosses her hair back sensually.

Holy shit.

I need to get this tattoo done so I can be with her. Four hours is too long away from her.

The buzzing of the machine echoes through the room as I work to finish the tattoo, fueled by my newfound motivation.

Walking up behind her, my hands greet her first, then my lips. Wrapping my arms around her lush figure, my lips press to the side of her neck. Jill's head tilts to the side to allow me better access, a soft sigh escaping her as I taste her sweet skin.

"I brought you something." I place the box on the counter in front of her. Jill reaches for the box while I feast on her.

"I'm supposed to be working." There's not an ounce of conviction in Jill's voice, making me grin against her neck.

"You're on a break," I inform her. She lifts the top off the box to reveal the jewelry inside. A short gold chain that matches one of her favorite necklaces sits inside with the gold letter L hanging in the center.

"Is this an anklet?" she asks. "With the letter L."

"For Lawless," I reply, trailing my nose up to whisper in her ear. "I needed a way to get my other initial on your body. This way, I can have it dangling over my shoulders tonight."

"Wait, what is that?" Jill asks, feeling the clear bandage covering the fresh tattoo on my palm. She lifts my hand and flips it over to see her lips permanently branded on my skin in her signature crimson color. The color match to her lipstick is impeccable, if I do say so myself.

"Is that—? Did you—?" She asks, looking up at me. "Did you really?"

"Abso-fucking-lutely. It's a work of art that I want on my skin forever," I reply. "Besides, it's only fair." She looks down at the tattoo again, gently tracing over it with her finger.

"You think this makes us even?" she smarts, making me bite back a grin. I love her defiance. "Those lips could belong to anyone. It's not like it's my initials."

She has no idea.

Taking my hand from hers, I cup her face in my palms.

"I'll tattoo 'property of Jillian Hart' across my forehead right now. Just say the word."

"You would not," she argues.

"Try me." I'm dead serious, and once she sees that, her expression softens. She only gets sweet with me, I fucking like it.

"Don't do that. I like your forehead the way it is."

"Do you?" I murmur. She nods against my hands.

"Yes, it's a very nice forehead," she says, an amused smile tugging at her lips. "Plus, imagine the hassle of having to fix the tattoo when my name changes to Lawless." Her words have my grip on her face tightening possessively, making her grin. This radiant smile of hers could sustain me for the rest of my life, and I'm determined to keep it there for the rest of hers.

"I like the sound of that," I inform her, stating the obvious.

"I'm warming to the idea." She leans up to kiss me, our lips moving together sensually before she pulls away. She gazes up at me for another minute, and I can see the moment she realizes where we are. "My break's over. Now go away so I can focus."

With one last kiss, I leave her to do her work. On my walk back to my office, there's a swagger to my steps that has me feeling like a giddy schoolboy who got to hold hands with his crush at recess. Only this is a million times better. Jill is letting me in, letting me see every part of her.

I never expected it to be easy. Up until now, men have been nothing but disappointments in her life. But I'm nothing like her abusive ex, pathetic excuse of a father, or her leech of a brother. Jill is mine to protect, to care for, and baby. She just needs to realize it.

For months, I planned and fantasized about how I would win her over once I got the chance. And now that it's working, I have no intention of stopping.

CHAPTER TWENTY-EIGHT

JILL

"Come with me tonight, the game's gonna last until tomorrow. I don't like being away from you that long." Gage steers the car with one hand, the other resting on my upper thigh as he drives us across town towards the Halfway House. His thumb traces mindless circles in my skin, sending tingles between my legs.

We're meeting up with a few of Gage's friends at the bar, and he's already spent the entire drive trying to convince me to ditch my plans for tonight to join him at The Raven for a big poker game. But I'm not having any of it.

"I have plans with Lana. I'll be sleeping over at her place tonight," I remind him.

"You really need another girl's night?" he counters. I flash him a look of disapproval.

"I've been having these girls' nights for a long time. Don't think I'll start ditching Lana for you just because we're together. I'm not one of those girls who forgets about her friends for some guy."

"I'm not *some guy*, little devil. I'm yours." His grip on my leg tightens, his fingers digging into the ample flesh as his fingertip press closer to my wet pussy. "And you're mine."

"Are you gonna hit me over the head with your club and drag me back to your cave next?" I ask flatly, unamused.

"You want my club? I'd like to pound you into submission, and I know just how good your head is." Turning into the parking lot, he uses one hand on the wheel to whip into a spot. It's fucking hot.

"I'm going to strangle you." Irritation mixes with the desire swirling through me.

"Oh yeah?" He grins at me like the devil. "What else?"

I lean closer to him, stopping over the center console. Crooking my finger, I gesture for him to come closer. "Come here," I murmur. Gage obeys without hesitation, stopping less than an inch from me. I cup his face in my hands and pull him closer until his lips are just barely brushing mine, his facial hair tickling my chin.

"You piss me off," I say softly, my eyes flickering to his lips.

"You turn me on." He matches the softness of my tone, his eyes gazing at me deeply.

"We're going inside the bar now, and I want you on your best behavior." His brows jump, his expression darkening. "Pretty please."

"Since you asked so nicely." He pushes closer to press a soft kiss on my lips. Pulling back, his gaze touches every inch of my face tenderly. "I'm obsessed with you."

"You're going to give me space to socialize," I state expectantly. "Right?" The edges of Gage's face sharpen, his tender gaze on me turning intense. Predatory.

A thrill runs through me like a hit of dopamine, it's intoxicating.

"Don't forget who you're talking to, Menace. If I can't have my hands on you, there's no escaping my eyes." He stares at me for a long moment, watching my defiance war with my attraction. "Let's get inside before I turn this car around and take you back home."

The Halfway House is fairly busy for a Tuesday afternoon. Chained Saints and locals mingle at the bar and around the pool tables. Rock music plays from the old jukebox in the corner. When Gage and I enter, there's a chorus of greetings, mainly for Gage.

Stevie stands with two other women on the other end of the bar. I recognize them from the barbeque—Alexis and Ruby. Stevie's smiling and waving me over as soon as she catches my eye. Moving to peel myself away from Gage's side, I don't make it more than two steps before he catches me by the belt loop and tows me back in. When I turn around to face him, his hands wrap around me to plant firmly on my ass.

"So quick to run away from me," he murmurs teasingly with a smirk.

"Best behavior, remember?"

My tone is casual, but my eyes dare him to misbehave. His smirk grows into a grin.

"I'll let you go socialize," he promises. "But not before this." He leans down to kiss me soundly, our lips dancing in a passionate give and take. This kiss is more than a display of affection. It's public branding—though I'm not sure of whom, him or me.

His tongue slips in to taste mine, making me moan softly.

Definitely both.

Not trusting him to end it before we go further, I pull back. My teeth catch his bottom lip, giving it a sharp tug that pulls a shuttered breath from his chest. When I look up at him, I can feel every set of eyes in the bar on us. On me.

It's thrilling.

"Go spend some quality time with your brother." I tilt my head to the left at a table where Rio sits with Orion, Saint, and another Chained Saints member named Gunner.

"I'll be watching you, little devil."

"Aren't you always?" With that, I'm slipping out of his grasp and strutting away. Approaching the trio of girls at the bar, Stevie waves over the bartender when she sees me coming.

"Hi!" She greets me with an excited hug. "Can I get you anything? A martini? A cold shower?" I can't help but laugh, glancing over my shoulder to where Gage has taken a seat next to his brother against the wall, his eyes trained on me as he accepts a beer from Orion. I don't let our eyes connect, knowing I'll be sucked into our connection.

"He's pretty intense," I say, biting back a smile as I turn back to the girls. I address the bartender. "I'll take a bloody mary."

"You both are," Stevie comments with a knowing smile. The bartender hands me my drink, and I can't help but notice that he refuses to look me in the eye. But his glance over my shoulder tells me why. I refrain from the urge to roll my eyes, refusing to look back at the man I know is still craving my attention. He doesn't get what he wants, not right now.

"So what are we talking about, ladies?" I ask, taking a sip of my drink.

"Ruby was telling us what she heard from one of her

clients today," Alexis says. Ruby is a hair stylist, a job that lets her hear all the hot gossip.

"Her sister's husband was having an affair with their mom. She just had twins, and she found them in bed together after coming home from visiting the babies in the NICU."

"That's crazy," I say, taking another sip.

"He'd be a dead man walking. I swear," Alexis states.

"Both of them would be." I think about the level of betrayal. If someone took advantage of me and broke my trust like that, I'd peel their skin off like an apple and feed it to them. "I don't think they'd ever walk out of that room again."

"Tell me about it," Ruby agrees. "And get this—the husband and the mom moved in together after the wife left. They claim they're in love, and now the mom insists on co-parenting with her and the ex-husband."

"Grandma thinks she's gonna be the step-mom to those babies?" Stevie asks, taken aback.

"Over my dead body," I state. Ruby nods in agreement.

"Exactly what she said. She's fighting for sole custody, and I'm ready to start a lawyers fund to help her with the legal fees."

"Count me in. Where do I send my check?" Alexis comments.

"Why go through all that trouble? We know people who have ways of dealing with worms like that. Nice and quiet." Stevie's eyes look pointedly at the table in the back corner where Gage and his friends sit. They're a ruthless group, each one of them dangerous in their own right.

"I hinted at that," Ruby says with a shrug, taking a swig of her beer. "She says she'll see how the court hearing goes first. But I gave her my personal cell number just in case."

My body perks up, and I can sense Gage's energy behind me. Out of the corner of my eye, I notice the group he was sitting with passing behind us. They move towards the back door that leads to the Saints' clubhouse. As he passes, Gage leans in close to me, brushing up against my back— his hands skimming the sliver of exposed skin on my back above my jeans. My body comes alive with that simple touch, my heart skipping a beat as butterflies flutter in my stomach.

As fast as it happens, it's over. He moves past me, following the group out the door. Leaning against the bar, I watch as he walks away. Before he disappears out the door, he turns to meet my eyes. The wink he flashes me has warmth spreading through me like wildfire.

True to his word, Gage keeps his distance while I chat with the girls and make my rounds with Stevie. He's only out in the clubhouse for twenty minutes before he's back inside to meet Anders when he comes striding in. After they greet each other and grab some drinks, the two of them settle themselves against the back wall to chat.

My shadow's eyes follow me for the rest of the afternoon, watching my every move as I talk, smile, and laugh. His attention hums over my skin, fuelling my soul. Before too long, I'm being drawn back to him with our magnetic connection.

CHAPTER TWENTY-NINE

JILL

Making eyes at Gage as I saunter past him, he follows me to the back of the bar room—like a moth to a flame. Walking through the doorway, we enter the empty pool room. The rowdiness from the group at the bar fades into the background now that it's only the two of us back here.

"You wanna play a game?" I ask over my shoulder as I approach the table.

"Something tells me we already are." Gage snags my hand to turn me around. I don't bother to bite back my devious smile as I look up at him through my lashes.

"Billiards," I state, my tone chiding him for assuming otherwise.

"Hmm," Gage's voice hums deep in his chest as he gazes down at me. His fingertips gently brush a tendril of hair from my face before his strong hand cups my cheek. "You play pool?"

"Like you don't already know," I tease, but he simply tilts his head with an expression that insists he's not sure what I'm referring to. We both know better, but I play along. "I play a little."

A little is an understatement. I've been playing pool since I was tall enough to reach over the table. My dad basically lived on barstools growing up, and my mom worked nights, so I was practically raised in dive bars like this. Tommy taught me how to play pool to pass the time.

"I'm not going to let you win," Gage says arrogantly with a smirk. I bite back my own smile and maintain my innocence—I'm sure he can see straight through me.

"You better not." I lean up to press a soft kiss on his lips. "It'll feel so much better when I do it myself." Pulling away from him, I turn to start racking up the billiards.

I've never considered playing pool a sexual experience until I played with Gage. Watching the man lean forward to line up a shot is hypnotic, with his gorgeous arms flexing, and every ball he sinks into a pocket is like an aphrodisiac. I can feel his ravenous eyes on me every time I bend down to do the same. Our banter is a mix of trash talk and flirting until the air around us remains charged.

I play it cool for the first few shots, keeping my hits simple and even throwing a few so he doesn't realize exactly what I'm capable of. But that only lasts so long until my competitive nature takes over.

"I never figured you for the kind of girl who would play dumb to appear weaker to a man. It's beneath you," he comments. I drop the pool stick with one hand to flip him off, making him throw his head back and laugh. Still grinning, he saunters towards me.

"Duh-dun, Duh-dun," Gage starts singing the *Jaws* theme song under his breath as he walks around the table behind me while I bounce my cue ball off the side and sink two balls with one shot. "Duh-dun."

"I'm not a pool shark," I argue, biting back a smile, but it's pointless. "You're just not as good as you thought you were. That's not my problem." Lining up my next shot, I take out another two balls. At this rate, I'll win in the next three shots.

"Oh, I'm good," Gage counters. "I just don't pretend I'm bad to mess with people's heads."

"Fuck you," I mutter, leaning forward to cue up the ball. Only I don't make it very far before a muscled arm is yanking me around, and a body is pressing to mine until my ass hits the pool table.

"You wanna try that again?" Gage asks deeply, getting in my face to check my attitude. His dominance is so fucking hot—it makes my pussy throb and my heart flutter.

"I love you." My tone pretends like it's what I said in the first place, but the words have his expression sharpening. When I move to turn back to the game, one of his hands grips my jaw to halt my movements and force my eyes back to his.

"Don't fucking play with those words, Menace. If you don't mean them, don't say them." His voice rumbles with conviction, making my humor drop as I really look at him. That's when I see it—an image in the ink on his chest.

"Is that my switchblade?" My fingers tug at the neckline of his shirt to get a better look. I've seen a lot of tattoos, and it could be any knife. But it's not, I'd recognize my blade anywhere. There aren't any coincidences with Gage. The tattoo is hidden amongst all of his others, and it makes me wonder. Are there more?

Gage allows me to tug at him—pulling his shirt down, and lifting both of his arms to search the sleeves of ink covering them. That's when my gaze catches on a pair of pretty eyes inked on the inside of his forearm. They're green and feminine.

And mine.

He has my eyes tattooed on his body?

One glance up at his face confirms it, his gaze on me never wavering in its intensity.

"Take off your shirt," I demand, pulling at the fabric in my way.

There have to be more.

Gage obeys without hesitation, lifting the shirt over his head and tossing it on the pool table behind me, leaving his magnificent chest bare. His rippling muscles jump beneath my hands as I trace over the images painted on his skin in search of anything else recognizable.

And I find them.

Black cherries, a red lipstick, a pinup devil that looks exactly like me—The more I look, the more I see pieces of myself woven into his tattoos. My favorite things and little pieces of my personality intertwined with his.

"Are there more?" I ask, my eyes trailing down to where his ink disappears beneath the waistband of his pants, before my gaze clashes with his. He nods. "Why?"

"I needed you with me." His words have every muscle in my body stilling with realization. His hand reaches up to cup my face, caressing it sweetly before lowering to tow me in by my jaw.

"You love me, don't you?" The unspoken truth calms my restless soul as the question leaves my mouth. My eyes gaze into his, searching for confirmation. What I find is so much deeper, it rocks me to my core.

"Love you? From the second I laid eyes on you, there has been an itching in my veins that only the sight of you can ease. Without you, the world has no art, and I have no purpose." I swallow hard against his hand, the breath halting in my chest as his words seep into my bones. "I don't just love you, Jill. I worship you. I bleed you. I *am* for you."

My eyelashes flutter slightly as this revelation washes over me, taking a moment to revel in the feeling of complete and pure devotion. The sensations touching every nerve in my body are like nothing I've ever felt before.

His thumb strokes my jaw against his tight hold on me, his all-seeing eyes unrelenting on mine. He's not letting this moment go until he's sure I believe him, that I know the truth. And I do. There's no denying something so certain.

"I love you, Gage," I state, my eyes telling him just how much I mean it. "I don't exist without you to see me."

There's a moment of silence between us, the world going still. Gage stares down at me like I've given him the answers to the mysteries of the universe. His eyes look into mine so deeply that I'm positive he can see his own soul intertwined with mine. Several seconds pass, the tension between us growing so thick it's almost palpable. As we stand here, just gazing into each other's eyes, our bodies slowly draw closer and closer with our irresistible magnetism.

Until the dam breaks and our mouths desperately clash.

This kiss is a tornado, a reckless give and take as we devour each other with all of our passion pouring into our connection. I don't know how I ended up on the pool table, but I'm suddenly seated on the edge of it with Gage's body between my thighs, his unforgiving lips never leaving mine for even a breath. With his arms wrapped around me, his hands on my back slide lower until they're pushing under the waistband of my jeans on my ass. One of my arms snakes around his neck to anchor him impossibly close while the other holds his face to mine.

"Gage, we have to go—" Anders' booming voice cuts off abruptly with a muttered, "Oh shit."

"Hey boss, don't shoot the messenger, but tweedle-dumbass locked the keys in the shop last night. So we're gonna need your spares." I briefly register Stevie's voice as my mouth moves against Gage's. His arms lock around me, hands palming my ass, and unrelenting lips tell me he has no intention of separating from me, no matter who's watching.

Until the third voice sounds in the doorway.

"Hey, no sex on the pool table! We just had it re-felted after the last time." Gage pulls away from me more than reluctantly, turning a murderous glare on the three people keeping him from me. Anders, Stevie, and Rio stand in the doorway of the pool room, each with a different expression.

Anders is looking at us as if there's nothing to see—like he didn't interrupt us almost fucking on the pool table. Stevie looks guilty, her eyes full of apology as she looks between me and her boss. Rio's knowing smirk couldn't look more like Gage's if he tried.

"All of you, get the fuck out of here before I pull my gun." The threat edging Gage's tone could inflict serious physical damage.

"Sorry, not gonna happen. We have about half a billion dollars in the form of douchebags wearing boat shoes waiting for us at The Raven right now. That's not money we're walking away from. You two can mess around later," Anders states, holding his ground.

"And I have a client coming from out of state who expects to be in my chair in the next forty-five minutes, so I'm gonna need those keys." Stevie's eyes apologize as she shrugs. Jaw clenched tightly, Gage stares down the three people who intruded on our moment like he's considering cutting his losses and taking them all out by a bullet to the head. Placing a hand on his cheek, I turn Gage's head to look at me in an attempt to deter any bloodshed.

"There are very few people I actually like, and those are three of them. You're not going to kill them," I say, making Gage's eyes narrow on me slightly. "I'm going with Stevie to get the keys from the club. You're going to your poker night. And when you come home to me tomorrow morning, you're going to fuck me on the pile of money you took from those preppy asshats."

Gage lets out a harsh breath that sounds dangerously like a growl. He pulls me in until my chest is pressed against his, and I'm gazing up at him through my lashes.

"Tell me again," he demands, and I know exactly what he means.

"What, that you're going to fuck me?" I ask, playing dumb, a mischievous smile tugging at my lips.

"Jill." My name is a warning, making me grin.

"I love you, Gage Lawless. I didn't know I could ever be this in love with someone." I let the humor fall from my face to let him see my sincerity. Leaning up, I kiss him deeply, letting our passion linger for a moment before pulling back. "I love you. Now go."

Releasing his face, I press my hands against his chest until he takes a step back, large enough for me to get off the pool table. My body slides down his as I lower to the floor, plush curves against solid muscles. Dark eyes pin me where I stand like they never intend to look away.

"When I get home, you better be in my bed ready for me. Because there won't be any negotiating, and I don't plan on being gentle with you."

"I love it when you talk dirty to me." I give him a smile full of promiscuous promises. With that, I'm pulling out of his embrace and turning to address the pink-haired woman across the room. "I hope you brought your car because I just came with Gage."

"We hadn't gotten that far yet, but we will soon," Gage says deeply behind me, making Rio and Anders laugh. I roll my eyes at Stevie, who gives me a smile that laughs at the men, not with them.

"I can drive us." Turning to follow me through the doorway, we walk out of the bar.

CHAPTER THIRTY

JILL

"You know," Stevie says, pressing on the clutch to shift the gears of her Mini Cooper—a cute little yellow car that feels like we're riding around in a ray of sunshine. It suits her perfectly. "I never really thought much about the idea of soulmates or whatever. And it literally never occurred to me that there was a woman in this world who could match Gage, edge for edge. But then you strutted into the shop, and it made me question everything. You guys are like a matching set."

I smile at the thought, picturing just how well Gage fits with me. In every sense. Leaning back against the headrest, I tilt my head to look over her. "I felt the same way. It's kind of crazy how that works, isn't it?"

"Seriously. If you weren't such a ridiculously hot couple, it'd be creepy." She flashes me a smile as I breathe out a laugh.

I instruct Stevie to park in the spot reserved for Gage in the employee lot right next to the club entrance, and she follows me back to his office. Stevie gets excited about being in the employee-only area of the club, and she tries to poke her head into every doorway we pass along the way. If she weren't in such a hurry, I'd show her around and tell her all the drama that goes on behind the scenes. Walking into Gage's office, I promise to give her a full, in-depth tour the next time she's here.

Opening the top drawer of the desk, I pull out a small set of keys with a flaming heart keychain on it. I lift them up to show Stevie. "These are the ones you need, right?" If not, I can call Gage. He's busy right now, but I know he'd drop everything to answer my call before the second ring.

"Yes, those are the ones. You're my savior," Stevie sings as she accepts the keys from me. "I swear, if Saint screws around with my work because he decided to be an idiot again, I'm going to riot."

"I'll bring the gasoline," I add, making her grin. A ding on her phone has her checking the time.

"Shit, I gotta go, or I'm going to be late. Do you have a ride home?"

"My car is parked in the lot," I say.

"Okay, cool. Thanks again, I'll see you later." She catches me off guard when she leans in for a quick hug before she's off in a flurry of pink. Looking around the office, something occurs to me.

I'm here by myself.

Without any eyes on me.

For the first time in months, I'm completely alone. My shadow is currently occupied elsewhere, and I know for a fact he doesn't allow cameras in his offices. No one takes their privacy more seriously than a man who's doing the watching.

Walking over to his desk, I sit down in the chair and hit the space bar on the keyboard. His computer comes to life, the cursor blinking on the login screen as it waits for a password.

What would Gage use as a password?

My name is too obvious. Anyone who knows him would try that first. He wouldn't choose a date for this, it's not long enough for a computer login. My fingers hover over the keys for a moment before I finally start typing.

LittleDevil.

When I hit enter, the box turns red to tell me it's incorrect. But something in my gut tells me to try again. So I type again.

MyLittleDevil.

Hitting enter has the login screen disappearing to show the desktop. A wave of pride and giddiness ripples through me at the small victory. Not only am I Gage's password, I'm also his screensaver.

A black and white photo of us takes up the whole screen, making my heart flutter. It's a picture I took in the reflection of the hotel elevator. I'm smiling wickedly at the mirror while Gage is standing behind me with his arms wrapped around me. He has his head buried in my neck as he whispers naughty things in my ear. I remember the moment this picture was taken like it happened a minute ago, not a few weeks.

Refocusing on my task, I start my search. I'm not sure what I'm looking for, but I'll keep looking until I find it. Because with the men I've had in my life, there's always *something* to find.

I trust Gage with my life, with my soul, and with my heart. I want to know what he has on me more than anything else. Does he know things about me that I don't? How far has he dug into my life, and what skeletons has he unburied in the process?

Scrolling through his files, I find one titled "Menace," and I click on it. Hundreds of files pop up, each one labeled with a date, some with a specified time. Clicking on it, I find myself looking at surveillance photos and videos.

Photos and videos of me.

Me working. Me dancing with Lana. Me shopping for groceries. Me in my apartment. Even me getting changed in the club dressing room. Every new photo of me that flashes across the screen has another spike of adrenaline coursing through me until I'm high off it. And with every image, the same message is pounded into me over and over.

Gage Lawless is madly obsessed with me.

After reveling in that truth for a few minutes, I finally shut down the computer and stand to leave. Since Gage has been driving me everywhere lately, my car is still parked in the lot from a few days ago. I won't have to order a ride home.

Grabbing my purse off the desk, my bag catches the corner of a cigar box and sends it clattering to the ground. An irritated huff escapes me as I crouch down to collect all of the expensive cigars that have fallen out and scattered across the carpet. Lifting the cigar box off the floor, a heavy thump catches my attention as something else falls out and lands at my feet. Looking down at it, my brain glitches as I try to process what I'm looking at.

It's shiny and metallic.

And very familiar.

The breath stills in my chest as I lift the short, heavy gold chain off the floor and stare at the charm hanging on the end.

Double aces.

Flipping the charm over, the hand-scratched heart on the back stares at me. The edges of my vision blur, dread falling over me like the weight of the world. This can't be happening. Why would I find this hidden in Gage's office? Why would Gage—the man I love—have my dead brother's bracelet?

My mind races with a million questions, my head spinning as things slowly start to click into place. Emotions flurry through me until I'm a wreck, and only devastation remains.

There's only one way Gage could have this bracelet. The bracelet I've been looking for, the one my brother never took off. There's only one explanation for why he would be hiding this from me.

Gage Lawless killed my brother.

CHAPTER THIRTY-ONE
JILL

I can't sit in my car for much longer, and yet I can't seem to move from this seat. My hands firmly grip the steering wheel as I stare at nothing in particular. The entire drive over to Lana's apartment building, my head was a complete mess. The shock of my discovery threatened to break me until I was questioning if what I found was real.

I'd sat there in Gage's office for almost an hour, just trying to process the gold bracelet in my hand. And then I stood up, put it back in its hiding place, and replaced the box on the desk like nothing had ever happened.

But something did happen.

The man I loved—the man I fucked, the man I let pull my walls down, the man I finally decided to trust—is also the man who killed my brother.

It all makes sense to me now. Gage got rid of Tommy so I would be forced to repay the massive debt to Jonas. Then he found a way to take the club and my debt from Jonas so he could own me. He wanted me where he could see me, control me, and manipulate me.

And it fucking worked.

Because he had me.

The thought has me sick to my stomach, and the waves of nausea have anger storming inside me. Climbing out of the car, I walk inside on unsteady legs. It's a relief that no one else is in the elevator to see as I ascend to the seventh floor. As soon as the doors slide open, I'm moving again. I don't stop walking until I see her door.

Pulling out my phone with shaking hands, I call Lana. She answers on the second ring. "I was just thinking about you. I swear we share half a brain."

"Are you home?" I ask, praying she's not on a date or something. I'm not supposed to be here for another few hours, but I desperately need my best friend right now.

"Yeah, I'm home." Completely missing the anguish in my voice, she continues. "Christos has a business dinner, and I couldn't be bothered to go to another one of his meetings. Last time, they wanted me to take my top off to prove I wasn't wearing a wire, and Christos almost shot up the place over it. It was nuts," she rambles. "Why?"

"Come let me in," I state simply, stepping up to her door. A few seconds later, the door swings open, and my gorgeous best friend stands on the other side with her megawatt smile. The instant her eyes land on me, and she sees the misery in my expression and the tears streaming down my face, all happiness vanishes.

"What happened? What's wrong?" she asks, ushering me into her apartment and closing the door. Just being in her presence, my walls start to crumble, and I fall apart. A sob escapes me, my tears streaming freely. Lana doesn't hesitate to wrap me in her arms and hold me while I cry.

After a few minutes I pull away and allow her to lead

me to the couch. Sucking in deep breaths, I start to push back the tears in an attempt to regain control.

"Babe, what is it?" Lana asks, concern written all over her face.

"Gage did it."

"Gage did what?" She's confused.

"Tommy," I say through a rattled sob. "Gage did it." It takes a second for Lana to piece together what I'm saying, but I can see when it clicks. A million emotions cross her face in the same order I felt them when I found the evidence of Gage's betrayal. First the sheer shock of it, then the confusion and denial. Lastly, the outrage—the anger so potent you can taste it.

"Gage killed Tommy." She's still processing. "Fuck, Jill. Tell me everything."

Telling her how I found Tommy's bracelet in Gage's office has me getting worked up all over again—this time, Lana feels it too.

"I'm going to fucking kill him." She shakes her head, her thoughts racing. "I'm going to murder that psycho bastard, chainsaw-massacre style."

"No, you're not. And neither am I," I say, putting an end to that idea. "Killing someone like Gage is too kind. I want him to live and suffer. I'm going to rip away every ounce of happiness in his life and make him drown in so much misery that he chokes on it. And I'm going to need your help." I thought about it on my way over here, but my mind was too big of a mess to come up with a concrete plan.

"Anything, you name it."

"Gage watches my every move, and I don't want him to realize that I know the truth until it's too late. I'm going to distract him, and I need you to go to my place and pack a few bags for me. You know what I'd want."

"Done," Lana agrees eagerly. "Where are you gonna go?"

"I need to go dark for a while," I say, earning an understanding nod. It's going to suck leaving Lana behind, but I need to get away from my stalker soon-to-be ex. And creating a plan on how I'm gonna lose him and stay gone for however long is going to take some strategy. Luckily, Lana and I are both as smart as we are pretty.

"Are you still going on Christos' yacht next week?"

Lana nods. "We leave Friday."

"I need to borrow your arms dealer."

The sound of the front door slamming shut is followed closely by the metallic click of the lock. I stay in place, sitting back on my knees in the center of the bed, watching the bedroom door. The sound of heavy boots striding with a purpose grows closer, sending a thrill through me.

Gage is about to walk in here to find me basically naked and waiting for him in his bed. He's going to fuck me and tell me how much he loves me. And I'm going to let him. Not only will I let him, I'm going to enjoy it.

This sex is about to be the best sex of my life. I'm going to use every inch of Gage's body to wreck me, tear me in two, then put me back together. His skilled fingers, starved tongue, and big, desperate cock are going to destroy every inch of my body until I'm a breath away from death and ready to be reborn.

Then I'm going to rise up from the ashes and scorch the very earth Gage walks on.

I'm going to smile as Gage tells me how much he adores me. Every time I tell him I love him, I'm going to picture a new way to make him wish he'd never laid eyes on me. Each orgasm will come with the thought of severing our soul ties as brutally as possible.

"Holy fuck, you're a goddamn vision." Gage stands in the doorway, his large frame filling the space. His eyes move over me so slowly and meticulously that I can feel them touching every inch of my bare skin.

Showtime.

The lingerie set I put on just for him is in full effect, and his erection is already pressing against his jeans. The bows on each of my hips beg for his teeth to tug away the string thong, the underwire of my cup-less bra lifting my bare breasts to offer my hardened nipples to him. The black thigh-high stockings attached to my garter belt cut into my thick thighs, calling for Gage's hands and lips.

The lust pouring through me gathers between my thighs until I'm soaking a spot on the comforter. Anticipation grows inside me until my chest is heaving with breathless pants. When Gage steps towards me, I smile at him with thoughts of everything I have planned.

Gage Lawless doesn't know what's coming for him.

Me.

CHAPTER THIRTY-TWO

JILL

I've never been this calm before.

Sitting here in Gage's chair behind the desk in his office, staring at the door while I wait, my body and my mind are still. I feel at peace with what's about to happen. There's no doubt or turmoil in my soul for the first time, maybe ever. Only resolution. Knowing the truth—now, *finally*, after all this time—the chatter in my head is finally quiet.

If this is what being calm feels like, I've never been truly calm before. But I am now, in this moment. It's not going to last very long, but I'm soaking it in while I have it.

The last four days have been spent pretending and planning. Pretending that I don't hate Gage with every fiber of my being and planning my escape. I've come to terms with what I have to do, and I've meticulously organized my exit strategy. And with a little help from my best friend, I'm about to cut all ties with my life—and maybe gut a liar in the process.

The door to the office opens and a large figure steps through. Gage walks in, head bent as he types on his phone.

When he looks up, and his eyes land on me, he halts mid-step in surprise. The way his eyes light up at the sight of me has anger chipping away at my calm.

Here we go.

"What are you doing in here, baby?" Gage asks, step-ping into the office and closing the door behind him. When his gaze connects with mine, he stills. He can sense the dark storm coming.

"I'm sitting here thinking about how, out of all the piece-of-shit men I've dealt with in my life, you take the cake. Hands down."

"What the fuck are you talking about?" Gage's expression darkens until the room around us seems to dim. Anyone else would be scared shitless, I'll admit he's got the intimidation factor. But I'm not afraid of the dark.

"I'm talking about this." I stand from my seat and toss the bracelet onto the desk between us. The gold hits the wood with a heavy metallic thump that rings in the silence. When Gage's eyes land on the jewelry, tension ripples through his body until he turns to stone, some of the color draining from his face.

"It's not—"

"It's not what I think?" I cut him off bitterly. "All this time, I've been crying about the monster who killed my brother and how devastating it was that I'll never know what happened to him. Turns out that not only did I seek comfort in the arms of the monster I was hunting, I even let him fuck me."

"Baby—"

"Call me that again, I dare you." The threat in my tone couldn't be more clear, or less empty.

"*Jill,*" he growls, frustration evident, "let me—"

"Another word, and I'll cut out your *fucking tongue!*" The

rage in my voice builds with my volume until the last two words lash out violently, punctuated by my hands slamming down on the desk between us. Anger surges through me until I'm shaking. I suck in a harsh breath and close my eyes.

Taking a moment, I force myself to reign in the fury engulfing my entire being. The potent need to see the life draining out of him, to feel his last shuttering breath, is all-consuming.

Desperately needing something to ground me, I reach into my back pocket and pull out my knife. The sound of the blade clicking open is calming enough for me to see through the blinding rage and shelve my lethal urges.

If I kill Gage, this will be over way too quickly. As much as I want to—and I *really* want to—I have other plans for him.

Letting out a calmer breath, my body shifts from fiery hostility into cold contempt. When I open my eyes, I settle my frigid glare on him. The arctic breeze coming from my icy death glare could give the man frostbite—and I hope it does.

Gage's gaze on me is swimming in such deep yearning that it threatens to swallow me whole. The muscle in his clenched jaw ticks tellingly in his tortured silence.

"I don't know what's more disappointing—the fact that I let you convince me that I could trust you, or that you turned out to be the worst life lesson I've ever had to learn."

"You don't know what you're talking about. This changes nothing."

"This changes *everything*."

"Your brother wasn't who you thought he was."

"Tommy was flawed and fucked up, but he was my

brother—my family." I raise my knife and point it at him. "You're the one I got wrong. *You* were my mistake."

"Hit me," Gage demands, tossing his phone onto the desk. His large hands fist the material of his shirt and, with one hard pull, he tears it down the middle until it hangs in nothing but tatters before spreading his arms out wide. "Punch me, cut me. Slice me open and gut me until I'm nothing but a pile of skin and bones. Destroy me." He takes a step forward until the tip of my knife is pressing into his skin.

I inch closer, allowing the tip of the blade to pierce the skin of his chest. Watching the bead of blood spring to the surface has me pressing harder, dragging the blade across the brawny flesh. Gage stands still as a statue as I carve my initials over his heart. I don't stop until I've left a permanent mark, ugly and twisted, on his heart.

Just like he did to mine.

Blood drips down his ink-covered chest, but it's not enough. Not even close. I pull my gaze away from the carnage to the eyes that have been burning a hole through my skull. Gage's dark gaze stares down at me, eyes trying to suck my soul straight out of my body. I stare back, unmoved and unblinking.

"Sit down." I gesture to the chair behind his desk.

"I was going to tell you everything." Gage says, and his words have white-hot anger flashing through me.

"*Sit. Down,*" I seeth.

He obeys without another word, sitting in the desk chair. His unrelenting eyes track me as I walk over with the zip-ties I pulled out of my bag. Using two ties per arm, I cinch his wrists to the arms of the chair—pulling the ties so tight that they dig into his skin.

I don't want him getting out of these too soon, and I want them to hurt until he does.

"I can only imagine how dumb you think I am. You didn't even bother to hide the bracelet in the safe. Not like all that cash you have piled up in there."

"Take it, all of it," Gage's voice is so rough with desperation that I almost don't recognise it.

"Oh, I've already helped myself. The contents of the safe are the least you can do. But don't worry, I left you a little something to remember me by," I say flatly. "Figuring out the combination was too easy—the day we met? Not very original. Then again, I fell for all of your bullshit, so you never expected me to figure anything out, did you?"

"This isn't over, Jill. Don't for a second kid yourself thinking it is."

I ignore his statement, watching as the blood drips from my mark on his inked chest until it disappears into the waistband of his pants. I could kill him—right here, right now. It's what he wants. But that would be an act of grace, and I have no intention of showing him any mercy.

None.

"You know what the only consolation in all of this is? That you had it. You finally got what you really wanted in the deepest part of you. You had me. Because I fell for you, so hard, and so completely—without abandon. I fell for you in ways you could have only dreamed about. *You had me.*" The malice in my tone is almost palpable. "And now, that's gone. Done. You'll go the rest of your life knowing exactly what it felt like to have everything you wanted and then lose it. Forever."

"It's not done. We're not done. Not ever."

His words slide right off me, my body going still as I let the finality settle through me.

"I regret ever loving you."

Gage reacts like I've hit him with a sledgehammer. The devastation on his face would be enough to break my heart if he hadn't already ground it into the dust.

"Any last words before you never see me again?"

Gage leans forward in the chair until he's pulling against his restraints, his eyes spearing me with conviction. "Wherever you go—it better be far, and you better go fast. Make yourself invisible while you're at it. Because I'm coming for you, little devil, and there's nowhere on earth you can run that I won't find you," he says. "We're forever, Jill. There's no getting rid of me. Even if you kill me right now, my soul will find yours in every lifetime. I'm your shadow under a never-setting sun."

My gut clenches, and my heart threatens to pound right out of my chest. Ignoring my visceral need to collapse into his arms and let him make everything okay, I lean down until I'm just out of his reach. My soul tears in two as I gaze at the man who I thought was my forever.

Using the painful ache in my chest where the love used to be, I allow my voice to shake with all the anguish that's ripping me to shreds. "Shrivel, wither, and rot in hell. Just like the rest of them."

When I grab the bag of loot from the safe off the floor next to the desk and turn around to leave, I don't look back. But I do lock the office door behind me. It won't stop Messer or Anders when they inevitably come to let Gage loose, but it'll slow them down.

I stride through the club with a purpose, evading every familiar face as I make as fast an exit as possible. A large black luxury SUV waits in front of the building for me. As soon as I climb in and close the door behind me, the vehicle is pulling away from the curb and weaving into traffic.

"How did it go?" Lana asks from the seat next to me. I toss the duffle bag onto the floor at my feet and clench my shaking hands. There's blood on them—it's not much, but it's there.

His blood.

I'll have to scrub my hands when I arrive at my destination.

"I almost killed him. I could have, but I didn't." My voice is trembling, and I hate it. I feel like I want to laugh and cry at the same time. Maybe I need to scream or punch something.

"I'm proud of you," Lana's tone gets softer, and it makes tears mist in my eyes. But I force back the waterworks. I can cry later. "Are you okay?"

I look over at my best friend, and I know she can see that I'm absolutely devastated. I give the slightest shake of my head no, and that's all she needs.

"We'll be at the marina in seventeen minutes," The driver informs us from behind the wheel. Lana's hand creeps across the back seat to intertwine with mine and gives it a reassuring squeeze. I glance over at her but quickly avert my eyes to look out the window. If I keep looking at her, I'm going to lose my shit. I can't be a mess right now, not yet.

Soon, this will all be behind me, and that man will be nothing but a rancid memory.

CHAPTER THIRTY-THREE

GAGE

"Where would she go?" Anders asks, typing at my computer.

After Jill walked out, leaving me locked in my office and tied to the chair, I had to call for backup. Using my voice command on my phone on the desk, I called Anders in. He kicked the door down and cut me loose within fifteen minutes. But it's not fast enough.

Devastating desperation has me in a chokehold as I rewatch the security footage of Jill exiting the building and climbing into an anonymous car. The camera doesn't catch the license plate of the SUV before it disappears from view.

My body hurts—my wrists are raw and bloody from fighting against the zip ties, my chest hurts where the knife carved my flesh, and my head is pounding. But none of that registers past the soul-aching anguish that feels like all of my vital organs have been ripped out of me.

"Flights would be too obvious and unreliable," Anders adds. I shake my head. She wouldn't take her chances on a flight. Those are too easy to track, and she wouldn't take the chance of a delay or cancellation. She would only leave with someone she trusts, and that list is very short. Especially now.

"Lana," I say, standing from my chair and striding towards the door. "Lana left on a yacht this afternoon."

"I'll drive," Anders says, matching my pace. The drive to the Marina breaks all traffic laws—running lights, speeding, and ignoring traffic signs. Anders doesn't hesitate to drive his car down the boardwalk, only stopping when we run out of dock.

"Hey, what the hell are you doing? You can't drive your car here!" There's not a flicker of hesitation when I pull my gun and aim it at the whining middle-aged man standing in a boat to my left. His hands go up immediately, the words dying on his lips.

"We need your boat," I demand, gesturing to his speedboat. "Now." The man pales visibly, nodding and stumbling as he clammers out of the boat onto the dock.

"Tell anyone about this, and this entire clip will have your name on it." I don't bother disguising the vicious edge in my voice, and he nods numbly before stumbling away. Anders jumps down into the boat and revs the engine, and I'm right behind him. Anders doesn't hesitate to whip the boat around the dock and steer into open waters.

"How do you know where we're going?" I yell over the engine and wind.

"Let's just say I've seen Christos' anchorage plans."

He's been tracking Christos because of Lana. I could kiss my best friend right now. If there's ever been a moment his obsessive tendencies paid off, it's right fucking now.

Adrenaline courses through me until I'm shaking, my gut twisted in anticipation. I need to find Jill, I have to. There is no other option.

If not today, then tomorrow. Or the next day.

I won't live without her. I *can't*.

Fear tightens around my neck like a hangman's noose, but I refuse to let it take me. I won't lose her. I don't care what it takes to get her back. If it means locking her up, kicking and screaming.

After slicing through the water for a good twenty minutes, we finally spot the yacht off in the distance. As we approach my body shakes with all of the emotions thundering through me. My grip on my gun adjusts and readjusts as I anticipate what will happen once we get there.

They're expecting us. Four armed men stand on the main deck of the boat, their firearms trained on us. My gun is drawn before Anders even cuts the engine to pull his out. Christos walks closer to us while his three-man security team stays at the ready.

"You shouldn't have come out here," he calls.

"You know why I'm here," I state darkly, my trigger finger itching. If I weren't out-gunned I'd have already taken him out and climbed onboard to search the yacht by now.

"We knew you'd show up, so predictable." A female voice says. Lana appears at Christos' side, and his arm immediately wraps around her. The sight of the blonde has my heart rate spiking with hope.

"Where is she?" I demand.

"You'll never see her again unless it's from the business end of a Glock." Lana spits, disdain written all over her face. "I'd shoot you myself if I could. But that would be an act of mercy. And you don't deserve any mercy, just a long life of pain and suffering."

"I'm not gonna ask you again." My knuckles turn white from my grip on my gun. "Tell me where she is. Now." My eyes scan the deck for any signs of Jill—flashes of her dark chocolate hair, one of her designer suitcases, a whiff of her cherry blossom perfume. Anything.

Nothing.

"She's gone," Lana states, flashing me a smile of contempt. "Suffer." With that, she turns on her heel and walks back inside. She pauses next to Christos, placing her hand on his chest. "If he tries to board, shoot him."

With one last withering glance over her shoulder at me and Anders, she disappears inside.

"Jill's not here. And I'm not supposed to kill you, but if you try anything, my men won't hesitate," Christos bellows.

"Where is she?" I'll ask the same question a million times until I have answers.

"Probably halfway across the country at fifty-thousand feet by now." Christos' laughed words have my stomach dropping. She's on a fucking plane. "It's really too bad, too. I was rooting for you two. Now get the fuck away from my boat."

CHAPTER THIRTY-FOUR
JILL

The cityscape below me disappears beneath the sea of clouds. And as I leave my life behind me, my walls start to crumble. With the first tear that rolls down my cheek, there's no holding back. A sob wracks through my body, and my emotions overwhelm me.

For the next three hours, I can cry and sob and wallow in my misery. I can grieve the loss of the future I'll never have with the man I thought was my soulmate. My heart will break, and my stomach will churn.

But when the landing gear touches down on the tarmac, and I step off the private plane to start my new life, I'll pull myself together. I'll refocus, rebuild, and move on. As soon as my feet touch the ground in San Francisco, Gage will be nothing but a memory.

CHAPTER THIRTY-FIVE

GAGE

ight weeks.
Eight weeks of searching, hunting, and going out of my fucking mind. Two months unable to sleep, without being able to taste a single bite of food or craft any type of art. Eight weeks without my heart, Jill.

Tattooing is impossible without my muse. I haven't even been able to sketch a design since Jill walked out of my office without so much as a backward glance. When she left, she took my soul and my passion with her—ripped it right out of my body without hesitation or mercy.

I will find her, I have to.

I've been tracking everything—phone records, email addresses, spam social media accounts. Jill knew what she was doing when she left and she certainly didn't take it easy on me. She's effectively disappeared without a trace, which has left me scrambling for anything to cling onto, any fucking lead to follow. Even with Anders' help, we've found fucking nothing so far.

The *little something to remember her by* that she left in the safe was her phone completely wiped to factory settings—sim card included—and the tube of Crimson Sin lipstick. *My* lipstick. Neither of those items can help me find her, they just remind me of what I've lost. Every time I lay eyes on the tube of lipstick, the knife in my heart twists painfully.

I need to get her back.

An alert sounds across my office where Anders is working on his laptop. Awareness trickles through my body when he glances over at me. "I just got a hit on that stolen credit card you wanted me to track."

"What's the location?"

"Aguadilla, Puerto Rico." Anders' voice is heavy with skepticism, but I'm already up and reaching for my keys. Looks like I'll be on the next flight out.

"Send me the address, I'm going to Puerto Rico. Stay on Lana, she's still our best bet." Energy spikes through me, forcing me to let out a heavy breath. "Finally, we're getting somewhere."

I knew tracking that credit card would pay off eventually, and now I have a thread to pull. It won't be long before it leads me straight to who I'm looking for.

You can run, Jill. But you can't hide. Not from me.

The address leads me to a weathered little building that's more like a hut than a house. I look past the broken wind chimes swaying in the breeze and the faded, colorful stencil around the front door as I pound on it. Hard. I don't want the person inside thinking they have an option when it comes to answering the door.

As soon as I hear the scrape of the lock, I'm crowding the door. Blocking the resident, I push into the house and lock the door behind me. Staring at the familiar face, I grin as excitement floods my veins. "Did you miss me?"

CHAPTER THIRTY-SIX

JILL

I've only been home for the night three minutes before there's a knocking at my front door. My heart races at the aggression behind the pounding, apprehension tensing every muscle in my body. Holding my breath, I can't help but brace myself before I open the door.

"Medium supreme pizza with breadsticks?" a delivery woman drawls. I confirm, and she offers me the two food boxes before power-walking back to her car.

Forcing a cleansing breath, I close the door and lock is soundly behind me, before heading toward the living room. Huffing out a deep sigh, I walk through the dark house and drop my purse and the food boxes on the coffee table before tossing down my keys. It's been a long day, I'm tempted to fall onto the couch without bothering to turn on any lights.

Living off of the cash I took from Gage's safe was easy in the beginning, but it's proving more and more difficult as time goes on. The digital age isn't built for anonymous, cash-only transactions. Everything wants you to create an account with a paper trail. Funny how actual paper doesn't usually leave any trails.

San Fransisco only lasted for a few nights while I got myself completely off the grid, then it was time to find someplace quieter. I got lucky when I found this little two-bedroom house in southern Georgia being rented out by a sweet Southern woman who prefers cash. All I had to do was pay the minimal deposit, and she was happy to let me sublet under her name. She didn't even notice that I initialed the paperwork instead of writing my full name. If only everything else could be so easily managed.

I spent most of the day trying to set up an internet provider, but I wasn't able to find one that would let me sign up without creating an online account with my personal information and showing proof of address. Modern times are really making hiding from a psycho ex nearly impossible. I even had to reach out to Lana a few days ago about getting me a fake ID. But if I have to go to the public library every time I want to use the internet, that's what I'll fucking do.

"You're a hard woman to find when you want to be. But not hard enough." The large shadow looming in the corner steals the breath from my lungs. "I'll always find you."

The switch of the lamp floods the room with light, revealing Gage standing in my living room like the shadow of death. The cold shock that freezes every muscle in my body is quickly melted by the hot anger that pours through me like molten lava.

"You clearly have a death wish. Maybe I was being too kind when I let you live. Now I'm going to have to kill you. And I'll make sure it's slow and painful to pay you back for what you did to Tommy."

"Your brother—"

"What about my brother? You needed to track me down to explain in detail how you killed—?"

"Jillybean."

All words die on my tongue at the familiar voice. My eyes widen, jaw dropping, as I turn to look at the man standing in the doorway.

Is this real?

"Tommy?" The name is barely a whisper. He walks closer, stepping further into the light until I can see him clearly—husky build, dark brown wavy hair, green eyes. "Tommy!"

I throw myself at him, and his arms wrap around me in a tight hug. I breathe in the smell of his Old Spice as I press my face into his bulky chest.

He's real.

"You're alive." I pull back to look at him—excitement, confusion, and outrage swirling through me. *"You're alive?"*

I glance at Gage, my eyes clashing with his and momentarily getting caught in their intensity. I rip my gaze from his to refocus on my brother when he starts talking. Tommy breathes out a breath of relief like he'd been worried this was all a trap. "I'm alive. It's a long story, Jilly. I—"

"A story he's going to be telling without sparing any details," Gage states darkly. My eyes dart over to glare at the man burning a hole through my forehead. His demanding gaze latches to mine, forcing me to avert my eyes before I'm being sucked in.

"Tell me." Taking several steps backward to create space between me and the two men, I focus on my brother. The weight of my stare makes him fidget in a way that has me narrowing my eyes. I know all of his tells. "What did you do?"

"Nothing! I didn't actually do anything." Tommy says defensively. His eyes cut over to Gage nervously before he continues. "Okay, so I got in too deep with Jonas."

"I already know that part."

"I know, I know. You were never supposed to have to take over my debt like that. I was going to win enough to pay him. I just needed a few more good games. You know how good I am when I'm on a winning streak." Tommy's eyes glaze over like they always do when he's talking about his addiction. "And I was doing it. I was winning. I won over fifty grand, but I knew I could do better. I was going to double it. But then Danny Cordon won the pot. He's always been a fucking cheat—I *had* him. He shouldn't have had that pair. It didn't make any sense." My brother starts rambling, veering off track as he starts spiraling to himself.

"Tommy, focus," I say, snapping him out of it.

"I lost the money. All of it. And Jonas wasn't happy about it, so he sent his guys to...remind me of what happens if I didn't pay. I had to get the money another way. I didn't have a choice." Something in his tone has my gut clenching with dread. He pauses for a moment that spells trouble.

"Then I heard about the reward money." My stomach drops.

"What reward money?" I bite out slowly. Tommy winces.

"Carter's parents. They were offering a lot of money to know what happened to him. A *lot* of money." I remain silent, my stare turning cold as he continues. "I wasn't gonna tell them everything. Just enough to get the payout."

"How did you even know about Carter?"

"I saw you. Carter was at the dock that night to meet me. I was going to convince him to spot me some cash, but you got to him first."

My head is swimming with a million thoughts all at once, anger and denial swirling through me. But one feeling pangs through me without question. Betrayal.

"You were going to sell me out?" My eyes rip from my brother to look at Gage for confirmation. His deep gaze holds mine easily as he stands unmoving.

"I was going to tell the truth. You made your choices, and I had to make mine. I wasn't happy about it." Tommy spreads out his hands defensively.

After all I've done for him, Tommy was going to betray me. Turn me in for a paycheck. He was just using me. Again. My entire life, all I've ever been to him was a card in his hand to play whenever it suited him. He didn't give a damn about me, he never has.

He still doesn't.

I've been avenging a brother I never had. A man who never saw me as family or even a friend. A person who's only ever been out for himself.

Anger simmers inside me like molten lava brewing. I'm a fucking volcano ready to erupt and cause total devastation. My eyes move from the pathetic excuse of a brother and look at Gage. His eyes lock with mine like he's just been waiting for me to look his way again. His entire body is tensed, corded muscles in his arms bulging against the tight fists clenching at his sides. I can't tell what urge he's currently fighting—the need to touch me or the impulse to throttle Tommy.

"You knew about this?" I ask, the angry words coming out as an accusation.

"I stopped him."

Gage's statement says so much.

"After beating me to within an inch of my life," Tommy interjects. He takes a step closer to me, his tone changing like he's trying to reason with me. Gage takes a step closer in response. "This guy is a violent lunatic, Jilly. You can't trust him, he's fucking crazy. Let's get rid of him, and we can go back home. Just the two of us."

"Just the two of us?" I scoff. "You were going to rat me out. Throw me to the wolves to save yourself."

"Hey, you're the one who killed a man. I was just cashing in before you did your time. The cops would've found out who did it eventually." Realizing that he's not helping his case, Tommy changes his tune. "Look, I'm really sorry. Okay? I never would've gone through with it—you're my sister. I'm sorry for even thinking about it. We've gotta stick together. We're all each other has."

"He called to make an appointment with the detective." Gage's deep voice cuts in. Tommy throws him a glare before turning his pleading eyes back to me.

"We've both made mistakes. But we can move on from all this." I stare at him, listening as his sweet talk and negotiations slide right off my back without making a dent. There's no going back, the damage is done. What little faith I had in this deadbeat is long gone.

My brother is standing right in front of me, the brother I've spent months going crazy looking for. But it feels like I'm looking at a stranger.

"Let's go pack your things. You have the bracelet, right?"

"The bracelet," I repeat bitterly. Tommy nods, looking around the room like he might catch a glimpse of the gaudy gold jewelry.

"Yeah, I'm gonna need my lucky charm now that I'm back. Where is it?"

Now that I'm back.

Something about those four words slices painfully into my chest like I'm being stabbed by realization. He thinks everything is the same as before, like nothing ever happened. Like he didn't try to betray me on the deepest level for his own benefit. He doesn't care about that, and why would he? He sees nothing wrong with it.

Tommy is never going to change. He's going to stay who he's always been, who I've allowed him to be my entire life —a selfish, greedy asshole who's only ever out for himself. A bloodsucker draining the life out of anyone he can sink his teeth into.

I've always known who he is. But for the longest time, I thought that being his sister—his family—somehow meant I was safe from him. I'm not. I'll never be safe from his self-serving egotism. He'll turn on me without a second thought the moment it turns in his favor.

And what's to stop him from cashing that reward check from Carter's parents the second he gets back to Chicago? Nothing. He's got his ammunition now, and he'll pull the trigger on me every chance he gets.

I look at my brother, who's been waiting with bated breath, to see how I'll react to all of this. "Wait here, I'll be right back." Tommy's shoulders sag with relief, but Gage isn't so happy.

"Jill—" I hold up a hand to cut off his protest.

"Just wait here. Both of you." Striding out of the room, I head down the hallway to the bedroom. Pulling open my nightstand drawer, I find what I'm looking for. The weight of the metal in my hand as I stride back toward the living room carries the heaviness of this entire situation. When I walk through the doorway, Gage is standing with his arms crossed, staring Tommy down. My brother is trying to stare back but can't help but fidget.

His tell has gotten even worse than the last time I saw him. He's losing it.

Walking over to my brother, I lift my arm to dangle the

ugly gold bracelet in the air in front of him. "Is this what you wanted so badly?"

Tossing the jewelry at him, he reaches out both arms to catch the damn thing like it's a fragile heirloom. I wait for both hands to wrap around the metal, his arms raised, to make my move. My knife pierces him just under his ribcage with all of the anger that's been building inside me my entire life. All of it comes to a head in this one moment as I shove the blade through his muscular wall as hard as I can.

Tommy wheezes out a grunt as the wind is knocked out of him, his eyes bulging in his head at me in shock. "What are you—?"

"This is what I want. Badly."

White hot anger flashes across Tommy's face, his expression morphing into hateful contempt. His arm raises to swing at me, but he doesn't get the chance. In an instant, Gage has Tommy in a chokehold with both arms pinned behind his back.

"You don't fucking touch her," Gage growls menacingly. Tommy wriggles against his hold, But it's useless against Gage's unshakable hold. Tommy's eyes glimmer with disdain as he sneers at me.

"You worthless bitch. You're just as useless as Mom was. It should've been you who died in the accident, not Dad. You're nothing but a fat fuck that no one will ever really care about." Tommy's practically frothing at the mouth. Gage's arm around his neck tightens painfully until his face is turning red and his breathing is labored.

"I wouldn't bet on that," Gage growls darkly, making butterflies flutter in my stomach.

"He shouldn't bet on anything." I lean in, enjoying the warmth of the blood covering my hand as I hold the knife that's still four inches deep in Tommy's abdomen. "Do you know why you never won, Tommy? Hmm? Should I tell you why? Because you're a loser. It's what you are, what you've always been. All your life, you've been running from the truth, trying to convince yourself and anyone who will listen that you're worth something. That you can win. But you can't, you never could. You're nothing but a failure.

"The other men I've killed had it coming, but you're the person who stole my life from me. You never made anything happen for yourself. You had to drag other people down with you. But you're done dragging me." I twist the knife in his gut, making him groan in agony. But against the torture, he barks out a bitter scoff.

"You were so easy. *'Jillybean, you can't let them hurt me.'* You just couldn't help yourself, you kept coming back for more," he sneers, fueling my rage.

"And this is how it all ends. With you losing one last time. And the biggest thing you've lost yet." Using all of my strength, I yank the blade upwards to drag it through his stomach. "Your life."

The yell of agony that leaves Tommy is one of irreparable damage.

"All you've ever wanted was to be relevant, to be something," I say calmly between his screams. "But you're nothing. No one missed you when you were dead before, and no one will miss you now." The knife is slippery with the blood it's coated with when I pull it out of him, inflicting as much damage as possible in the process. When I jam the knife back in, this time piercing his heart, my hand slides down the handle with the force of it.

Tommy's eyes widen in pained panic before his entire body stills as the life leaves it. He stares at me with lifeless eyes as Gage's hold keeps his now slack form upright. My chest heaves with my amped breaths as I stand, unmoving, in front of my dead brother.

Tommy is dead. Actually dead. And there are no more questions about what happened to him.

I killed him.

I stay there for a moment as the adrenaline courses through me—my hand on the knife that took Tommy's last heartbeat, blood dripping down my arm. I'm sure I'm covered in it.

My brother's blood.

Seconds stretch into minutes as I allow my body to calm and take stock of how I'm feeling. Once the high of the adrenaline wears off, the sense of power remains. It's sweet, with a bitter aftertaste that might never go away.

This kill feels different.

Out of all of the men I've killed, this one feels more final. Like a weight has been lifted off my shoulders. The weight of my brother's disappearance, the heaviness of who he was in my life. Now that's all gone, leaving something new settling through me.

Freedom.

My eyes drift closed and the ghost of a smile crosses my face as the sensation flows over me. I soak in the sense of peace and calm, so potent and comforting that quiets my mind—until the deep voice speaks.

"Are you okay, baby?" My eyes snap open to clash with the man gazing at me intently.

Gage hasn't moved an inch while I've been reveling, his eyes fixed solely on me as he holds my now dead brother. His words slap me back to reality, and my fiery emotions kick back into gear. The passionate look in his dark eyes drill me with so many turbulent feelings until I'm overwhelmed.

And just like that, the peace is gone.

"Don't think that this just fixes everything between us," I snap, yanking the knife from the dead man. Gage doesn't seem the least bit put off by my remark.

"But there *is* an *us*," he states, like it's the only thing he cares about. I don't have the energy to argue with him about this right now. At least, that's the excuse I'll be giving him if he presses the matter because I don't currently know how I feel about him or where we stand.

"I can't do this right now."

Gage releases his hold on the body and quietly lowers it onto the floor. There's blood everywhere, and one glance down at me confirms my early assumptions. Gage takes a step closer and looks tempted to touch me, but he refrains. Just barely.

"Go take a shower, and leave your clothes and the knife in the tub. I'll get things cleaned up in here." Gage speaks as if he's just about to do a load of dishes instead of disposing of a body. The gentleness in his voice is startling, and it makes my chest ache.

I nod and turn towards the doorway, but Gage steps into my path and forces my eyes to meet his. "Don't leave this house. I'll find you, you know I will. I'll *always* find you."

I don't bother refraining from rolling my eyes. "Fine, whatever."

"Jill." The authority in his commanding tone has my heart doing damn near cartwheels as I meet his eyes again.

"I won't leave," I say more seriously. I don't plan on going anywhere, at least not tonight. It would be pointless anyway. I don't have another escape plan in place. And I'm not dumb enough to think I could shake my shadow so easily a second time.

Gage holds my gaze for a moment, trying to decide if he can believe me. The muscle in his clenched jaw ticks tellingly when he finally steps back and allows me to pass. I look down at the body lying on the floor as I leave the room one last time.

I won't miss Tommy. I know I'll see him again.

In hell.

CHAPTER THIRTY-SEVEN

JILL

I hold my head under the spray of the shower head long after the suds are gone. The hot water ran out three washes ago, leaving nothing but the cold to rain down on me as I scrub away any remnants of what I've done. I've already scrubbed every inch of myself clean three times over, and my hair has been shampooed and conditioned four times. But it doesn't feel like enough.

I want no part of Tommy or his death touching me. After I leave this house, I don't plan on thinking about him ever again. He doesn't deserve to reside in my head, cross my lips, or stain my hands. I might let him red my lips, but that's for me. Not him.

After tonight, I'll finally be free of him. Of his habits, his incessant neediness, and his greed. No more questions about him will plague me while I'm falling asleep, and the compulsive familial urge to help him disappeared with the light in his eyes when I extinguished it.

I won't be mourning Tommy Hart. No one will.

Reaching for the faucet, I turn off the water. Pulling

back the shower curtain, a gasp of surprise escapes me at the man silently standing a few feet away.

"What are you doing? You scared the shit out of me."

Gage stands in the doorway, leaning against the doorframe with his arms crossed. His eyes rake over me like a man dying of thirst in the desert, staring at an oasis. His attention surges through me like a sugar rush, giving me the high I've been craving. The one only he can give me.

Holy fuck, he's so attractive it hurts to look at him.

My pussy throbs at the mere sight of him, my arousal joining the moisture already dripping down my legs. Gage drops his arms and pushes off the doorway to offer me the towel I hadn't noticed he was holding.

"You've forgotten what it's like to be watched already, little devil? I'm disappointed. I had to make sure you hadn't run out on me again."

"I told you I wouldn't." I accept the towel and use it to wring some of the water out of my hair before drying off my body.

"I would have to be an idiot to believe you," he states. "And I'm not taking any chances. I won't lose you again." I do my best to ignore how hungrily the hot tattoo god is looking at me, his eyes devouring every inch of my naked body like I know his mouth wants to.

Fuck I want him to.

"Don't assume that I'm yours to lose, Gage. I haven't decided how much I hate you yet." I don't bother to wrap the towel around my body, I know it won't reach all the way around. I miss the oversized bath sheets I left at my place in Chicago—these dinky regular towels aren't designed for bigger bodies. Instead, I reach for the bathrobe hanging on the back of the bathroom door.

"Then let's talk." Finally closing the distance between

us, he takes the robe sash out of my hands to tie it. He sinches the robe closed, pulling me closer in the process. "Because I have no intention of ever walking away from you."

I want to kiss him. I want to punch him. But instead, I just turn around and walk out of the bathroom. I'm not having this conversation next to the damn toilet.

I rush down the hallway with all of the pent-up animosity brewing inside me, with Gage right on my heels. "You want to talk?" Reaching the middle of my bedroom, I whirl on him. "Go ahead, talk. Tell me why I shouldn't still kill you for lying to me. Tell me why I should ever trust you again after how you used my own brother against me. Or maybe you can tell me how you plan on convincing me that you're not a no-good sack-of-shit like every other man I've had in my life—including the one I just killed."

"Let's cut the shit, Jill." Gage storms closer until he's crowding me, the air around us crackling with tension. "You don't care that I lied to you. And you're not some doe-eyed innocent who had the wool pulled over her eyes. You're mad because you feel like you betrayed yourself by not seeing what was right in front of you. We both lie to get what we want. And I wanted you, *needed* you. I'm not sorry for what I did to have you, and I'll do whatever it takes to keep you. You know exactly what I'm capable of. It's why you love me."

His words piss me off, the truth of them digging under the walls erected around my heart. When he's no longer able to restrain himself, his hands unclench at his sides to wrap around my waist and yank my body flush against his.

Staring up at him, every fiber of my being screams for his touch. I want him to kiss me, to fuck me, to mark me. I want his cock to split me in two before his lips bite away the pain.

Rearing back an arm, my hand lashes out until my palm strikes his face with the force of my torment. The strength of the slap jerks Gage's head to one side, and he takes it like a hit of his favorite drug. A rumbling groan ripples through him as he slowly turns his head back towards me, his eyes on fire. The heat in his gaze sparks me from the inside until I'm going up in flames.

Leaning up, I pounce on him. My hands grip his face as my lips clash with his. His arms around me tighten their hold painfully until there's no telling where his body ends, and mine begins. His mouth devours me—desperately, self-ishly—like a man devouring his last meal before he meets his end.

I meet him at every turn, taking my own pound of flesh. My hands slide from his face to wrap around his neck to secure my hold as our tongues tangle and explore.

"I don't forgive you," I state breathlessly.

"You don't have to," he mutters between kisses. "You love me."

"I'm not going to fuck you tonight."

"I don't care. You love me."

"I love you, but I don't like you."

"You're going to marry me."

"Don't push your luck, Lawless."

"You will."

"I'm going to bed, and you're sleeping on the couch."

"Get your rest. You're gonna need it." Strong fingers gently brush a wet strand of hair from my face, his hand threading through my hair to fist it at the nape of my neck. "In the morning, I'm going to fuck you the way you deserve to be fucked—first hard and fast, then soft and slow. Then I'm packing you up and taking you home."

CHAPTER THIRTY-EIGHT

JILL

The Chicago skyline is a beautiful sight through the plane window. The last time I was on a private plane, I was flying in the opposite direction and couldn't get away fast enough. But I've missed my city.

"Welcome home, baby." My eyes leave the window to find Gage watching me. He hasn't taken his eyes off me once since I woke up to his face buried between my legs.

Gage had eaten my pussy this morning like he'd never get the chance again. Once he'd had his fill, and I'd come on his tongue three times, he fucked me so roughly and thoroughly—talking so dirty it made me blush—that my body still aches deliciously from the power of it. Then he made love to me, soft, sweet, and slow, as he took me to heights of pleasure I'd never experienced before. And while he was worshiping every inch of the body he'd just completely destroyed, he'd showered me with praise and words of adoration that I'll never forget.

Gage Lawless is madly in love with me. And as much as I'd still like to fight it—*and fight him*—I'm just as devoted.

Exhilaration washes over me at the thought of it all. I'm home with the man that I love. Everything is as it should be. Well, almost. It's going to take more than a morning of sex and five orgasms to make things up to me. Gage still has a lot of groveling to do.

I don't forgive so easily.

He didn't tell me what he did with Tommy's body, and I didn't ask. Honestly, I don't give a shit. My brother wouldn't care what happened to me, so why should I worry about his eternal resting place?

Gage's car is waiting for us on the tarmac when we arrive. I allow him to help me down the plane's stairs, but I refuse to let him hold my hand as we walk in silence to the car. I wait in the passenger seat as Gage and the flight crew load my luggage into the trunk.

When Gage climbs behind the wheel, I don't offer my hand to hold as I look out the window. But when his large hand reaches over to rest on my thigh as he drives us away from the small airport, I make no move to remove it.

I'm still not happy with this man, but damn did I miss him. I missed his touch, his voice, the smell of his cologne. I missed the weight of his eyes on me and the way my body responds to his presence. I even missed that damn smirk of his.

Half of me—the angry, vindictive half—refuses to let my guard down with him after the deceit. I know what type of man he is, and I'm still bitter that he used it against me. He was a weapon I thought I had a handle on, but it blew up in my face. So, while he might currently be allowed in my presence, I'm not gifting him my attention.

"What are you doing?" I ask as we turn in the opposite direction we should be going.

"I'm taking you home."

"This isn't the way to my apartment. Where the hell are we even going?" I look around as we make our way through an unfamiliar part of the city.

"Do you trust me?" Gage's question has me cutting him a look that says he must think I'm an idiot. So he clarifies. "Do you trust me to keep you safe?"

Yes.

The answer echoes through my mind clearly and without hesitation. I don't have to say it out loud for Gage to see it on my face. He flashes me a knowing smirk, and I barely refrain from rolling my eyes like a petulant child. That has me settling back against my seat with an annoyed exhale. "I'm already starting to regret coming back with you."

"It's too late now, baby. There's no going back."

We weave our way further and further away from downtown, towards the suburbs. The distance between properties grows wider as the houses grow bigger. My brows knit in confusion when we pull up to a fancy gated community. With the click of a fob on his keys, the detailed metal gate swings open to allow us entry.

Winding through the ritzy neighborhood, Gage finally turns into a greenery-lined driveway that leads to a house tucked away from the street. Although house isn't the right word to use for what's waiting at the end of a circular drive. Manor is more like it.

The massive white colonial mansion stands in the center of immaculately manicured grounds, with detailed white pillars reaching the full two stories on either side of the front door. Gage pulls up to the front door and cuts the engine. I can feel his heavy gaze on me as I stare out the window, taking in every detail of the gorgeous home. When I pull my eyes away from the house to look at him in confusion, I find him staring at me with such passion it makes the breath hitch in my chest.

"Come inside, I need to show you something."

I open my mouth, but before I can ask him any of the questions racing through my mind, he's climbing out of the car. I watch him round the car, my eyes narrowing as he pulls my door open and offers me his hand. I stare at the offered palm for a second, trying to decide if I'm willing to play his little game.

Finally, curiosity wins out and I place my hand in his. He helps me out of the car and refuses to let go of my hand as we talk towards the front door. I expect Gage to knock or ring the bell, but instead, he walks right in, taking me with him.

The grand foyer opens up with an imperial staircase leading up to the second floor, with two-story vaulted ceilings and original detailed woodwork. From this standpoint, I can see a parlor on the left, a dining room to my right, and a large kitchen past the staircase. The walls are painted in rich, moody colors, with panels of ornate wallpaper decorating the spacious entryway. My heels click on the checkered flooring made up of black and white marble tiles.

"What do you think?"

"Of what? How you just broke into someone's house?"

"The house. What do you think of the house?"

"Why? Are you thinking of buying it or something?" I look over at him to find him staring at me expectantly, so I relent. "It's a beautiful house. Absolutely gorgeous."

"Good. I think so too." He grins from ear to ear as he uses our connected hands to pull me through the entryway towards the kitchen, passing a library full of gorgeous built-in bookshelves on the way.

"Did you drag me all the way here to ask me what I think about a house you're thinking of buying?"

"It's not for sale, baby."

"Then, what? Don't tell me you won it in a poker game. I swear those idiots don't know when to quit."

"This house isn't mine."

"Then who's is it?"

"It's yours."

I stop dead in my tracks as my stomach does a fucking cartwheel. Gage looks back at me and grins, his hand tightening around mine.

"What did you just say?" There's no way I heard him right. I must have hallucinated or something.

"It's yours—sell it, gut it, keep it. Whatever you want."

"You bought me a house? Why would you do that?" I'm in utter disbelief.

"Your dick of a landlord wanted you out of the apartment so his idiot son could move in. I knew I'd bring you back before too long, and I wanted you to have somewhere to come back to." I listen to what Gage is saying, but it doesn't seem to compute. I simply stare at him, bewildered, as I try to process what's happening. Gage takes advantage of my stillness to tow me into him.

"I can see that you're trying to decide between kissing me or killing me, so let me show you the place before you decide. Deal?" I slowly nod, my eyes narrowing slightly.

Gage takes me through the house, showing me the sunlight-flooded forest green kitchen—with its black quartz countertops, walk-in pantry, and top-of-the-line appliances. I follow in silence as he tells me about each room, pointing out details and the history of the building.

Next comes the butler's pantry, a large dining room, a massive living room with a gorgeous fireplace, a sunroom, the library, two powder rooms, and a home office. Following him upstairs, he takes me through four large bedrooms, with two full bathrooms, and finally, the primary suite.

Walking into the spacious bedroom, I feel like I've stepped out of my body. The arched floor-to-ceiling windows flood the room with natural light, with high coffered ceilings and stunning crown molding that looks original to the house. A king-size bed sits perfectly made in my bedding, and a second glance shows me my nightstands on either side. The rest of the room is empty until we walk into the closet of my dreams.

Gage flips the switch, and the room fills with light, revealing rows and rows of clothes, shoes, handbags, and other accessories. I step further inside, I can't help it. My hands brush along some of the neatly hanging clothing, and I recognize them as the clothes I left in my apartment. But then, as I round to the other side of the closet, I realize the clothes are unfamiliar and still have tags hanging from them. Designer, luxury materials, gorgeous custom pieces. They're all for me.

My head is swimming, and I barely register the glorious primary bathroom with a giant soaking tub, steam shower, marble tiles, and double vanity sink.

Gage takes me by the hand and leads me back downstairs, through the kitchen to the sprawling backyards with an Olympic-sized pool and jacuzzi. We don't go down into the finished basement, but Gage tells me about the theater room, wet bar, and wine cellar. And in the three-car garage, my car sits waiting for me like I left it here all along.

When we finally make it back to the kitchen, I'm in a daze. A million thoughts are swirling around in my head, but there's only one that makes it out of my mouth.

"You bought a house?"

"It's your house, Jill." Pulling his key ring out of his jacket pocket, Gage places the house key and gate fob on the kitchen counter. "Everything has been paid in full under your name. This place is yours, not mine or anyone else's. No strings."

"No strings," I repeat. He takes my tone as wary, and maybe it is.

"I won't pretend that I'll ever let you walk away, Jill. But I can take a step back until you're ready for me again. If watching you from afar is what it takes to keep you in my life, I'll do it."

Gazing at him, everything comes crashing down on me all at once—our fight, the plane ride, the house. And the thought of Gage leaving that key for me and walking out the front door, leaving me in this big house alone, feels like a punch to the gut.

I don't want him to leave.

I don't want this house to be just for me, I want it to be ours. My chest aches at the idea of having to live in this mansion without the man I love.

Rounding the counter, I walk over to press my chest against his, my arms snaking up around his neck. Gage doesn't hesitate to wrap me in his arms, pulling me in so close that there's no distance between us. Raising up on my toes, I kiss him. His eager lips move with mine desperately, drinking me in with an unquenchable thirst.

"Ok, fine," I say between kisses. "Yes."

"Yes, what?" Gage asks against my lips, his tongue slipping in to tangle with mine. I let him devour me until my head is spinning, and my knees are threatening to buckle.

"Yes, I'll marry you." Gage pulls away abruptly to look down at me, a glorious grin spreading across his face. He stares down at me, looking like a man who's just won the lottery. Then he slowly shakes his head, his brilliant smile never faltering.

"I'm not asking you to marry me, little devil." He gestures around the kitchen. "This isn't a proposal."

"But you will. And when you do, I'll say yes." I pull him back down to recapture his lips with mine. "But you better ask me very nicely." Gage inches back to rest his forehead against mine, our breath mingling between us with our proximity.

"Oh, don't you worry your pretty little head. When I ask you to marry me, there won't be any choice but to say yes." One of his hands cups my face, his thumb tenderly stroking my face. His dark eyes remain connected with mine so deeply I can feel our soul ties tighten. "Cut me, fight me—hell, you can even kill me—but don't ever fucking leave me again. You are my soul, Jillian Hart."

"I'm not going anywhere." I've never meant anything so strongly in my entire life. "I love you, Gage Lawless. Forever."

EPILOGUE

GAGE

Paradise isn't a place, it's a person.

Jillian Lawless.

Watching her walk towards me—bikini-clad, my diamond sparkling on her ring finger as she carries her drink, dark hair swirling around her in the tropical breeze with her eyes set on me—it's my wildest fantasy come true. Even from across the beach, she's a fucking vision.

Her dark red string bikini does little to hide her voluptuous curves, a black mesh mini skirt hanging low on her full hips. The small triangles of fabric display her gorgeous tits and the marks covering them.

My marks.

Lovebites and hickeys cover most of Jill's perfect body, declaring her mine like the ring on her finger and her new last name. She's finally mine, and I'll do everything in my power to stake my claim on her so that she, and the rest of the world, know exactly who she belongs to. Just like how I've been hers from the moment I laid eyes on her.

The wedding was an intimate ceremony in a Gothic church. Jill wanted what she called 'romantic elegance' with hundreds of white candles, blood-red roses, and all of the guests wearing black. I'll never forget when the church doors opened to reveal Jill standing in her ivory wedding gown, a black layered veil, and a bouquet of red roses. When she walked down the aisle, eyes locked with mine, her stunning smile brought attention to the red on her crimson lips.

Me.

Standing in front of our closest friends and family, declaring our vows, and committing to each other for time and all eternity—not even will death do us part—was the happiest moment of my life.

A honeymoon in St. Barths was Jill's idea, one I happily agreed to. Sun, sand, and my gorgeous wife strutting around in tiny bikinis? Easiest yes of my life—after saying 'I do.'

As Jill walks closer, I'm reminded again just how lucky of a bastard I really am. Lifting up a hand, I gesture with my pointer finger for her to give me a little spin. She flashes me a look and rolls her eyes but pauses a few feet from me to turn around, giving me a full three-sixty view of her in all her glory. That bikini was made for her, and the little mesh skirt adds coverage while still showing off the thong bottoms being swallowed by that lush ass of hers.

"Goddamn," I groan, making her bite back a smile.

"Do you think I'm pretty?" she asks, closing the distance between us to walk into my awaiting arms.

"The most beautiful woman to ever walk this earth," I state without hesitation.

"Do you want me?" She melts into me, her eyes softening like they do only for me.

"More than my next breath."

"Do you love me?" The softness of her tone gives me

life, a glimpse at who she is just with me. Seeing her be sweet and vulnerable is a privilege—one I plan to earn every fucking day.

"Like it's my reason for existing." I lean down to press a kiss on her forehead.

"Mmm," she hums softly. "I love you."

"I have a present for you." I can't help but grin at the way she perks up.

"What is it?" she asks, her eyes scanning around us for a package or a clue. Not seeing anything, she turns her narrowed eyes back to me. "You better not be playing with me."

"Oh, I'll be playing with you very soon," I promise with a salacious grin. "Follow me, I'll bring you to your gift."

Taking her by the hand, I lead her away from the bar down a secluded path to a private beach. I can feel Jill's eyes on me as we walk, growing more and more curious. A small maintenance shed sits tucked away in a grove of trees. Opening the door, I let her enter first before I latch the door securely behind us.

The interior of the hut is mostly empty—with a few rakes, sandbags, and some landscaping equipment tucked off to the side. But that's not what I brought her to see. A man stands in the center of the room, his wrists bound above his head and tied to the support beam on the ceiling. He stands, body taut against his restraints, his ankles tied together tightly with a cord. He starts making noise against the rag stuffed into his mouth that's been secured with duct tape as we enter, hoping we're his chance at being rescued. When his eyes land on me, his tone changes to angry desperation.

Jill stops just inside the door and takes in the whole scene as she processes. When she looks back at me, I can see the confusion dissipating as the excitement starts to settle in.

"Is that...?"

"The man who groped you at the bar last night." The memory has my tone darkening.

"So this is what you were doing while I got my facial?"

"I had to keep myself busy somehow," I reply with a smirk. She leans up to capture my lips in a sensual kiss, allowing my tongue to dance with hers. She tastes like everything I've ever wanted. When she leans back, an amused smile tugs at her full kiss-swollen lips as she swipes her lipgloss off my mouth. I'm tempted to pull her back in, to indulge my insatiable craving for her, but then she pulls away to get a closer look at her present.

Walking over to the pathetic asshole, she stops just a foot away from him. His eyes, wide with fear and glassy with pain, dart between me and my beautiful wife.

"He looks like he's been crying," she comments, tilting her head at him. I walk up behind her, wrapping my arm around her waist to pull her against my side.

"I may have shattered every bone in both of his hands," I say, my hold on her remaining nonchalant despite the violence edging my voice. She looks up at me with those gorgeous green eyes of hers, and my anger at the fucker spikes all over again. "He touched you."

"He did." The sharp edge to her voice speaks to my violent urges. "I wonder what color he bleeds."

"Fuck, I want to watch you find out." *I need to*. Reaching into my pocket, I pull out the knife I sourced for this very moment. Jill's face lights up with a radiant smile when she sees the switchblade, its warmth touching the deepest, darkest parts of me.

I'll do whatever it takes to keep her smiling like that for the rest of her life.

When she reaches out for the switchblade, I keep my hold on the knife to tow her close enough to kiss—I can't help myself. I don't want to. My mouth clashes with hers to pour all of the passion and attraction I feel. I'm so turned on right now, it's all-consuming.

Jill is all-consuming.

My wife.

"You look so pretty with my ring on your finger," she comments. "My husband."

One of Jill's hands grasps mine left hand, lifting it to her mouth. Her lips press to my wedding band, eyes on me, as her teeth nip at the metal—the sign of my devotion. I all but nut in my pants at the sight of it, an inebriating cocktail of potent lust and unadulterated love surging through me until I feel invincible. With this woman, I can do anything.

For this woman, I *will* do anything.

Letting my hand drop, she turns to the man awaiting his fate. The resounding metallic chink as her switchblade springs open makes the man start to panic, pulling at his restraints. With Jill's step closer to him, my anticipation rises, adrenaline coursing through me. I'm so hard right now, so ready to watch my soulmate indulge her dark urges.

She glances at me over her shoulder, eyes bright with excitement with a smile that's all for me. My adoration for this woman is overwhelming, it threatens to swallow me whole like a black hole. There has never been anything more beautiful than my wife, unapologetically twisted, sensually dark, and mine.

Forever.

ACKNOWLEDGMENTS

There are a few people who made this book possible that I'd like to thank. First, is my sister Hannah—who let me talk myself in circles while I tried to figure out my characters and plot. She's the reason this book makes any sense at all. Next is my friend and fellow author, Shannon Elliot, who was gracious enough to answer all of my questions, share her guidance, and help me over the publishing finish line. And I can't forget to thank my readers, who took a chance on my debut novel and encouraged me to keep writing. None of this would be possible without all of you.

ABOUT THE AUTHOR

Lila Herron is a writer and avid reader of spicy romance. As a plus size woman, she realized there's a lack of big body representation across all genres, especially in dark romance. Lila is intent on showing up for the plus size community with confident, vibrant, fat main characters who know their worth and feel comfortable in their skin.

When she's not writing, you can find Lila in Chandler, Arizona watching trashy reality tv shows surrounded by house plants and playing with her puppy, Honey. She always has a her phone open to a graphic she's designing or social media app she's exploring for her work in digital marketing.

With her second novel, Red My Lips, Lila has stepped out of her comfort zone to publish the kind of story she wants to see on her bookshelf. Her writing combines tension and incredible banter in a dark romance where a fat babe gets the spicy ravaging she deserves.

Made in the USA
Columbia, SC
22 December 2024

50461886R00195